STAR BRIGHT

BRIGHT YOUNG THINGS, BOOK 1

STACI HART

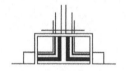

TO THOSE OF YOU
SEARCHING FOR A PLACE
TO BELONG.

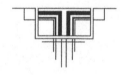

"THERE IS TO BE A FANCY DRESS PARTY. HOW EXCITING IT SOUNDS.
ONE'S HEART THUDS. IT ALL SOUNDS SO DIFFERENT TO ANY OTHER PARTY,
THOUGH IN REALITY IT IS MUCH THE SAME ONCE THE DRESSING UP IS
DONE. INFINITELY DARING IT SEEMS."

—CECIL BEATON

STAR BRIGHT

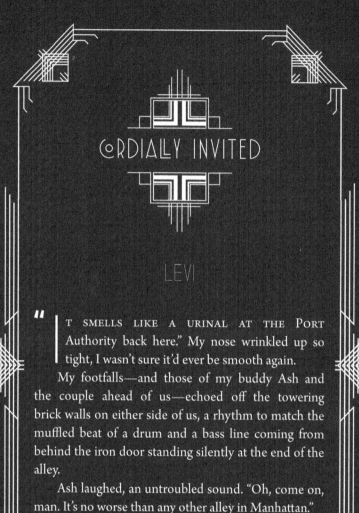

CORDIALLY INVITED

LEVI

"IT SMELLS LIKE A URINAL AT THE PORT Authority back here." My nose wrinkled up so tight, I wasn't sure it'd ever be smooth again.

My footfalls—and those of my buddy Ash and the couple ahead of us—echoed off the towering brick walls on either side of us, a rhythm to match the muffled beat of a drum and a bass line coming from behind the iron door standing silently at the end of the alley.

Ash laughed, an untroubled sound. "Oh, come on, man. It's no worse than any other alley in Manhattan."

"This can't be the location of the party. I swear to God, Ash—if I got all dressed up just to get mugged, I'm gonna beat the shit out of you."

Again with that laugh, coupled with a flash of teeth that made it almost impossible not to smile back.

I somehow managed to resist.

He clapped me on the shoulder and snapped my suspenders like a dick. "Come on. Be a good sport."

A derisive noise from somewhere in the back of my throat was my only answer.

"Listen. You wanted me to get you into one of these parties—"

"After you badgered me for months to come with you—"

He shot me a look. "Not on one of the nights I had Lily James on the hook—I've been waiting five years for her to be single. But I'm a good fucking friend, so I brought *your* ass instead. So live it up, bucko. Next time, you won't be so lucky. So wear your suspenders and quit bitching, would you?"

I jerked my chin at the couple ahead of us as they approached the door. "They didn't dress up in '20s gear." When the guy turned his head, I leaned toward Ash and said under my breath, "Wait—is that who I think it is?"

"You'd think he'd play along with the '20s theme. He played *the* Gatsby, after all."

Some commotion went on at the door, and Leo turned, blowing past us, mumbling swear words with his date trotting behind him, trying to keep up. Out of nowhere, he whirled around, jabbed a finger at the door, and yelled, "Bullshit!" His date plowed into him, and the two spun around before he righted them, snagged her hand, and stormed toward the mouth of the alley.

Ash's sideways smile noted his pleasure at the sight. "Not even Leo gets in without a costume, golden ticket or not."

At the mention, he reached into his inside coat pocket and extracted the invitation, printed on heavy black paper with gold foil deco detailing and our instructions:

The Bright Young Things
do cordially invite you
to ruckus and rebellion
by way of jazz and whiskey.

The brighter, the better, darling.
Password: The Tattler

The address, which wasn't so much of an address as it was a general direction, was printed underneath, the words catching what little light shone in the dim alley, glinting like a promise.

It was typical of the Bright Young Things—vague, melodramatic, and undeniably intriguing. Since the recent turn into the modern '20s, the enigmatic social group had taken over—first New Yorkers, followed quickly by gossip columns, and then the country as a whole. Copycat parties had swept the nation, but none were so extravagant as the trendsetters'. Presumably founded by a pack of anonymous socialites, the parties had become a topic of voracious interest. Where would they be? What spectacle would follow? And most importantly, who was Cecelia Beaton?

The name was a play on the illustrious Cecil Beaton, an icon in fashion photography and notorious member of the original Bright Young Things. The infamous, irreverent youths had overtaken London newspaper headlines through the late 1920s for all the same reasons as their namesake: they were wild, rebellious, and glamorous with exclusivity that was almost impossible to break into.

Cecelia Beaton signed her name to any contracts and invoices for parties, paid in cash, and generally flummoxed everyone regarding her real identity. If she even was a she. No one knew, and none of the fifty or so core Bright Young Things would talk. The mystery of it ate the general populace alive. So they wondered and watched and salivated in unison at the sight of celebrities' Instagram posts from the parties and stalked Twitter for any sliver of gossip they could inhale. Two hundred invitations went out for every party, and not one single attendee would risk their coveted spot by leaking any important details leading up to an event. Just enough to whet the appetite of the public, amplifying the intrigue exponentially.

As far as I knew, I was the first reporter to actually make it into one.

And I intended to make the most of it.

The steel door we stopped at was imposing, set under an unassuming tin-topped light in the brick wall—a rusty, bolted, ten-ton affair with a metal slide at eye-level. When Ash knocked to the beat of "Shave and a Haircut," the slide rasped open, and a pair of suspicious eyes glinted from the shadows.

"Password," he growled.

But Ash flashed that smile he flung around so easily, along with his invitation. "The Tattler."

The slide slammed shut, and with a creaky grind, the door slid open.

I wasn't a small guy—six-four with no shoes on, my shoulders broad enough to intimidate most anybody into submission. But the man behind that door wasn't so much a man as he was a rhino, with a jaw like a brick and a neck like a tree trunk. He could have pounded us into the ground like a stake with nothing more than a hammer swing to the skull. But instead, he stepped out of the way and let us pass, watching us as he rolled the door back in place and lowered a metal arm dense enough to stop a battering ram.

"They don't fuck around about security, do they?" I asked, glancing once more over my shoulder.

"Don't want the rabble getting in, do we?"

"Anything but that," I answered flatly as we trotted down a set of narrow stairs as black as pitch.

The stairwell dumped us into a long, dimly lit hallway, and at the end was a doorway, a portal to decadence, a glittering window to music and laughter, gold and velvet. Luxury incarnate.

In a rare act of nerves, Ash grabbed his homburg hat by the indentations, lifting it just high enough to run his free hand through sandy-blond hair. Where he wore a double-breasted three-piece suit, complete with pocket square and pocket watch,

I'd decided on the '20s workingman. Shirtsleeves cuffed to my elbows, no tie, slacks with a higher waist than I preferred for authenticity, suspenders, and a tweed newsboy cap.

Never was one for suits. Ash, however, had been born in Armani with a silver spoon in his mouth and a G & T in his hand. Just like almost everyone on the other side of that threshold.

Though I had plenty of rich friends—and I mean, filthy rich, old-money friends—their extravagance always made me uncomfortable. Not for the underscoring of what I didn't have, but for the sheer lack of normalcy, the flippancy at which they'd spend twenty grand in a night while there were so many who had nothing. That sort of grandeur was so out of touch, it bordered disrespect.

But that was what it was and happened to be exactly why I was here. For a fairy tale of riches no commoner would ever see.

I tried to put away my disapproving frown, lifting my chin and straightening my spine. My lungs expanded with a fortifying breath.

And we stepped through the doorway to be thrust into fantasy.

A jazz band played on the stage at the other end of the space, lights shining on glistening skin as they played their goddamn brains out. A fiddle and a bass, a trumpet and a trombone, a sax player next to the clarinet. Behind them was the drummer, looking slick as all hell and cool as a fucking cucumber, despite his soaked shirt. The dance floor before them was a glittering thing, sparkling with beaded dresses and feathered fascinators and fringe and pearls. A swirling mosaic of mirrors covered the low ceiling, the grout golden. And the rest of the space was a symphony of textures—red velvet and brass, mahogany and exposed brick.

Ash grinned like an idiot from my side, eyes hungry and bright as he watched the dance floor bounce in time to the beat of the drum. Blindly, he slapped me on the chest.

"We need a drink. And then we're finding somebody to dance with whether you like it or not."

With a laugh, I followed him to the bar, where we ordered scotch from a guy with an undercut and a handlebar mustache. And when we turned around to make our way to the edge of the dance floor, I took a moment to appreciate the feast laid before me.

It was, as everyone had said, rich and indulgent, from the decor to the people who filled the establishment. I spotted faces that would have been recognized by even the most devoted recluse—actors and actresses, musicians and models—and some many wouldn't have a clue about, from photographers to artists and even a few writers. Not a single person in the place was out of costume, the effect both unnerving and immersive. We'd gone back in time to enjoy the night to the fullest before the cops busted down the doors and threw us all in paddy wagons.

It wasn't a far cry even now, a hundred years after the Prohibition. If the police commissioner had anything to do with it, every Bright Young Thing in the joint would be locked in said paddy wagon and on their way to having the truth about Cecelia Beaton's identity wrung out of them.

His obsession with the group of seemingly harmless youths was its own spectacle, and everyone was curious as to why. Why was the commissioner on a crusade to disband the movement? What did he want with the group, and why had he decided to grandstand? Something about it felt personal, though no one knew what'd happened to instigate the attack.

But that wasn't what I was here to find out—not officially, at least. The scheme was simple, concocted over several gallons of coffee in a writers' room at *Vagabond*, where I was a staff writer. We were the '90s answer to *Rolling Stone*, created as the new generation's music and culture magazine. Almost overnight, we'd stepped into their role, starting a rivalry that still went on thirty years later.

Everyone wanted to know what it was like to be a Bright Young Thing. The public was thirsty as fuck for details, for deeper insight into the fantasy the group provided. Was there some higher purpose, or were they just a bunch of disparaging youths, parading their elite and exclusive group around to tease the masses?

Since I was the only one at the writers' table with an in, the gig was mine, and with it came a substantial pay raise on delivery. The plan was simple enough: convince Ash to bring me to as many parties as I could in order to write a big overview article for the magazine feature.

But to get what I needed, the necessity for secrecy was imperative. Ash knew—I wouldn't have asked without his knowledge of what I was really doing. But otherwise, I'd have to keep my profession to myself or risk being blacklisted from the parties. Or worse—I could Ash down with me.

And if I could draw out Cecelia Beaton, I might just earn myself a hefty bonus.

The suspicion was that it was the whole lot of them, or at least the fifty or so core members. The secrecy drove people mad, and though they never really caused trouble beyond some red tape here and there, serving minors on occasion, noise violations and the like, Commissioner Warren didn't care. Never mind drug dealers and sex traffickers—Warren put the Bright Young Things on his banner and waved it around like they were everything wrong with the younger generation. The generation of waste and sloth and irresponsibility. A brood of whiners, soft and useless.

He might as well be shaking his fist and shouting, *Damn millennials! Get off my lawn!*

Where some called him out for wasting resources on something so harmless, he insisted it was just as important—he wouldn't let the rich kids get away with flagrant disrespect for the law. And beyond all logic, the louder voices agreed, ready to hunt down Cecelia Beaton and give her the old Marie Antoinette.

Truth be told, I thought they were all assholes. But at least *these* assholes threw a great party.

Ash hit me in the chest with the back of his hand, but when I shot him a look, he wasn't looking at me. He was staring in front of us.

At her.

She floated toward us like a north magnet through a sea of norths that parted as she approached and closed behind her, a bubble of force keeping them just out of reach in deference or awe or both. Eyes, bright as glittering diamonds, were locked on mine, her lips touched with the ghost of a curve at the corners, the promise of a smile. Everything about her shone—the finger waves in her golden hair, the crystals dotting the band of her fascinator, the reflective beads on her dress.

That dress. White chiffon and silver lace, twinkling beads trimming the deep V, the ghostly fabric hugging the curves of her body from rib to hip before cascading to the ground. Tiny strands of silver beads capped her shoulders like a draping spiderweb, heavy with sparkling dew.

But my eyes snagged hers again, lustrous blue eyes lined with smoky kohl and long lashes, her skin pale and perfect but for the rise of color in her cheeks and the blood red of her narrow, lush lips.

A tug somewhere in the expanse of my chest urged me to meet her as she drifted toward me.

Not Ash.

Me.

Because if she was a north magnet, I was a south. And it seemed both of us knew it.

Time lurched to a start and picked up speed, like turning on a record player when the needle already rested in the groove.

She smiled.

I smiled.

Ash saved us from having to speak. "Stella Spencer. Aren't you a vision?"

She laughed, the sound plucking a thread in me. "Flatterer."

She reached for him with long, pale fingers, brushing his bicep as she leaned in to press her cheek to his. "I thought you were bringing Lily," she said as she backed away, her eyes flicking in my direction.

I didn't miss the flush of her cheeks from whatever she saw.

"I was, but Levi here is a nonbeliever, and I felt compelled to show him just what it was all about."

"Levi," she said, almost as if it were a sound she'd never heard before. "Stella." She extended a hand, which I took, my thumb absently stroking her skin, charting the fine bones that rested beneath.

"Welp, look at that." Ash held up his empty glass with a dramatic flair. "Time for a refill. Need one, Stella? Levi?"

"I'm good," she said on a laugh, removing her hand from my grip. I hadn't realized I was still holding it.

"Me too," I answered. Or mumbled.

Ash said something smart before walking away, but I didn't hear him.

You'd think I'd never seen a pretty girl before.

You'd think I'd never seen *Stella Spencer* before.

Not in person, of course, but everyone knew the socialite, heiress to her father's unbelievable real estate fortune and one of the core Bright Young Things. But the dozens of photographs I'd seen of her were nothing compared to the real thing. A picture could never capture the sheer allure of her, the charm of her presence that existed by nature alone, without a single word of encouragement.

It was no wonder everyone wanted to know her. I counted myself among them for the first time whether I liked it or not.

I took a sip of my scotch to fortify myself, gathering up my wits and lining them up like soldiers. When I lowered my glass, she was watching me with her head cocked.

"I'm surprised you bumped Lily off Ash's arm," she said. "How big of a favor does he owe you?"

"Big enough that this doesn't even begin to cover it."

"Well, I'm glad you managed it. Where's he been hiding you?"

"Nowhere. Never wanted to come before."

One of her dusky-blonde brows arched, tugging the corners of her lips up with it. "Oh? And what changed your mind?"

"Ash can be very convincing." I glanced around the room in appraisal.

She moved to my side to assess the room with me. "And what do you think? Does it live up to the hype?"

I glanced at her with a smirk on my face and a thud of possibility in my sternum. "Exceeds all expectations."

Another laugh, another pretty blush, her gaze moving back to the crowd. "Glad to hear it."

"Why? You didn't throw this elaborate shindig, did you?"

She laid an amused, mildly patronizing look on me. "That's cute."

"You didn't say no. Should I call you Cecelia?"

"You can call me whatever you'd like," she answered with a smile. "But those of us who are at every one of these parties have a certain ownership to the thing, even though we didn't put it together. We're just the pieces that make up the whole, but don't mistake it for more than it is. We have the distinguished Cecelia Beaton to thank for our good time."

"Hear, hear." I raised my glass, and she lifted an imaginary one in salute, eliciting a frown. "You don't have a drink. How about I rectify that?"

But as I slipped my hand in the small of her bare back to guide her toward the bar, she stepped into the crowd, turning to face me as she went. "I think I can manage. Nice to meet you, Levi."

"Not as nice as it was to meet you."

With hot eyes and a lovely smile, she headed away. The crowd parted before swallowing her up again.

And I gave myself a new mission, one that superseded my reconnaissance.

On the wings of a smile, I knocked back my scotch and turned for the bar.

There was something about that girl. A curiosity, one I found myself compelled to unearth. I wasn't easily struck, and that alone was all the reason I needed to find her again tonight. So I picked up my metaphorical shovel and made a vow to find out just what it was about her that obliged me to dig. Maybe I'd learn more than I bargained for.

And if I was lucky—very, very lucky—I would kiss Stella Spencer, well and thoroughly, to see just what all the fuss was about.

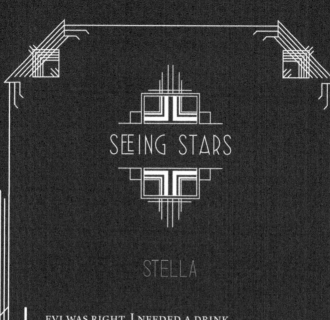

SEEING STARS

STELLA

L EVI WAS RIGHT. I NEEDED A DRINK.

I was a little ashamed of the extra sway in my hips as I walked away, but I couldn't help but want him to watch me go. Doing my best to cover my deliberate grab for his attention, I nodded and smiled at the faces I passed, scanning for Betty and Zeke. One of them would have a spare drink. I didn't care what it was.

If I didn't cool down, I was likely to burst into flames right there in front of everyone.

I could feel Levi's eyes on me, eyes as dark as the shadow of his beard on a jaw cut from stone, dark as his hair, long enough to curl around his ears and lick the collar of his shirt. Something in my chest shuddered at the memory made just a few short seconds ago, and it took an excessive   amount of willpower to stop myself from looking back at him, just to make sure he was still there.

Unknown faces—especially faces as gorgeous as his—were a commodity at these parties, which must have had something to do with the intrigue. Maybe it was that in all the years I'd known Ash, I'd never seen Levi before. Maybe it was in the way he'd looked at me, as if I were a juicy, rare steak, and he hadn't had a meal in a week.

I had a feeling he'd devour me. All I had to do was give him permission.

Permission granted, I thought in his direction with my smile on the rise.

The thought sent a delectable shock of heat from my stomach to the juncture of my thighs. I wasn't one to sleep with random guys at these parties—that was more Betty's brand. But it'd been a month since my steady, Dex, had gone off and gotten himself a girlfriend, and a serious one at that.

Dex and I had been a convenient thing for years. When either of us needed a date, the other was there. Two in the morning *You up?* texts were always answered, no questions asked. I couldn't call it a fling. That would imply it was here and gone. I couldn't say it wasn't a relationship either—we partook in cuddling and pillow talk and genuinely enjoyed each other's company. But he'd told me from the start that not only was he not looking for a relationship, but he wasn't even interested in being monogamous, citing monogamy as a societal expectation that defied our human nature or some bullshit like that.

And I'd told myself I wasn't in love with him. But it seemed, in the end, we'd both been lying.

It's fine. Who even cares? There are plenty of fish in the sea, and I'm pretty sure I just snagged a hammerhead.

I pursed my lips to stifle a laugh.

A trickle of sweat rolled into the hollow of my throat. It was as hot as the inside of a furnace, and though my dress was airy, the heavy beaded details stuck to me like flypaper. My smile widened with pride as I looked around the party, taking it all in. The music.

The atmosphere. Their happy faces that told me exactly what I wanted to know.

I'd thrown one hell of a party.

Being Cecelia Beaton had become a full-time job, one spent planning and dreaming and imagining the next party, the next good time. Other than Genie—the event planner I'd snagged while she was still in college and paid buckets of money to keep quiet—very few people knew, though it still felt like too many.

Legally, I was fully protected. Cecelia Beaton was the business I'd set up in Delaware, where the records were sealed. Money was paid into the business from an offshore account, and Genie and I talked on WhatsApp under fake numbers. We hadn't even seen each other face-to-face in months, not with the paparazzi staking her out. But enough nonessential people had interfered that I'd had to do my fair share of bribing, and a few members who had fallen out of line or disobeyed our credo had been publicly shamed—a task Betty and Zeke took great pleasure in. It was the only time we used our powers for evil and happened to be the most effective way to keep everyone on their best behavior.

I spotted Zeke, not only for his formidable height, but that said height was topped off by platinum-blond hair in perfect finger waves. With a sigh, I beelined for him.

Or tonight, her. Rather than come in full-blown drag like I'd figured she would—I'd expected the Ziegfeld Follies getup, complete with a sparkly four-foot headpiece—Zelda Fitzperil had come as in a smart three-piece suit with no shirt beneath the three-button vest. A man dressed as a woman dressed as a man in a cheeky nose thumbing at gender as a whole. The V hit just beneath her impressive cleavage—a magical combination of contouring and creative taping. The second Zeke put on falsies, he became Zelda, and Zelda was always onstage with a bottomless bag of jokes and an, *Oh, honey*, for us all.

Z smiled at me with luscious red lips, extending her extra drink in my direction. "You look like you need this," she said.

"Thank you," I answered in relief as I took the longest pull of her old-fashioned that I could manage, grateful for the chill of the glass in my hand.

Betty smirked. "What's got you all bothered?" One of her dark brows rose, and she elbowed Z in the ribs. "Look, she's flustered."

"You mean besides it being a thousand degrees in here?" I said.

Z shifted in my direction, hip first. "Who's the boy, Stell?"

"What boy?" I asked innocently.

Both of them rolled their eyes, and a laugh busted out of Betty. "Mr. Tall, Dark, and Broody. He looks like he could work on a railroad."

"*All the livelong dayyy*," Z sang. "He could lay tracks on me all night long."

"Me too," Betty said, inching up onto her tiptoes to catch a glimpse of him. "Pound some stakes."

"Nine-inch steel." Z looked over everyone's heads at Levi. "How big do you think his hammer is?"

"Fucking sledgehammer, no doubt," Betty said before donning an accusatory look. "How come you didn't climb him like a gym rope?"

"If I'd stayed any longer, I would have."

"It's about time," Z said, three words of straight attitude.

"I'll drink to that." I nodded and waved in return when another of our friends caught my eye.

"You're due. When was the last time somebody snaked your pipes? Dex at Under the Sea? If I remember right, you almost got arrested for rubbing your parts all over each other in the Washington Square fountain." Z shuddered. "I don't know how you were so drunk as to have *any* parts in that fountain. Should have been arrested on a health violation."

"I've been busy," I answered lightly.

"Busy wondering why Dex is dating Elsie Richmond instead of you?" Z laid a look on me.

I gave her one right back. "It's fine. I couldn't give a good goddamn who Dex is seeing."

"Then how come he's not here tonight?"

I shrugged. "I sent him an invitation like I was supposed to. I don't care if he comes."

Z snorted a laugh. "You are so full of shit."

"We have a silent agreement that he won't show his stupid face. Anyway, I've been *busy*. You two know better than anyone why."

"Busy partying," Betty amended. "And if you can't get laid partying, you're doing it wrong."

"So maybe I've been feeling a little picky," I said.

They looked at each other for a protracted moment before breaking into laughter.

I pinched the back of Z's arm and twisted until she yelped and slapped my hand. "Ow, bitch. If that leaves a bruise, I swear to God—"

"We're just concerned about your well-being," Betty said.

"And the well-being of your vagina," Z added. "I get Dex fucked like a porn star, but that asshole is emotionally bankrupt. What you need is a good old-fashioned nailing, and who better than the big, beefy sledgehammer? Get yourself a rail job." We must have looked confused because she added, "A rim job with more steel."

"Maybe for you," I said on a laugh. "No steel is getting near this rim. At least, not without a lot more booze than I've had tonight."

"Amen." Betty clinked her glass to mine in solidarity.

"Amateurs," Z said into her crystal glass before taking a drink.

"Where's Roman?" I asked, surveying the crowd for Z's boyfriend.

"Who the fuck knows?" Z said with a wave of her hand. "He'll pop back up when you least expect him. Like herpes but cuter." Her eyes hung on something behind me, something that had her both appraising whatever she saw and amused by its approach. "Chugga-chugga *choo-choo*."

A glance in the direction of Z's gaze knocked the breath out of my lungs.

Because Levi was winding through the crowd toward me.

He was all broad shoulders and corded arms, his chest wide and waist narrow. Thick forearms dusted with dark hair led to very large hands, which were wrapped around two drinks. A tilted smile accompanied a look that set that fire in my belly again. Another droplet of sweat rolled down the valley of my spine, and I wasn't entirely sure it had anything to do with the temperature of the room.

"He is gonna fuck you *up*," Z said into my ear.

That's what I'm afraid of, I thought.

Levi climbed the few steps to meet us, and I stepped back to make room in the circle. He took up so much space, not just for his daunting size, but for the gravity of him, pulling me toward him like a black hole. I wondered if that gravity affected everyone or just me.

"Couldn't let you go until I knew you had a drink in your hand," he said, his voice rumbling and low. His dark eyes shifted to the glass in my hand. "Looks like you found one after all."

Z snatched the drink from my hand with a smile. "Actually, that's mine." When my brow furrowed, she said, "What? You've got another one, thanks to your big, hairy wolf." She swiped his second drink, put it in my hand, then extended her elegant hand in Levi's direction. "Zelda Fitzperil. Who are you, and what are you doing with Ash?"

Levi took her hand. "Call me Levi, and Ash and I went to Columbia together. He owed me a favor."

"Must have been some favor," Z cooed and released his hand.

"I'm Betty," she said with a wave.

"Betty Vance." Levi raised his glass. "Vic Vance's daughter. Man, my dad had all the Hell's Bells records. Gotta say, I'm a big fan."

"I'll let old Vic know." To her credit, she tried not to sound bored.

"What a gentleman," Z said, sliding closer to Levi. "He brought you a drink, Stella, and I'm almost positive it doesn't have a roofie in it."

"Who needs roofies when you've got a smile like this?" Levi joked, laying a smirky, smoldering look on Z.

Z slipped her arm into the hook of his. "I like him."

Levi looked pleased with himself. "Works every time."

Betty rolled her eyes. "Come on, Z. Let's go find Roman."

"He's not a lost puppy, Betty, even if he is a dog. Ten bucks says he's doing lines off a toilet seat."

Betty threaded her arm through Z's free one. "Well, let's go make sure he doesn't end up facedown in the shitter, shall we?"

Z pouted and let Levi go. "Fine, fine. See you around." She caught my eye and started singing about the railroad again before taking off toward the dance floor.

The temperature in the room rose by a dozen degrees the second I was alone with Levi. Looking for a reprieve, I pressed the cold glass to my neck and smiled at him.

"Thanks for the drink. I mean, even though I said I didn't want one."

He rolled one massive shoulder. "What can I say? I'm persistent." A cool stream of sweat from the glass rolled down my neck and into my cleavage, and he watched it all the way down before catching himself. His gaze shifted to the crowd. "You really come to all of these?"

"Ever since I got my first invitation." I didn't mention that I'd sent it to myself.

"New Year's Eve, right? The White Party?"

My lips quirked with a smile. "Just like the original Bright Young Things. It was unseasonably warm, and we drove upstate, danced all night in an orchard on a white dance floor. Raced champagne corks in a stream. The whole deal."

"I've heard the stories." He looked over the crowd. "These parties are a national treasure, and you're all American royalty. Guess nobody should be surprised you caught the negative attention too."

"Like what?"

"Warren, for starters."

My lip curled at the mention of the commissioner's name. "He needs to get real problems. You'd think he'd be worried about *actual* crime in the city instead of busting perfectly legal themed parties."

"That's everybody's question, isn't it? I figured something personal happened, something to get him fired up. Out for revenge maybe."

They were the same questions all the new people asked. Everyone wanted to know about the scandal, even though I didn't have any more of a clue than they did.

So, unfazed, I answered, "I think he's just angry about his lost youth or bitter about his years as a beat cop—who knows? I do know he's a big fan of being a pain in everyone's ass."

"Well, I know you don't know who Cecelia Beaton is, but I bet if you figured it out and served her up, he'd shut up."

A laugh shot out of me, and I looked over to find him unamused. "Oh, you're serious." And then I laughed again. "You really *are* new, aren't you? None of us knows who Cecelia is, and even if we did, none of us would tell."

"Not even to save your own necks?"

I frowned at him. "We're not doing anything dangerous. No one needs saving. But in your hypothetical, no, we wouldn't do it. It might seem like we're nothing but lushes and degenerates, we're here for more than just what you see. It runs deeper than dancing and booze and costumes."

"Does it?"

"It does. I … it's hard to explain."

"Try."

I thought about it for a second. "Have you ever felt alone in the world? Like you don't belong anywhere? To anyone?"

Something flashed behind his eyes, a certain sadness or regret. "I have."

"So have we. So has everyone. These parties are proof positive that we have a place to belong and people to belong to. It's not ... it's not *purpose*—that's too productive a word. More like family." I looked over the crowd, greeted with faces I knew so well. "And we're just like any family. There are squabbles and scandals, but in the end, we always have each other's backs. Most of us don't have anyone else."

When I met his eyes again, they were sharp with cynicism even though his smile was light.

"A sad pack of poor little rich kids? Must be tough." He took a drink.

"Probably looks like that from the outside. But not all of us are rich. And money doesn't solve anyone's problems."

"But it sure can't hurt."

I cut him a look, not bothering to hide the offense. "Shows how much you know."

But then he laughed, his face softening. "That's fair enough. I'm sorry. As an orphan raised by a cop and someone who went to college on an academic scholarship, seems like money is the answer to just about everything. All of this"—he gestured to the crowd—"is the exact opposite of what I know."

"Then maybe it's time to visit the other side and discover its merits," I challenged with a smile. "Keep coming and you'll see for yourself that it's not so simple."

"And duke it out with Ash's dates?" he scoffed. "That's no easy task, and the odds of me landing an invitation of my own is pretty slim. I don't exactly fit in, do I?" There was the slightest bite in his voice, and I hated the sound of it.

"I figured you were cynical, but I didn't take you for a snob."

Unaffected, he shrugged again. "It's all right—I don't feel the need to fit in. But the divide between your kind and mine seems a little deeper in a place like this."

"Maybe it only feels deeper because you dug it that way."

A chuckle. "Maybe. It makes me wonder."

"Wonder what?"

"If there's any merit to that. Especially since you're so adamant that I'm wrong. I'm not usually wrong. I wonder if you could change my mind." He turned his molten gaze on me, and it weighed a thousand pounds, not at all lightened by that crooked smile of his. "I have to say, this is not how I thought tonight would go down."

"No?"

He shook his head, casting a glance toward the bar. "I figured I'd come once or twice, see what it was about, and that'd be that. But I find myself surprised."

"These parties will do that," I said on a laugh.

Once again, he looked straight at me, into me, through me until I was hot and cold all over. "It's not the party. It's you."

Something pulled at me, some wicked desire that lived on his lips, in his mouth. I took an unknowing step closer, close enough to feel the heat of his body even though he was still feet away. "You're not like the rest of them."

"Neither are you."

I laughed, not knowing how I'd gotten closer or even when his hand had first cupped my hip. "Where did you come from?"

"Hell's Kitchen," he answered with an uptick of his smile.

"Do you ever take anything seriously?" I asked with a smile of my own.

"Not if I can help it."

My hand rested on his chest, a solid plane of muscle. I stood between his legs, felt the bulk of his thighs outside mine. When I leaned into him, pressed the length of my body to the long stretch of his, another bulk greeted me.

"I came to find out about the party," he said as his hands

charted the curves of my hips, the words brushing my lips. "But now I have another intention entirely."

"Oh? And what's that?" I breathed.

"To find out how you taste."

A hot shudder slid through me. I inched closer. "Then shut up and find out."

For a heartbeat, he savored the anticipation.

And then I saw stars.

Utter blackness and flashes of light and his lips against mine. Hands, hands on my face, my neck. His noisy breath, or maybe it was mine, the sound of his stubble rasping my palms, louder than the music or the crowd. But those lips, demanding and insistent, devouring, consuming, swallowing me up as if part of me belonged to him and he wanted it back.

It wasn't until I nearly climbed up his body that one of us regained our senses, and I realized it had to have been him. Because although the kiss slowed, the rest of me didn't, my body stretching to cover as much of his as I could and my hands fisting his shirt, bringing us as close as we could get without getting arrested.

We popped apart, lips parted and chests heaving and eyes wide, like we'd seen a color neither of us had laid eyes on before.

A crack like a gunshot whipped our heads in the direction of the sound as a wave of laughter rose, followed by more cracks and snaps as the crowd grabbed balloons and popped them, though some were left bouncing over the crowd, kept afloat by a bodiless hand here and there.

I stepped back, needing and hating to put space between us. My smile said more than I wanted it to.

"You've had your taste," I said blithely, ignoring my racing heart. "Now what?"

"I'll take the bottle."

He reached for my hand, but I drifted back, my fingers sliding through his.

"Come to the next party and maybe you'll get a glass."

"And if I can't get an invite?"

But I smiled at him over my shoulder as I turned. "Oh, I'm sure you'll find a way."

The determination on his face told me I was right.

SOMETHING ELSE

LEVI

"**Y**OU'RE A SWEET BOY, LEVI." PEG SMILED AT ME from behind the fluff-and-fold counter at the Laundromat.

"Don't tell anybody." I leaned in and lowered my voice. "You're gonna ruin my street cred."

She laughed that husky sort of laugh only achieved with the help of fifty-some-odd years of Marlboro Reds. "Taking care of Billy like you do? You could be off, having fun. Living it up. Chasing tail."

"Who says I'm not?" I took the offered laundry bag full of my foster dad's clothes and slung it over my shoulder.

She waved a hand at me. "I mean it. I don't know what Billy'd do if it wasn't for you."

"Eat microwave dinners and bowls of cereal for sustenance."

"Nilla Wafers for dinner."

STACI HART

"Only on Tuesdays."

That earned me another laugh. "How come no girl's locked you down yet? If I were forty years younger, it'd be me."

"If you were forty years younger, I'd have already beaten you to the punch, Peg."

The color in her cheeks rose when she laughed again. "Quit makin' old ladies blush."

"You started it." I turned for the door. "See you next week."

"All right, and you tell Billy to come on by when he's out for his walk."

"Why, you gonna take care of him when I'm gone?"

She waggled her brows. "If I have my way."

With an unamused shake of my head, I pushed the door open. "Bye, Peg."

"Bye-bye, honey." She waved a gnarled, old hand at me as the glass door closed behind me.

It was as hot as a frying pan, the sidewalk sizzling in the mid-day sun. But even the sweltering heat and a full smoke-free year couldn't stop the itch for a cigarette. I gnawed on the stir stick between my lips to keep them occupied instead.

Poor substitute, if you asked me.

The familiar block was already bustling, but it didn't look much like it did when I was a kid. So many of the old businesses were gone, bought out by fancy hair salons and cheese shops and hipster cafés and Starbucks as Hell's Kitchen gentrified, but some of the old staples remained, holding out against the surge. Like Peg's Laundromat, Gino's Subs, the Fareedis' liquor store—which didn't have a name, just the word *Liquor* in big red letters over the door. The Li's bodega was still up and running, but a developer was after them—I had a feeling they were ready to fold. And who could blame them? The kind of cash these developers threw around was more than any of us had ever seen in one place at one time. It'd be bad business to pass up that kind of opportunity, and everybody knew it.

26

But seeing the neighborhood change still sucked. Everybody knew that too.

Money changed things, changed people, and most of the time, not in a good way. The neighborhood was an easy example. I had my fair share of filthy rich friends, and though their extravagance frequently made me uncomfortable, they were old money—multimillion-dollar trusts was the life they knew. But through journalism, I knew plenty of people who'd been made, and they rarely stayed who they were before. Especially the ones who hadn't had to really work for it.

It was hard to fathom. All I'd ever done was work for it, scraping and scrabbling for everything I had, even Billy.

I popped into Gino's to grab Billy his usual and headed back out into the heat, adjusting the bag on my shoulder as I went over an unofficial list of things I needed to do this weekend. Grocery shopping for Billy, some meal prep tomorrow. Tidy up the apartment, vacuum and dust, since he didn't see messes. Not that he saw a lot of anything—he refused to wear his glasses, preferring blindness to the indignity. He'd practically kicked me out in college, insisting after my mandatory dorm year that I live on the Upper West, near school. He also insisted he was able to take care of himself, which was mostly true, so long as he had somebody to run his errands and help with bills.

But with this article, I would earn myself a step up the ladder.

Just like *Rolling Stone*, *Vagabond*'s circulation had been in steady decline for years, and as such, we'd been pushing hard to rebrand over the last few years to make the shift from focusing primarily on music to reaching for a broader audience with politics. And not just national, but issues around the world. We were looking to make a new name for ourselves—an opinion-slanted culture magazine with an edge, the voice of young America.

An opportunity had opened up—a war correspondency in Syria—and if I did my job with the Bright Young Things, I'd land my dream gig covering the war. The money would take care of Billy for years—his city pension and Social Security checks barely covered his bills, never mind what would happen when he couldn't live on his own anymore. I needed money in savings to pay for in-home care if he wouldn't let me live with him.

Everything I did now was to pay into that future.

I'd been putting off finding someone to take my place when it came to Billy, not trusting anybody to care for him the way I did. But he'd threatened me with disownment if I didn't take the job in Syria with the magazine, fueled by the astute assumption that I didn't want to leave him. But he was pushing eighty, and his age, combined with an old gunshot injury—the same one that had ended his long career with the NYPD and left him hobbled—made me hesitant to go anywhere, even the next borough over. Hell, I'd move in with Billy if he'd let me.

Stubborn old bastard.

I trotted up the steps to the building, setting the laundry bag at my feet so I could unlock the heavy green door. The stairwell smelled like old paper and musty wood, the familiar scent following me as I climbed two flights and turned for the apartment.

When I entered, Billy glanced over with a crooked smile on his weathered face. "Don't take this the wrong way, son, but you look like shit."

"You should talk. Brought you Gino's—don't get up."

"Don't tell me what to do," he said as he used what looked like a vast amount of his strength to haul himself up. "How's Peg? She ask about me?"

"Always does." I set the bags on the table and moved to the cabinets for a plate. "Said you should come by on your walk."

"Heh." He shuffled over, leaning on his cane. "I don't brave two flights for the fresh air, that's for damn sure." He pulled out a chair and lowered himself into it. "What'd you do last night? Looks like you got two black eyes and liver disease."

I set his lunch in front of him, and he licked his lips as he unwrapped the sandwich. "Went out with a buddy of mine, one of those Bright Young Things parties."

One of his brows rose. "Those kids Warren is all bent about?"

"The very same." The sink full of dishes called, and I answered, flipping on the water. "I'm writing a piece about them. Nobody will really talk about what goes on or how any of it works, so I've been sent in to infiltrate."

"Some code of ethics you've got," he snarked with his mouth full.

"Don't act like you never went undercover."

"Different."

"Is not. And anyway, it's not an exposé. Just an opinion piece."

"So you're not covering Warren's part in the whole thing? He's out to light those kids up."

"Not officially, no. It's just about the parties and the culture. But I won't lie and say I'm not itching to find out what his beef is and, if I can figure it out, who Cecelia Beaton is."

"Got any leads?"

A smile tugged at my lips. "One, and she's something else."

"So much for objective journalism."

"Hey—there's a reason I'm a literary journalist and not a reporter."

"Authority issues or truth issues?"

I shot him a look. "I tell the truth as I see it instead of a cold regurgitation of facts. How I obtain that truth is at my discretion, which is the sum total of my code of ethics. Why, you callin' me a liar?"

"You tell this little bit of something else what you were there for?"

My brows furrowed.

"Didn't think so." He took a spectacular bite of his sandwich.

"I'm leaving, Pop. It's just a fling. An interesting diversion and an inside look at the group as a whole. One that's not Ash—getting him to help with anything is like trying to put pajamas on an octopus."

"So lemme get this straight," he said when he swallowed. "It's all right to lie, but only if lying gets you the information you want?"

"You act like I don't do this all the time. All I do is lie about my last name and my job. Jesus, nobody ever gave Hunter S. Thompson shit for it."

He gave me a look.

"Okay, fine, he caught some shit over it, but he was a genius, and everybody knows it."

"You might do this all the time, son, but not usually when a girl's involved. I'm just sayin', it changes the game, and pretending it doesn't will only get you in trouble."

"I got it under control—don't worry."

"The line you ride between being honest and lying for the sake of your work makes you a contradiction in boots. I just want you to admit it."

My brows stitched together. "It's a necessary evil in pursuit of visionary truth. *That* is the truth that trumps everything."

"All right, all right." He raised his palms in surrender. "Don't shoot."

"I'm just going to a few parties so I can give the public some sort of insight into what the group is like, and then it'll be done."

"Buncha rich kids with no jobs."

"You'd think, but there's maybe more to it."

"Out all night on a Thursday? Working people don't party like that."

"The young ones do. It was a real spectacle though—whoever's running it has a disgusting amount of disposable income."

"Rich kids with no jobs," he said again before taking another bite.

I stood a plate in the drying rack. "We'll see. If I can convince Ash, I'm going to another party next week."

"So who's this something else? Think she'll come to the next party in the buff?"

A single laugh shot out of me. "Dirty old fucker."

"I know it defies your sense of space and time to believe I was once as young and vital as you, but that doesn't make it any less true."

I set the last glass in the rack and turned to face him, leaning against the counter as I dried my hands. "Stella Spencer."

He swallowed hard. "Dean Spencer's kid with that model? She's got more money than God, if the rumors are true."

"I'm sure they are."

"Kiss her?"

"Yup," I answered as my smile tilted.

"Anything else?"

"I don't kiss and tell."

"You *just* told me you kissed, dipshit."

I shrugged. "Fine, I don't fuck and tell."

He rolled his eyes so hard, I think he saw Jesus. "Youths."

"I know, we're the worst." I pushed off the counter. "Want me to put your clothes away?"

"Do I look like an invalid?"

"You really want me to answer that?"

"Wiseass. I can do it myself."

"Fine, but I'm taking them into your room at least. Last thing I need is you bustin' your hip."

Ten years ago, he'd have punched me in the arm as I passed, but as it stood, he just glared at me, maintaining eye contact as he took another bite of his sandwich.

The apartment hadn't changed since I'd moved in twenty years ago—same old couch, same old curtains, same old everything. In fact, I didn't think it'd changed since his wife died in the '80s of ovarian cancer. They'd never had any kids, and Billy never remarried.

He was part of the DCFS crew that had picked me up when

I was eight. I didn't know how long my parents had been gone at the time—off on a bender, I figured. It was summer, so there wasn't any school, no way for me to measure time, but Billy said they figured it had been at least three weeks. I'd been living on cereal and ramen noodles, wondering when they'd be back. Wondering if they'd ever come back.

They hadn't.

I didn't know what it was that had inspired Billy to take me home. But who knew where I would have ended up if I'd been put in the system. Certainly not where I was now, with an Ivy League degree and a highly competitive job in journalism.

Once I unloaded the stacks of clothes onto his bed—which I would absolutely catch shit for—I headed back out.

"Need anything before I go?"

"Nah. Thanks for Gino's. Sure hit the spot."

"Anytime, Billy." I clapped him on the shoulder as I passed. "Tell Peg I said hi."

"In your dreams. She'd pick you over me twelve times over ten."

I laughed, opening the door. "Bye, Pop."

"See you tomorrow, son."

Down the stairs I went and back into the street, pointing myself toward Midtown and work, where I'd already turned in my recount of the Gatsby party. It had poured out of me the second I opened my laptop, the remains of the party still fresh and clear and eager to fill pages. The spectacle of it all. The familiar faces.

Stella Spencer.

I'd left her out for obvious reasons, leaning into the atmosphere. That was what people wanted to know, to feel. They wanted to *be* there, and I hoped I could usher them through the portal I'd been so fortunate to pass through. And with every party I was able to attend, the layers would peel back to uncover the truth, as they always did. Because I already knew there was more going on than it seemed.

I couldn't stop thinking about the look I'd find on Stella's face when I rose to her challenge and finagled my way in again, looking for that glass she'd promised me after the taste I couldn't forget.

It was shaping up to be one of the more memorable assignments I'd taken on.

I'd gone from Columbia to freelancing, submitting articles to everything from the *Times* to *Washington Post* to *Esquire* and *Vagabond*, hoping to impress someone enough to give me a permanent job. And for five years, that paid the bills. But it was a piece I had done about sex workers—three months of deep on-the-streets research, a broken nose and near stabbing by a pimp, and too many fights with johns to count—that had gotten the attention of my editor and won me the coveted staff writer title. And when I was through with the Bright Young Things, I'd hop a plane and fly into a war zone, so I could experience the pain of those who were stripped of everything in the hopes that maybe, if I did my job well, I could incite some change in the world.

Heat wafted off the pavement as I traversed the six blocks to the office. By the time I walked into the cool, crisp lobby, sweat had dampened my shirt, and I patted myself on the swampy back for deciding on shorts and Vans over jeans and combats.

It seemed like there was music everywhere—from the rock playing in the common areas to our personal preferences playing in our small, glass-walled offices. There were no suits and ties, no pencil skirts and pearls. We weren't one of those hippie tech companies who didn't believe in chairs or had Segways to ride through the private dog park, but we were the height of casual. Nobody gave a fuck what you were wearing, and we had everything from bonkers, off-the-runway getups to shredded jeans and Ramones tees. But it was a *live and let live* sort of place, one that valued originality and beauty in words and imagery above all.

My editor's assistant, Kendall, rolled her chair over and stuck her head out of her office. "Levi, Yara wants to see you. About the BYT."

I frowned. "She already read it?"

"Uh-huh." She winked before rolling back to her desk.

Whatever the hell that means.

I had a hard time believing I was about to get praised. She was going to slash the shit out of my prose, no doubt. Remind me I wasn't Truman Capote. Tell me the article was canceled. But whatever it was, I doubted it would be good.

I knocked on Yara's doorframe, interrupting the intense eye contact she had with her computer screen. She blinked and smiled.

"You wanted to see me?" I started.

"I did. Have a seat." When I did, she snapped her laptop closed and leaned back in her chair. "I read the piece."

"I heard."

"You look surprised."

I shrugged. "When was the last time you read an article of mine within an hour of me sending it?"

A laugh. "Never. But I'm as curious as the next girl about what goes on at those parties. When's the next one?"

"Next week. You pulling the plug?"

"Nope. I'm here to push you full steam ahead."

Relieved, I smiled. "Good, probably would have still gone."

"If you hadn't, I'd have happily taken your place. Because if it's anything like you described, it defies imagination. I'm not ashamed to say, I'm jealous as fuck that it was you and not me who got to go. What's the next theme?"

"Don't know."

"Oh, come on. The secret's protected by our confidentiality agreement."

"What confidentiality agreement?" I said on a laugh.

"Don't make me beg."

"Sorry, boss," I goaded her even though I really didn't know the answer. "Guess you'll find out when I turn in my next piece."

Yara sighed. "Asshole."

I smiled. "Anything else?"

"Just that. This is good, Levi. Really good. Like, cover-story good."

My heart skipped again, this time for new reasons. "You think?"

"It's what I'm pushing for. Mind if I send notes? If you can send revisions today, I can put it in for proof."

My brows pinched together. "It wasn't meant to stand alone. I just needed it out of my head. Material for the big piece."

"I know, but it never hurts to have something this good locked and loaded. Cool?"

Against my better judgment, I said, "Yeah, cool."

She offered a winning smile. "If Marcella doesn't flip her shit, I'm kicking her out and taking her job."

I laughed at the image of Yara literally kicking our editor in chief out of her chair and sinking her skinny ass into it. "A coup?" I asked as I stood. "You're gonna need rebels."

"Good thing I've got a whole office of them to enlist. Now get out so I can get your notes together, and don't leave for the day until you send them back."

"Yes, sir."

She snorted a laugh, and I left her office on a track for mine. Yara had put a little swagger in my step with the praise, and by the time I sat down at my computer, I found myself with an abundance of hope.

A cover story. My dream gig when it was done. More parties, where I would see *a lot* more of Stella, if I was lucky.

And I was feeling real lucky.

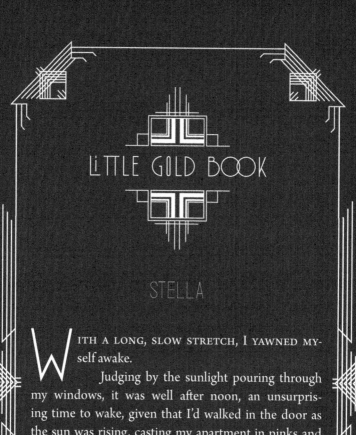

LITTLE GOLD BOOK

STELLA

WITH A LONG, SLOW STRETCH, I YAWNED MY-
self awake.

Judging by the sunlight pouring through my windows, it was well after noon, an unsurprising time to wake, given that I'd walked in the door as the sun was rising, casting my apartment in pinks and purples.

Apartment was perhaps an understatement—a five-thousand-square-foot loft in Tribeca was a coveted real estate purchase by anyone's standards. A gift from my father when I'd graduated from high school with my name on the deed. His name was on the deed to the building.

My parents' divorce when I was a little girl had been very ugly and very public, though I didn't catch the worst of it—my time was spent in the company of nannies and tutors. Dad left our Upper East penthouse on impact, and Mom was as present as ever, which meant I saw her a few times a week in passing. But the upside to their chaos was a newfound level of freedom—I was allowed to have sleepovers whenever I wanted.

Which was how Betty became the closest thing I had to a sister.

Her dad was always on the road, and her mom went with him, leaving Betty's grandma, Sheila, in charge. So I spent most nights over there, so happy for the company, I'd have moved in if they'd let me. I found a place there, a happy place where straight As were celebrated with Funfetti cupcakes and breaking curfew got you a talking-to. Theirs were the faces I looked for in the crowd at dance recitals, the people I celebrated my life with.

It was then that I'd learned I could choose my family. And I'd chosen Betty and Sheila.

I know, I know—poor little rich girl. Don't get me wrong. I didn't hate my parents, and we never fought. Never once had they raised their voices to me in fact, and I'd never even been grounded. Mom was pleasant and always seemed happy. Dad was distant, but his job was so demanding, we barely knew each other. I didn't hate them or even resent them. Because I wouldn't have had Betty and Sheila otherwise.

When she died a few years ago, Betty and I were lost. We spent a solid month in bed, nurturing each other's grief. But nothing could mend the empty space she'd left, the only mother figure we'd ever known. But we still had each other, and that was something. Something that tempered our friendship to steel.

My father, whom I hadn't seen in years, put an obscene amount of money in a trust for me before the divorce—strictly to keep it from my mother's bank account, I was certain. Not that it fazed her. She jumped straight into the next handsome Italian leather wallet. Then the next. Six weddings I'd attended—the seventh around the corner—and as a result, I had enough stepsiblings to make a baseball team.

I thought Mom was in Malta. Or was it the Riviera? Mostly, I kept up with her through her Instagram as she yachted her way through the Mediterranean with her silver fox du jour. Occasionally, we texted. Once a year or so, we called. Every couple of years, I saw her for another of her weddings. But we hadn't spent a Christmas together since I was in high school, and my birthday gifts always came by way of a courier.

Though I would have given just about anything to have a mother, a family, their absence hadn't bothered me so much after I found Betty. I'd made a home for my heart where my best friend loved me and my surrogate grandma cared for me. A place where I could escape what might hurt me, a place where I was safe. And we'd made that place perfect, never without a plan of attack for fun and foe alike. Whenever we had to do something we didn't want to do, we'd reward ourselves with something fun. Concert tickets. Shopping sprees. An epic night out when we were older. Sparkle Bombs, we called them. Because everyone knew if you got hit with a sparkle bomb, you'd never get the glitter off. And that was exactly how we liked it—we wanted to be covered in happy forever, thankyouverymuch.

We chose to be happy instead of sad, much preferring to ignore the bad and focus solely on the good. Life was so much easier that way, so much more fun.

Even in high school, we partied with the same crew we were with now. Prep school friends turned into college friends—Betty and I graduated from NYU a few years ago, and no one else strayed far from Manhattan. Our core group spanned ages from mid-twenties into early-thirties, the overlap bridged by siblings and mutual friends. Plenty of people had come and gone, but in the end, we were a unit, a force, a familiar space.

And the creation of the Bright Young Things had only brought us closer together. We were a big, unruly family, a gang echoing the idea of a chosen family. The experiences we shared were some of the best in my memory.

Just another reason why I slipped into Cecelia Beaton's shoes. We wanted to take things bigger, and I didn't do anything halfway.

I rolled over with a sigh, pulling a spare pillow into my chest. Last night's party slid into my mind, replacing lingering shadows with glitter and shine. It'd been a smash, and we'd hit no trouble with the cops, thank God. The constant badgering by Commissioner Warren had stopped being cute months ago, and though we always had our permits in place, some things were just unavoidable. Like serving underage kids.

You might tell Billie Eilish she couldn't have a drink, but I wasn't going to.

But last night had been perfect, utterly and completely.

Including the kiss.

A smile spread on my face, then through my chest, and I sighed again. *That Kiss.*

Levi and I had watched each other across the room for the rest of the night, though neither of us made a move. It was anyone's guess why he didn't, but as for me? If I'd gotten within ten feet of him, who knew where we would have ended up—a bathroom stall, a dark alley, any secluded corner we could have found. Certainly nowhere with a bed and definitely somewhere one of us would have gotten tetanus. Instead, we'd left the challenge I'd set hanging between us with anticipation on its tail. Because if he managed to get into a party again, it'd be tetanus or bust.

And God, I hoped he showed up again.

I took a long moment to recount my memories of him, from the first moment I'd seen him through *That Kiss.* Every time I'd spotted him, his eyes had been trained on me, his gaze locking me down like shackles. Hot, steamy shackles that did something tingly to my nethers. Poor, neglected nethers that tingled just at the memory.

He'd be the perfect diversion, the best kind of distraction. My very own Sparkle Bomb after the drudgery of spending the last month trying to get over Dex. Something casual and easy, something to make me feel good. I needed casual and easy. Complicated disinterested me on the molecular level.

With the flip of my covers, I rolled out of bed in search of coffee. A twist of my hair had it in a bun as I padded down the hall and into the open living space, walled in by floor-to-ceiling windows that overlooked a crosscut of Manhattan, with Midtown rising in the distance and the East River beyond.

I had just started the espresso machine when the door flew open, and Betty walked in wearing her dress from last night, hands in the air and heels hooked in her index fingers.

"I am the queen of the world!" she proclaimed as the door closed behind her.

"That good, huh?" I asked.

"Better." She tossed her shoes and reached into her cleavage to extract her ID and money. "How about you?" She glanced around. "Where's that beefcake who had laser eyes on you all night?"

"I told you I wasn't hooking up with him. But if he manages to show up to Cirque Du Freak next week, all bets are off."

"Zeke and I were really hoping you'd cave and hook up with him anyway."

"You're a terrible influence."

"Thank you," she said earnestly, laying her hand over mine.

The keypad on the door beeped, and I frowned in its direction, wondering which of my friends was on the other side just before the door flew open.

And Zeke blew in like hellfire.

He was light and dark, his face fresh and furious. Hair was combed back to expose his undercut in a streak of platinum, the rest of him swathed in black from his Chucks to his jeans to his tee. Even on a regular day, Zeke was quite possibly the most beautiful man I'd ever seen, but with his jaw filed steel and his eyes glinting with rage, he looked like an angel of death. Trailing behind him were two massive suitcases, one of them sprouting boa feathers from the zipper.

"Why didn't anybody tell me Roman was a useless shitbag?" The door slammed, and Zeke whipped the suitcases around before letting them go. They rolled several feet away before coming to a stop, but he was already storming to my liquor cabinet, ignoring the bar cart for the serious stuff. "I need a fucking drink."

Betty and I exchanged a glance.

"What did he do now?" I asked, watching him slam a bottle of whiskey on the counter and tear open the cabinet where the glasses were.

"What the fuck didn't he do?" He poured until the glass was three-quarters full. A dry laugh escaped him. "Drugs? Fine, what's new? Being an asshole? That's a fucking Tuesday. Getting blown by a twink in the bathroom? What-thefuck-ever. But fucking Magnus Dixon in *our* bed at *our* place in *my fucking clothes* is the end. It's the goddamn end of the motherfucking line." In one spectacular motion, he knocked back the glass, downed it, and set the glass down on the counter with an aggressive clink and a wince. "He even let that bitch wear my Marco Marco and then had the nerve to ask if I wanted it back. He's lucky I didn't fucking kill him."

Neither of us spoke, too shocked to know what kind of answer he needed.

He poured another drink. "They've been seeing each other for months. Months he's lied to me. I should have known. I'm so fucking stupid for not seeing it." A noisy breath through his nose nearly stuck his nostrils together. "I'm done. *Done*." He slammed the second and snapped the word, "*Fucker.*"

"I don't know what you were doing with that using whore anyway, Z," Betty said, shooting for detachment. "Know your worth!"

Zeke let out a laugh. "Bitch was lucky he had all this. Next time, do your jobs and don't let me move in with a liar." His smile fell. "One rule—that's all I have. *One rule*: do not fucking lie to me. So I'm moving in, Stell."

"I figured," I teased, nodding to his suitcases. With a couple of steps, I closed the gap between us to thread my arms around his narrow waist, pressing my ear to his chest where his heart thundered. "Stay as long as you want, Zeke."

He wrapped his arms around me, clinging to me as he took a shuddering breath. "I loved him," he said softly.

"I know."

A stretch of silence passed. "This is why I came here, Star Bright. It's impossible to be sad around you. You are the brightest, warmest, most sparkly star in the sky." With another breath, Zeke packed his feelings away and swiped at his cheeks with twin flicks. Like Betty, he glanced around, looking for Levi, no doubt.

"Where's your pretty boy? Tell me he's here. I need cheering up."

"God, you guys are the worst," I said. "I told you I wasn't going home with him."

Zeke made a face. "Wait—you were serious?"

Betty gestured to him with her brows up and a silent *see?* sitting in her upturned palm.

"Yes, I was serious."

He sighed. "You always were the moral one."

I snorted a laugh. "The bar's pretty low."

Zeke shrugged. "Think he'll come to the next one?"

"I sure hope so. I'm almost tempted to text Ash. Gentle pressure couldn't hurt." I picked up my double espresso and took a sip. "Wonder if he has a costume."

"Because who doesn't have Victorian circus attire in the back of their closet?" Betty asked with a dramatic sweep of her hands.

"What do you mean? That's not normal?" Zeke asked, mirroring her pose.

She giggled and threw an apple at him, which he caught. "Then can I borrow something?"

"As soon as I get all my shit from that dirty whore's place, be my guest." Zeke turned to me and took a bite out of the apple. "What's left to do for the next party?"

"Nothing. Genie said everything's confirmed, circus tent and everything."

"Thank God for that girl," he said. "Can you imagine having to plan all this shit on your own?"

"It would take about seven minutes for Commissioner Warren to figure it out if I did."

"Plus, it would just plain old suck," Betty said from the pantry. "Who wants to spend all day getting permits?"

"No one," Zeke answered. "But scheming it all up? Therein lies the fun."

"Speaking of, we should talk about the next scavenger hunt," I suggested.

Betty clapped, which was a feat with the bagel in her hand, but she managed. "Finally, the *Breakfast at Tiffany's* hunt. I have been waiting for this for months."

Zeke eyed her. "How about you shower before we have a family meeting? You smell like Drakkar Noir."

Betty made a *blah-blah* face. "I would insult you, but I'll give you a break since you just got dumped by *Homan*."

"Look at you, being all charitable." He headed to his suitcases. "I'm gonna unpack while Betty washes her parts off. Stell—order Thai, and let's Golightly this scavenger hunt. I'm starving."

"Yes, ma'am."

I listened to them rib each other down the hall toward their rooms with a smile on my face, glad for their company, grateful for the noise. Coffee in hand, I headed for my room where my planner awaited, unassuming, on my nightstand. It had no markings to distinguish what it was, no indication of its importance, just a simply bound planner in shades of pink and cream and gold foil.

My little gold book.

With a flip of the cover, I thumbed my way through the calendar to the sections I'd designated for each party. The planner had gotten so fat at one point, I'd been forced to take out the inserts for parties past, storing them in a photo box for safekeeping and reference. Honestly, I should have burned them, but the thought of torching all that hard work made my stomach crawl.

I slid my gold pen from its loop and jotted down a few notes for the *Breakfast at Tiffany's* scavenger hunt, but my mind was a thousand miles and a week away. Because if there was one thing I knew how to do, it was hope.

And my biggest hope was that I'd see Levi again.

HAVE THE CAKE, EAT THE CAKE

"COME ON, ASH. I THOUGHT WE HAD A DEAL?"

I walked the stretch of my living room with my phone pressed to my ear, sweaty first from the gym, then my run home, and eager for a shower. But first things first.

Ash answered through a yawn, "We did have a deal." He smacked his lips. "One party."

I rolled my eyes, heading for the stairs to the loft. "We never specified how many parties."

"I already lost a shot at Lily James—she's going to the circus party tomorrow night with that fucking beatnik poet, the Instagram famous one who writes with a quill because it's ironic. I blame you."

"Hadn't picked up on that."

"I'm at least eighty-nine percent sure I've got Grace Elizabeth convinced to come with me. You're cute and all, but you're no Guess model."

"And I won't sleep with you, so quit begging."

"Exactly." Sheets shuffled on the other end of the line.

I raked my free hand through my damp hair, pulling my tee out of my waistband to toss it in the hamper. "You owe me, Ash."

"I know I fucking owe you, but you're really interfering with my game, man."

"What game?"

"God, you're a real comedian, you know that? Listen—I can't be on the hook for this forever."

"Can't you? I'm pretty sure if Billy hadn't gotten you off the hook for your furniture-stealing shenanigans at Columbia, you would have been expelled."

A sigh.

"I've never called the favor in, not until now," I reminded him, "so here's the deal. You're going to bring me to all the parties I want to attend, and when it's all said and done, we're square."

He paused for a beat. "For good?"

"For good. If I'm being honest, I never planned to cash in on it."

"Do us all a favor and quit being honest. Some things are better left unsaid."

I chuckled, eyeing the leather chairs in my bedroom, wanting to sit but unwilling to ruin any furniture with the buckets of sweat the Manhattan summer had blessed me with. I opted for the bench at the foot of my bed instead, leaning to rest my forearm on my thigh.

"It's not that I don't want to help you, man. I do. But this is bigger than me just taking you to a party. You're lying about why you're there, and I've betrayed the sacred code by sneaking a reporter in."

"I haven't lied to anyone."

"Yet. At some point, somebody's going to ask you what you do, and somehow I doubt you're going to tell them there's a press pass in your pocket."

"You act like I don't do this all the time."

"Levi Hunt, professional liar."

"As far as anybody at these parties knows, I'm Levi Jepsen, the photographer—I've got a website and everything."

"Smart, since you are one, even if not professionally. And Billy's last name? Not totally a lie, I guess. I mean, except for the fact that you're writing about the group without their knowledge or permission. But hey, who am I to judge? Other than being the asshole sticking his neck out for you."

I rubbed the back of my neck. "Ash, you know I wouldn't ask you for this if it wasn't important. This is the gateway to—"

"All your dreams coming true or some shit—yeah, yeah. I get it. I do. And I know you've got this idea that I'll get to play dumb and not be implicated when they find out—because they will whether you tell them or they see your stupid mug next to the headline in the magazine. But I can't pretend like I didn't know you're a reporter, and I won't. The best I can do is say I didn't know that you were writing about us. And if they don't buy that, I'm throwing you under the bus."

"Please, throw me under the bus. Tell them I tricked you into it—I'll back your story up. Whatever I have to do to protect you, I'll do it. You have my word."

"The word of the king of bullshitters?"

"Oh, come on. What have I ever lied about but this? I don't have a choice. This is how I get places I'm not supposed to be."

He sighed again, and I thought I heard the scratch of stubble against his hand. "And what about Stella Spencer?"

My heart tha-dummed at the sound of her name. "What about her?"

"Somehow I get the feeling next time you see her, you'll exchange more than a kiss. Are you gonna lie to her too?"

"About what I do for a living? I don't see what other choice I have, do you?"

"No. Because if you tell her, you can kiss your admittance to the parties goodbye."

"I'm not looking for anything serious, Ash, not when I'm leaving the country for an undetermined amount of time."

"Which is just fine. But what about her?"

I had no answer to that.

"This group of us … I don't know if you understand what we are to each other. You've been around us, sure, but … well, we're family. We've been at this for a decade, and most of us have known each other since elementary school. Stella just got her heart stomped to pulp by Dex Macy, and I don't want her to get hurt by you too. Lying to the group as a whole is one thing. Lying to her when you're into each other is another."

I took a breath. Let it out. Thought it through. "You're not wrong. She's not interested in a casual thing?"

"Maybe. I don't know. I haven't read her diary or anything."

"So how about this? I'll play it casual, let her know I'm leaving before anything happens, and see where she's at. If she's just looking for a hookup, we'll be fine—"

"You think just because you hook up without strings, she'll be *fine* with you lying to her?"

"Again, you act like I haven't done this before. She'll be mad for a minute, but she'll understand when I tell her. Especially if I'm not ripping the group to shreds."

"You're a walking contradiction."

I ignored him. "I'll come clean the second it's over, well before anything is published."

"You make it sound like you know what you're doing."

"Because I do. Trust me."

"Beyond all reason, I do." Another sigh, this one resigned. "Fine, I'll bring you. Just watch your ass, all right?"

Relief took the place of my worry. "Always do."

And when I hung up, it was with the satisfaction that came with having your cake and eating it too.

FEED THE PYTHON

STELLA

"HOLD STILL, OR THE WING ON YOUR LINER IS gonna look like a heart monitor," Zeke warned.

With a sigh, I did what I'd been told and kept as still as I could, but it wasn't easy with Betty trying on wigs and performing monologues behind me.

I sat at Zeke's massive gold vanity, which took up a third of one of his bedroom walls. Over the last week, we'd gotten all his things moved in, and because Zeke was Zeke, the room was as good as home within twelve hours of the boxes and furniture delivery. Somehow, between shows at Supertramp and partying, he'd even found time to paint the walls emerald green. The room was huge, big enough for a queen-size bed to stand in the center of the room, housed in a gold frame that was likely meant to be a canopy, though he hadn't put one on. The only other color in the room was navy, and almost all of it was velvet, from his fluffy duvet to the bench at the foot of the bed and even the cylindrical tufted seat under my ass. Everything else was gold and deco and elegant. Just like Zeke.

I mean, if we didn't count what came out of his mouth.

One of the walls was covered in wigs so masterfully, it looked like an art display. It was this wall that Betty had chosen to occupy herself with while she waited her turn.

"God, I wish I had hair like this," Betty said, and when Z was finally finished with my liner, I looked over to find her stroking the gorgeous white hair that was so long and thick, it fell past her waist.

"Honey, everybody wishes they had hair like that," Z said, turning my chin back in his direction. "Look up."

I did, trying not to blink as he applied my mascara.

Zeke was already done up as Zelda—all she had left to do was to put on her costume. Her hair, which reached her chin when it wasn't slicked back, had been parted on one side, and over each ear were massive red roses attached to golden ram's horns and a headpiece of dangling tassels and golden coins. Dark shadow and smoky liner made her look like a bedouin, which was appropriate since she was going as a snake charmer—rumor had it that Zelda Fitzperil could tame any snake regardless of size or aggression. She even had a gigantic fake albino python that looked so real, I refused to touch it.

Where Betty and I came from the one percent, Zeke had grown up in Paris, Texas—a tiny town in the northeast corner of the state, close to both the Oklahoma *and* Alabama borders. They had a miniature Eiffel Tower and everything.

No one was surprised that a town named Paris had produced Zeke, not even if that town was in Texas. It was the best sort of joke cannon fodder, but those of us who knew him well knew those jokes covered up the unpleasant truths of growing up in Paris, Texas as a gay kid whose favorite pastimes included sewing elaborate costumes and doing everyone's makeup he could get to sit still for him, including his own.

"I wish Joss had made it back for this party. She's gonna be so mad she missed it—and by a day. What a dick punch," Betty said, inspecting herself in the full-length gilded mirror leaning against the wall.

"Our roommate, the romcom sweetheart of the silver screen. I can't wait until she's back. We need her mellow to balance out the two of you," I said.

"How long's she been gone?" Z asked. "Two months now?"

"Three," Betty and I answered in unison.

"Now all we need is for Tag to come and stay, and Zekey will be a happy girl." Z popped the lid off a liner pencil like she was unveiling the Crown Jewels.

Betty and I groaned at the mention of my stepbrother, who was the richest transient in the world and held the title of the most magnificent douche bag to ever live.

"Oh, stop it. He's not that bad."

Betty scoffed, "Easy for you to say. You've never had him shove his tongue down your throat without warning before."

"And what a shame that is," Z mourned. "Honestly, I'm shocked you'll still have two free rooms when Joss gets back," she started. "You collect friends like some people collect nesting dolls."

"Stella Spencer's Strays," Betty said, gesturing like she was reading a marquee.

"Boardinghouse of the stars," Z added.

"We should make a sign," Betty decided.

"And lucky for you two assholes," I said on a laugh. "God, I can't even imagine what it would be like to live here alone." My nose wrinkled.

"You could make a room for every occasion. Like a room full of tiaras," Z said with the flip of her hand.

"Or you could go the other way. Become a recluse and have

a room for every cat." Betty flipped her hair like a stripper and smirked at herself in the mirror. "Think Levi will find his way in tonight?"

"Oh, he's gonna find his way in, all right," Z said, looking down her nose as she lined my lips. "All the way in 'til he hits the end."

I tried to talk without moving my mouth, but Z shot me a look that shut me up.

"What you need is a fling," Betty said, exchanging her wig for another, this one a mass of auburn curls so thick, I didn't think you could get a hand in there if it wasn't attached to a pair of scissors. Maybe not even then.

"A fling." Z laughed. "Stella can't help but love any and everybody. It's one of the reasons everybody loves her right back." Finished lining, she booped my nose. "But casual sex? That's more for you and me, Betty. Not Star Bright."

"I can do casual sex," I argued.

Z and Betty locked eyes and burst into laughter.

"What? I can. I was in a non-thing with Dex for two years."

"Even if I didn't know you were in love with him, the fact that you just said *years* automatically excludes it from being even remotely casual," Z said.

"Maybe I just have bad taste."

"You have impeccable taste," Z assured me. "You just trust the wrong guys."

"Ugh, Dex," Betty started, never taking her eyes off the mirror as she posed for herself. "I hope he gets genital warts."

"It wouldn't have been so bad if he'd really believed his stupid creed about monogamy, but the whole line was bullshit." I said. "He didn't up and change his mind about monogamy. He didn't rewrite his rules for Elsie Richmond—he made up a bunch of nonsense to feed to me so he could fuck whoever he wanted."

"Be still," Zelda Fitzperil commanded, and nobody disobeyed Zelda. "Listen—you trust first and ask questions later. It's one of your great qualities, but sometimes our best qualities are flaws, and this, honey, is one of yours."

I sighed, held hostage as she dabbed on my lipstick.

"Right now you're asking me with your pretty little brain, *How do I fix it, Z? How do I become a savage bitch who gets what she wants? Teach me your wise ways. Impart upon me your sage wisdom.* And here it is—fuck the brains out of that boy tonight and do not, under any circumstance, exchange numbers."

My brows clicked together.

"Quit it. You're going to give yourself elevens, and you're too young for Botox. Blot."

I rolled my lips together before blotting them on a tissue. "What if I like him?"

"Then you *definitely* don't exchange numbers," Betty said as she approached with a French Revolutionary wig, swirled to look like pink cotton candy. "I don't know why you didn't go as cotton candy, Z. This wig is incredible."

"Because I wore it to the Candy party, and I'll be goddamned if I wear the same wig twice to our parties."

Betty sighed. "I don't know why I'm even bothering. It's not like I'm getting laid." She shot Z an accusatory look.

"Don't gimme that," Z warned. "You're the one who suggested I go man-free. It's only fair you should have to do it with me."

"You mean *not* do it," she corrected. "Whatever. You're going to cave, and then we'll both be free of the pact."

"That right there is exactly why I won't cave. It's like you've never met me."

"I know you too well, which is why I'm banking on you folding like a bad poker hand." Betty hinged to look at herself in the vanity mirror. "Sex or no sex, I still should have worn it."

"Probably. Because I'm about to tease your hair so hard, you'll be tasting Aqua Net for a week." Z leaned back to inspect her handiwork. "I'm a fucking artist. The end. Now, your hair."

Betty primped next to me. "This Levi guy is hot for sure, but you haven't dated anybody in the month since Dex, and before that, you were only with him. Even though he was fucking half of Manhattan."

I gave her a look in the mirror.

"I'm just saying that you're loyal and your heart is huge, which is why it's always getting bruised. Assholes are always bumping into it."

I chuckled while Z brushed my hair. "Last week, you two were practically shoving me into Levi's lap, and now you don't want me to see him?"

"That's because we thought it'd be a one-time thing," Z explained as we were swallowed up by a cloud of hair spray. "And anyway, we don't care if you see him. Just don't fall in love until you're sure he's not a scumbag. 'Kay?"

"You act like I fall in love every Wednesday."

Z backcombed my hair with what I could only describe as aggression. "No, it's that when it comes to you, what you see is what you get. You don't count on the other eighty-nine percent of people who only show you what they want you to see."

"We're just saying to watch out, that's all." Betty stood, cupping my shoulder and meeting my eyes in the mirror. "If you don't, we're afraid you'll keep getting hurt."

"Honestly, I don't want to fall in love. I just want to be happy, enjoy the company of someone without complications, and I think Levi might be that guy. I mean, assuming he shows up tonight."

But Z smirked. "If he doesn't, he's the dumbest motherfucker breathing air."

"Amen," Betty said with a praise hand in the air.

And with my heart afloat, I put all my faith behind that happy thought.

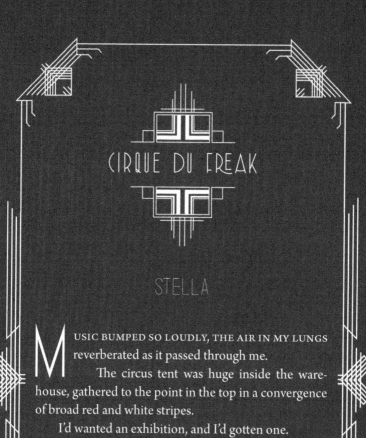

CIRQUE DU FREAK

STELLA

MUSIC BUMPED SO LOUDLY, THE AIR IN MY LUNGS reverberated as it passed through me.

The circus tent was huge inside the warehouse, gathered to the point in the top in a convergence of broad red and white stripes.

I'd wanted an exhibition, and I'd gotten one.

Strings of bulbs followed the upward curve of the tent and ran around the circumference, illuminating the scene with quiet golden light. From nearly invisible framework hung trapeze bars and tightropes, hoops and ropes for aerial dancers, strewn among sparkling stars and white crescent moons. The performers—secured via off-season Cirque du Soleil staff—rotated their talents, swinging and flying and dancing forty feet above the crowd, which was a sea of top hats and fascinators and velvet and black and white stripes. A spinning wheel stood where one could have knives thrown at them, if they were so inclined, and the crowd was interrupted by swirls of motion around performers, everything from stilt walkers to hoop dancers to fire-breathing jugglers. A fortune teller's tent stood in deep purple and gold and mystery near the back, and I made a plan to find out what was inside. I salivated at the scent of roasted peanuts and popcorn hanging in the air, and in the center of the tent, in the black-and-white checkered ring, was the bouncing dance floor.

It was happiness and hedonism, an escape into another world, another time. One where things were uncomplicated, simple. If only for tonight, we would all live in a moment we'd never get again.

I glanced at the entrance again to the jump of my heart, making excuses. Checking for a glimpse of Genie to give me a sense of how things were going behind the scenes. Or scanning for Dex, my nerves unready to see him for the first time since our split. He'd stayed away out of deference, I supposed, but I'd heard a rumor he would be here tonight and felt unprepared. Who knew if I'd ever feel prepared.

But the truth was, they were all excuses, nothing more. Because I was looking for Levi, no bones about it.

When I forced myself to tear my eyes away from the entrance, I wondered how I'd been so thoroughly distracted by Levi that I barely thought about Dex until today. I didn't even know Levi, didn't know his last name, hadn't exchanged more than a few minutes of conversation with him. But then I remembered *That Kiss*, and everything made sense again.

The anticipation of seeing him had been almost unbearable, my thoughts consumed with imaginings of him showing up, musings over what would happen if he did. I'd maintained my cool and refrained from texting Ash, but now that I was here—and had been here for well over an hour—my confidence waned with every minute that passed. Ash had probably turned him down in favor of Lily James. Or Levi wasn't interested and hadn't even considered coming.

"If you stare at that door any longer, you're going to set it on fire." Z handed me a whiskey and smirked.

I should have heard her coming with all the jingling chains and coins she wore in her headdress, circling her hips, and draped from the bra top she wore. Her arms were cuffed in gold, wrists and biceps, and her skirt flowed brilliantly, topped off by a tasseled sash and leather belt trimmed with—you guessed it—more jingly metal. Her snake draped around her neck and arms and watched me with what I was convinced was menace.

"I don't know what you're talking about," I answered lightly.

"You should go see the fortune teller. She can look into her crystal ball and tell you if you're going to get laid tonight."

"How'd you know she has a crystal ball?"

"What self-respecting fortune teller doesn't?"

I gave her a look.

She rolled her eyes, her insane black lashes brushing her carefully manicured eyebrows. "Obviously I went there first. You're not the only one who wants to know if they're getting laid tonight."

"Who said I'm hoping to get laid?"

"That look on your face."

That face flattened.

She looked me over. "I can't believe you went with ringmaster. Little on the nose, don't you think?"

I looked down at my costume—black vest with nothing beneath, red velvet coat with tails, bustled black hi-low petticoat, fishnets, black T-strap shoes. With a glance back at the crowd, I spotted a dozen more ringmasters in shouting distance.

"Take a look around, Z. I'm unoriginal tonight."

"Well, you're the hottest one, indisputably."

Betty bounded up the steps to the platform where we stood, one of many placed around the room—a perch from which to admire my work. She was dressed as the sexiest, least creepy clown I'd ever seen—black-and-white harlequin corset, black bloomers trimmed with stripes, her hair teased into a coiffure that was going to take her three days to untangle, her tiny top hat nestled in her black locks. Her face was painted with starburst eyes and bowed lips that stretched into a smile.

"Ash just got here," she said, a little out of breath. She stole a sip of Z's drink.

And my heart and stomach swapped places when I looked to the door.

Levi was scanning the crowd, his profile cut against red velvet. His costume was mellow, which I'd somehow expected, not pegging him for one to go over the top, particularly not for a costume party. He wore a black vest and pants, his white tailored shirt cuffed to the elbows and unbuttoned at the neck—basically what he'd worn last week. Tucked under his arm were three bowling pins.

A laugh shot out of me, my hand moving to my lips as if to erase it. And though he was too far away to have heard me, he paused, turned his face toward me, and looked me dead in the eye.

It happened again, that rubber band stretching of time, a flashbulb moment to burn a negative behind my eyelids. Slowly, we smiled in unison, interrupted by Ash smacking Levi's chest and rolling his eyes.

When I turned back to Betty and Z, they were laughing at me. I scowled back.

"*Somebody's getting laid tonight,*" Betty sang, and Z chimed in, the two of them skipping in place and doing their best to humiliate me.

"Oh my God, *shut up!*"

They burst into laughter again, mercifully cutting their shit out before Levi was on the platform with us and standing dangerously close to me.

I cocked my head, schooling my grin into a coy smile. "Look at that. You got in."

His hand slid into my waist. "I'm surprised you doubted me. I don't often give up. Especially not when lips like yours are involved."

I laughed, the sound breezy despite the buzzing excitement in my chest.

Before I could answer, a pair of girls somehow fell *up* the steps and into Z, spilling her drink.

She gave them a look.

"Oh my God, Courtney—I told you!" She turned to Z. "You're Zelda Fitzperil, right?"

Z somehow managed to both smile and look unamused. "And you're drunk, right?"

They tittered.

Not-Courtney listed a little and said, "Only a little."

"God, you're so pretty," Courtney cooed. "I paid two hundred bucks for a makeup artist tonight, and look!" She swiped under her eye and shoved the inky remains of her mascara in Z's face.

Not-Courtney pushed Courtney's arm down. "We just wanted to say you got robbed on *Drag Race*. You shoulda won. Everybody knows it."

At that, Z's smile was genuine, if not a little salty. "Don't worry, baby. Second place is just the bottom of the pair, and I can get off on either."

We chuckled, but Courtney and Not-Courtney doubled over. Not-Courtney snorted.

"He's so funny!" she said to Courtney, who elbowed her.

"She, you asshole." Courtney's face swiveled to Z, visibly confused. "Right?"

"You can call me whatever you want—I'll answer to just about anything. Especially the sound of a cash register."

Always on, always performing, always looking for a laugh. And Z got them.

Not-Courtney fumbled with her clutch. "I've gotta get a pic."

Courtney slapped the sparkly purse from her hands. "God, you are so tacky. I'm sorry," she said, holding Not-Courtney steady as she patted the ground for her lost accessory. "We'll leave you alone. We love you!"

"You and everybody," Z said, twiddling her fingers as they swayed away. Immediately, she turned, pinning Levi with the wickedest of smiles. "You just juggle bowling pins, or do you do balls too?"

"I can juggle just about anything the situation calls for," he answered with a sideways smile.

"How versatile." Z looked him up and down. "A ball juggler and a snake charmer. What a team we'd make."

Levi laughed, but if he had a comeback, he kept it to himself.

"Some party," Ash said as he looked around the tent. He was dressed as a strongman, his hair parted down the middle and a fake mustache under his nose. His outfit was a too-tight Lycra getup that looked like an old-timey wrestling uniform in red and white stripes. His junk bulged shamelessly, and he didn't seem to notice or care, even though I knew he did, the peacock. "Cecelia did good," he noted.

"There's cotton candy," Betty said excitedly, as if it wasn't her idea. "*Boozy* cotton candy."

He blinked. "How the fuck?"

She waved a hand. "Something about soaking the sugar in liquor before spinning it. Let's go get some."

Betty hooked her arm in Ash's and discreetly winked at me, but because she was drunk, it wasn't discreet at all. Levi stifled a smile, looking down at his shoes.

"Come on. You too." Betty grabbed Z, and she frowned.

"But I wanna watch Levi juggle the balls."

"Let him have a few drinks before the ball-juggling, would you?" she insisted, dragging everyone down the stairs. "We'll be right back," she called over her shoulder.

"Subtle," Levi said.

"As a grenade," I added on a laugh. And for a moment, we were quiet. "I didn't know if you'd come," I finally said.

"I'd have snuck in if Ash hadn't agreed."

"And faced the wrath of Cecelia Beaton?" I teased. Because we'd made it a habit of publicly ridiculing anyone who broke the rules, which proved an effective method of stopping infiltrators.

He rolled one shoulder. "If it meant seeing you again? Absolutely."

My smile was too honest, and I turned to the crowd, watching the trapeze artists fly. "So a juggler, huh? Can you really do it?"

"You think I'd bring these if I couldn't use them?"

With a laugh, I stepped back, folding my arms and popping my hip. "All right. Let's see what you've got."

My God, he was handsome. Ten-day beard and shaggy, dark hair. Looming height and broad chest. There was something about his eyes, an unknowable depth with an echo of mischief. Something about his lips, lush and wide and always poised to lift on that one side. Stepping back, he flipped the cuff of his sleeves one more time and grabbed two of the pins by the neck. He looked up, his tongue darting out of his mouth to wet his lips before they pursed in concentration. And then he threw one, two, three in the air just as he caught the first.

I bounced like a little girl, giggling my delight as he tossed one after the other, end over end into the air. And then he switched it up—rather than throwing them in a big circle, they wove in and out of each other. Higher he threw them, and when they reached their peak, he spun around, somehow managing to maintain his catch and pitch. His smile was full teeth at my cheering, though he didn't dare shift his eyes until he caught them and tucked them under his arm, one, two, three.

I clapped—along with those in our vicinity—as he rolled off his hat in a bow.

"You look surprised," he said when he set the pins on the ground and made it back to my side.

"Not every day I meet a juggler."

He laughed. "I'm not any good, just a thing I learned when I was a kid."

"I beg to differ, sir."

But he was too busy taking in the circus to argue. "This really is something," he said half to himself. "I can't even imagine what a production like this costs. These parties don't *make* any money, do they?"

I shrugged as if I didn't know. "No one pays to be here, so I can't imagine how."

"Incredible," he said to the trapeze artist as she spun twice and opened up like a flower just in time to catch her partner's hands. "What's over there?" He pointed at the purple tent.

"A fortune teller. I hear she has a crystal ball."

"You're kidding."

"Serious as a blood moon."

I earned a chuckle.

"What do you say we go grab a drink and see what it's about?" he asked.

"Only if you promise to let the knife thrower put you on his spinning wheel."

"I'm game. One condition."

"What's that?"

He leaned in, his lips at my ear. "You first."

With a flush and a laugh, I leaned into him. Too soon, he backed away, grabbing my hand to lead me into the crowd.

But all the warmth Levi had inspired left me in favor of an icy stream in my veins.

Because Dex stood in the crowd, staring right at me.

His expression was carefully blank, and I wondered what was happening behind those cool blue eyes I'd once thought were mine. And tucked in his side was Elsie Richmond, her face bright and pretty and earnest under the circus lights, unaware of my presence.

A tug of my hand snapped my gaze to Levi's back as he wound through the crowd, occasionally looking up at the performers. Aerial dancers on hoops spun around making artful shapes with their bodies, the trapeze artists gone. Around the center stage we went and to the bar, and once drinks were in hand, we headed to the perimeter of the tent. By the time we reached the fire breathers, I'd mostly forgotten Dex was somewhere under the big top. I had to avoid him. Either that or make a conscious choice to walk up to him, exchange niceties, and be on my way. Preferably with Levi on my arm.

The line at the knife thrower was crazy long, which somehow shocked me. People would do anything for a thrill, including letting a rough-hewn, possibly tipsy carnie throw knives at them. The girl on the wheel screamed bloody fucking murder as she went around and around, the sound punctuated by the thunk of the knife as it sank into wood.

I laughed, pulling a chunk of Fireball cotton candy off the cone to pop it in my mouth. My fingers were sticky and would be until I was done with the confection, but I licked them off anyway, preferring saliva to sticky clumps of sugar. I'd only gotten one finger before Levi stopped me with his hand on my wrist. I glanced up at him, puzzled.

"Do that again," he said darkly, defying his smile, "and I'm throwing you over my shoulder and taking you home with me."

A shudder of heat slipped through me. "Then you'll have to do it for me. They're all sticky."

He turned my wrist over in his hand, inspecting it for a moment with a look that was almost venerating. And to my greatest surprise and pleasure, he brought my finger to his lips, his tongue visible for only a flicker before his lips closed. The sweep of his tongue, the heat of his mouth were a promise. One I wanted fulfilled.

"Stella?"

I jumped, snatching my hand back at the sound of that familiar voice.

"Dex!" I put on my best fake smile and leaned in to kiss him on the cheek in the grandest of shows. "Good to see you," I lied.

He smiled down at Elsie, who was straight up beaming at me like a sweet, beautiful little fairy. So I directed the flaming beam at him alone. She'd figure out he was a garbage person. Eventually.

"I'd like you to meet Elsie. Elsie, this is Stella Spencer."

Plasticine smile in place, I lifted my hand. "I'd shake your hand, but ..." I held up the cotton candy in display.

"God, it's so nice to finally meet you," she said, her heart-shaped face upturned to mine. "I can't believe we've gone this long without a real introduction."

"You just moved here from California, right?" I asked with my heart pounding a rhythm that told me to run.

"San Fran," she answered. "New York is a culture shock, but Dex has made it easy." Again she was beaming, this time up at the snake himself.

But Dex's eyes shifted to Levi. The brightness from Elsie's shine flickered.

"Who's your friend?" he asked, something in the question possessive.

It was baffling. But then again, Dex had always been spoiled. And I didn't hate the idea of him regretting his decision to turn me out.

"Levi," he said with an easy charm, extending a hand.

Dex took it, giving it a hard pump.

And silence fell over us.

"Well," I started, "we were actually just wandering off. Can you believe how many people are in line? The thrill of danger or something, am I right?" *Oh my God, get out of here now.* Smiling, I waved at Elsie. "Nice to meet you, Elsie. You guys have fun."

With a set of goodbyes, we split up.

"Where to?" Levi asked, still calm and smiling at me.

I watched him for a second. "You know that was my ex, right?"

He shrugged. "Sure. Everybody knows about you and Dex."

The tightness in my chest eased on an exhale. "Just making sure. God, that was awkward. I've been dreading it for weeks."

"You haven't seen him? He hasn't been to the parties? I thought he was one of the regulars."

"He is. I think it was just a sort of … silent agreement. I got the Bright Young Things in the divorce," I joked.

Levi pulled us over to where a hoop dancer in red and gold stripes was caught in a tornado of hula hoops. A gentle tug, and I was flush against his chest, staring up at his lips. "For what it's worth, I always thought he was a douchebag."

"Wish you'd clued me in."

His hand rose to thumb my jaw, then clasp my chin, tilting it up. "Why'd you stay with him?"

"It was easy. Convenient. And he can be sweet. We were friends." *I loved him.* "I don't know."

A chuckle and a smile. "Well, I can't say I'm sad he's yesterday's news."

"Neither am I."

He laid a kiss on me, tender and brief, and even that brush of lips struck a match at my feet, the flames licking their way up my body.

When we parted, he was smiling. "Now what?"

"Let's get our future told by the charlatan in that purple tent."

Levi laughed, and I found I loved the sound. "You believe in fate and psychics?"

"As much as I believe in anything."

I pulled his hand as if I had a chance at moving a man of that size by force. But laughing, he let me drag him to the tent, pulling back the heavy curtain to enter.

The space was empty of people and bigger than it looked from the outside, the floor covered in carpets, and in the center of the room was a round table, a deck of tarot cards, and a crystal ball. A jingling of metal accompanied the fortune teller as she came out from the back, pushing the end of a fry into her mouth and dusting the salt off her hands.

"How is this empty but everyone's waiting in line to have knives thrown at them?" Levi whispered in my ear, and I stifled a laugh.

"Because people love danger more than the truth," she said, her accent more Jersey than Romany. "Please, sit."

We did as we'd been told. She eyed us, her lids lined in kohl. I couldn't peg her age—she wasn't quite old and she wasn't quite young, but her smoky, dark eyes knew a thing or two about the world.

"I would ask what you want me to read, but I know what you need. Give me your hands." She laid her hands on the table, palms up.

"No crystal ball?" I asked, disappointed.

"Feh, that thing's bullshit. It's for the suckers, not the skeptics." She gave Levi a knowing look before wiggling her fingers. "Come."

Levi and I exchanged glances before laying our hands in hers.

"Mmm," she hummed noncommittally, using her thumb to spread first my hand open and press the lines, then his. "This is new, hmm? It's strong but new."

We didn't answer. I held my breath.

"Dark and light, skeptic and mystic. One heavy, one light. One sees only good, the other what's bad. There's a place in the middle, where the sky kisses the sea. That's where you'll find it, but secrets will stop you. Trust is the only way. And if you don't …" She shrugged. But when she looked back at our hands, she frowned. "There is something else, another—"

The music went silent, replaced by a voice on a bullhorn announcing the NYPD's presence, telling everyone to stay where they were. By the sound of it, no one was listening.

"Oh fuck," she said, snagging her crystal ball as she stood, knocking back her chair. "Better run for it, you two."

We'd were already running for the tent flap that dumped us into chaos. My heart was a ticking bomb in my chest as I watched everyone panic, running in circles. The only ones who were calm were the carnies, and they seemed to just fade into the shadows and disappear.

"Come on," I said, grabbing Levi's hand. "I know a back way out."

"How do you know—"

"Shut up and *come on*!"

And thank God he did.

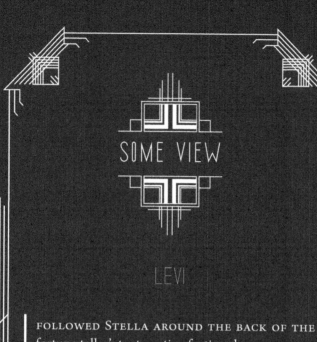

SOME VIEW

LEVI

I FOLLOWED STELLA AROUND THE BACK OF THE fortune teller's tent, casting furtive glances over my shoulder with the expectation of finding a cop with a nightstick. But they were occupied at the mouth of the tent with the cluster of youths scrabbling to get out.

Stella's hand ran along the wall of the tent, and when it disappeared into a fold, she let out a whoop of excitement. "Come on, this way."

She started to lift it, and I took the heavy flap from her, opening it enough that we could escape into the nearly pitch-black warehouse. Her heels clicked, her hand damp in mine as she moved with some certainty toward a back corner. Behind us, the tent was lit up, all red and gold and filled with pandemonium.

Stella slowed, feeling along the wall. "There has to be a door around here somewhere," she muttered.

I glanced around, looking for a sliver of light. "There," I said, pointing toward the corner.

We picked up our pace, panting as we reached the door.

Stella paused, hand on the handle. "Hope it's not an emergency exit."

"And if it is, get ready to run."

A curt nod, and she pushed, opening it just enough to peer out. I leaned over her to get a look of my own.

"We're good," I whispered as if someone could hear us. "Go."

Out the door we spilled, and she turned for the closest opening to the alley. But I spun in the other direction, pulling her with me.

"I've got a ride out of here, this way," I said.

And with the flash of a smile, she followed, and we ran for it.

There wasn't a person in sight as we rushed down the alley, the commotion at the front of the building echoing in the streets, the alley, everywhere it seemed. When we hit the other street entrance, we stopped, chests heaving from exertion. I kept her behind me, sticking my head out to scan for the cops.

"All right," I said, "let's go."

Without running, we hurried away from the warehouse, trying to look inconspicuous, which wasn't easy, given that Stella was in a bustle and top hat.

And we were just about to turn the corner where freedom waited in the form of an Indian Scout—salvation on two wheels and a hundred horses of power—when we heard an authoritative voice from well behind us shout, "NYPD! Stop where you are!"

"Fuck!" I hissed, and we took off in a full sprint around the corner.

I expected Stella to look afraid, to be worried or anxious—or worse, to stop running. But instead, she laughed, her face alight with the thrill.

It was unbearably hot.

We skidded to a stop at my bike, and she hopped on the back, her eyes wide but lips smiling, thighs spread—a detail I tried to ignore so I could effectively unlock my helmet and hand it to her. I didn't wait to see what she did with it before throwing my leg over the seat and starting the bike with a rumble that drowned out the footfalls and voices coming from behind us.

"Hang on," I shouted over my shoulder, and when her arms clamped around my middle, I took off with a thunder and a screech. The back wheel kicked sideways, my foot keeping us from toppling over while the rubber sought purchase.

The second it did, we were off like a shot.

I glanced back just in time to see a couple of cops round the corner—one of them on his radio, the other with his hands on his knees—the sight interrupted by my bowler hat flying off in a spectacular spin before landing in the street behind us.

Eyes forward, I leaned in, gunning it.

Through the streets I wound, knowing no one could catch us and hoping we were far enough away for the five to have missed my plates.

We were blocks away and finally obeying the speed limit when one of her arms let go so she could flip up the visor of her helmet.

"Franklin and Hudson," she shouted over the engine.

I nodded and took a left.

Stella fitted herself against my back, her arms tightening around my waist, bringing every curve flush against me. There was no way to speak, giving us time to think. To anticipate. The hum of energy in every little movement—the shift of her fingertips, the flex and release of her thighs as I threaded in and out of traffic. My hand wanted nothing more than to stay on her bare thigh, where it could note the softness of her skin and the long stretch of leg leading to an ass that vibrated on the leather behind me. Every moment that hand had a job to do on the handlebars was a moment mourned as I sped toward her place, eating up the minutes until I could get my lips on her again.

But first, I had to talk to her. See where she was, what she wanted. Tell her I was leaving.

Prepare myself to drop her off and go home alone.

Niggling dread snaked through my belly.

The lie I thought I could tell without upsetting my conscience felt bigger, sharper than it had even a few hours ago. Because I really liked her. I liked her enough that I wondered if I should go upstairs with her if she offered. And I had a good feeling she was going to offer.

But there had been a moment when I tipped up her chin and looked into her eyes that a thought struck me like lightning.

Stella Spencer wasn't the girl you casually fucked. She was the girl you held on to, basked in her shine as long as you could.

And if I lied to her, that wouldn't be very long.

I knew what I *should* do, which was deposit her on her front step and ride away before I got myself in too deep. If I stayed, I'd be making a choice I couldn't back out of. And if I fucked this up, I'd put my career and Billy's livelihood on the line.

My heart sank, sucking the joy out of me as it went. I couldn't do this with her, not now, not until the article was done and she knew the truth. Didn't matter how badly either of us wanted to. We'd both regret it, even if she didn't know it yet.

Fucking ethics. Being a literary journalist lent flexibility I wouldn't have at a newspaper—our pieces were more subjective, their foundation in truth rather than fact, our code of ethics vague and malleable. And though I covered music like most of my colleagues, my heart and soul were in bigger issues. The pieces that meant the most to me served as a voice for those who couldn't speak for themselves. Teen prostitution. Opium dens. Corner boys dealing drugs, poverty-ridden families, homeless kids. I wanted people to see beauty in the pain, to understand the world and themselves better after reading my work.

Not that covering the Bright Young Things was particularly deep or groundbreaking. But with this piece, I'd be set, my career goal achieved in the form of war coverage and a hefty paycheck to put into caring for the man who had raised me.

Which meant I couldn't have the story and the girl.

When we approached the intersection she'd directed me to, she pointed to a loft building. I pulled up to the curb, parked between two cars, and cut the engine, the instant quiet almost painful. Stella pulled off the helmet, laughing, her thighs still clinging to mine.

"God, that was good," she said breathlessly.

"Ever ride one before?"

"A couple of times."

"Like it?"

"Take a guess," she said with a wild smile.

With a laugh, I popped the kickstand and got off the bike first.

For a split second, she looked uncertain of how to dismount, but before she could figure it out, I grabbed her around the waist with one arm and picked her up.

God, how I didn't want to let her go.

Just one more kiss.

With a giggle and a squeal, she threw her arms around my neck. And with a twist of my body and well-placed shift of her weight, she was straddling my waist with her legs locked around me, her ass in my hands and her lips against mine. Soft and sweet, hot and determined, opened wide to grant me access I took. For a moment, at least. I lowered her to the ground when her legs went slack, letting go of her mouth last.

She took my hand and pulled, but I didn't move. Keeping ahold of her hand, I leaned on my bike, facing her.

Her face quirked. "You're not coming up?"

I sighed. "I want to—trust me, I do."

She stepped into the V of my legs, hanging her arms on my shoulders. "What's stopping you?"

I'm a liar. "I'm leaving for Syria soon. A work thing."

Her face remained carefully still. "What do you do?"

"I'm a photographer," I answered smoothly. *Lie number one.* "I've got a gig in foreign correspondence coming up."

"How long will you be gone?"

"Not sure yet. A few months at least."

A smile played on her lips. "Why is it so hot imagining you in combats and khaki with a bandana around your neck like a bank robber?"

I couldn't help but laugh. "I'll send pictures."

"Ooh," she cooed wickedly. "I accept. Sadly, I've been short on low-key porn since Tumblr shut down."

Another laugh, this one smaller, fading when I said, "But … I can't get into anything. I can't start something."

She smiled, the expression the picture of levity. "You really *are* a gentleman, aren't you?"

"I try."

"We're good," she assured me, answering the unspoken question. Her hands slid down my chest and to my shirt buttons. "In fact, I think you're exactly what I need. Especially if you take me on another motorcycle ride." The first button came loose.

I caught her hand in mine, stopping her. "You're not making this easy."

"Good," she answered with a smile. "I'm not asking for anything. No strings, no commitment. I'm not looking to fall in love. What I want is to enjoy your company until you leave. I've never met anyone quite like you, and I don't know if I could live with myself if I just let you ride off into the sunset."

"Stella, I don't think you understand—"

Her lips shut me up and held me captive, and for a long, hot moment, she did her best to convince me to abandon what I knew was right. I considered telling her who I was right then just so she could either forgive me or tell me to fuck off. But I couldn't.

You can't have the story and the girl.

She wound herself around me, and I held her as close as I could, already negotiating a way around my hurdle. She wanted something casual after all, told me this was what she needed. I wondered if I could really let *her* ride off into the sunset and knew with some certainty that I couldn't.

When she broke away, it was with a smile. "Did I convince you?"

"You drive a hard bargain, Spencer."

"We all have ways to get what we want, don't we?"

I laughed as she backed away and stepped up onto the curb, but a wave of uncertainty rose and fell in me. And I let it go, dog-earing the problem for later.

Because right now was occupied by her.

"You lost your hat," I noted as I locked up my bike.

"So did you."

She grabbed my hand and pulled me toward the door, then into the lobby where a security guard sat behind a desk. He nodded at us as we approached.

"Hiya, Frank. Have a good night?"

"It's been quiet. Best I can hope for, Ms. Spencer."

Stella laughed. "You're the only guy in Manhattan who wants a quiet Saturday night."

He shrugged. "How else will I finish my crossword?"

"Good point. Here's to hoping it keeps up," she said with a smile.

"And here's to hoping yours is noisy." Frank caught my eye, and his smile faded into a look of mild suspicion.

I raised a couple fingers at him in passing, which didn't seem to help my case. Oddly, it made me feel better that Frank was around to look out for her. I had a feeling he had a Taser and wasn't afraid to use it.

An elevator waited in the lobby, and the second the doors closed, she was in my arms again, my body pinning her to the wall in a flurry of hands and noisy breaths. Twelve stories passed too quickly, and when the ding of the elevator parted us again, she gave me a look that would have made a weaker man tremble, sucking her swollen bottom lip into her mouth as if to taste what was left of me there.

She led me out of the elevator and to her front door, her dress whipping behind her and into my legs. Once she punched a code into the keypad next to the door, she dragged me inside.

My feet slowed, but she kept going, our hands outstretched and trailing apart as I took in her place. Two of my apartments could fit in the stretch of space that constituted her living room and kitchen. Polished concrete floors, exposed brick and ductwork and piping painted a pristine white. The loft was on a corner, and two walls of floor-to-ceiling windows joined at the point. Brand new kitchen, all black and white and shiny. Understated, comfortable-looking furniture I was sure cost more than I made in a year. I wandered toward the windows as Stella took off her ringmaster's coat, then her shoes, hanging on to the island counter to steady herself.

The view was incredible—crisscrossing streets spread out before me, every block packed with buildings. Downtown rose in the distance like a mountain made of industry, and though I couldn't see it, I knew the East River lay just beyond. I wondered what it looked like at sunrise.

I hoped I'd find out.

Her arms slipped around my waist, bringing me back to her. I raised one arm and shifted to pull her into my side.

I liked the way she felt there.

"Some view you've got here." I nodded out the window.

She chuckled. "A gift from my father." There was approximately zero love in her voice.

"The view or the apartment?"

"He's so self-important, he'd take credit for both."

"So you guys are close then?" I joked, and she nudged me.

"He left when I was little, but the divorce left me with a

sizable trust fund. Honestly, I think he just put the money there so Mom wouldn't get it."

I thumbed her bare arm. "He sounds like a real delight."

"An absolute joy." She turned to face me, looping her arms around my neck. "What's your last name?"

There it was—the second lie.

I swallowed the knot in my throat. "Jepsen. Why?"

"Just like to at least know the last name of guys I bring home. Makes me feel more responsible."

A chuckle through my nose as I brushed a loose lock of hair from her cheek.

"You look worried," she noted with a smile. "Nervous?" Her hands moved to my buttons again, unbuttoning the one she'd left off on.

A laugh huffed out of me. "I was just thinking about you straddling my bike."

"And that worries you?"

"Only if it doesn't happen again."

"Tell me when we can ride again."

"Whenever you want."

"A dangerous offer." Another button.

"I've got more where that came from."

"I bet you do." With the flick of her fingers, the opening of my shirt widened. Red lips met the hollow between my pecs, the softest of kisses followed by a light sweep of her tongue that sent a shock straight to my cock.

When she made to move lower, I stopped her, slid my hands down her arms, to her wrists. I stepped into her, bringing her hands together behind her back, clasping her wrists in one fist. "How about I show you." With a tug toward the floor, she gasped softly, arching her back, exposing her throat to me.

And I took the offering.

It wasn't slow, but it wasn't careless, the open and close of my lips, the sweeping circles of my tongue against salty skin. She couldn't move, restrained by my hands and the extension of her body, her lips parted to the ceiling. My hand slid to her throat, holding it gently, thumbing her chin, my eyes on those lips.

And then they were mine.

My mouth and hers were a seam, and I kissed her as if I could swallow her. Breath loud and hard as if I could breathe her in. Tongues seeking as if we could consume each other.

If I could, I would.

Arm around her waist, I lifted her, not breaking the kiss as I took two steps and pinned her to the window with my hips. A well-placed shift pressed the length of me to her core.

She broke away with a hum of pleasure, her brows drawn, eyes closed, lip between her teeth. I watched her greedily as I exposed her thighs, only stopping the grind of my hips to slip a hand between us, her legs clamping tighter to bear her weight. My fingers hooked in the web of her fishnets and pulled, rewarding me with a satisfying tear of nylon. And with a stroke, my fingertip was met with the slick heat of her. A rush of desire sent a pulse to my cock.

I tested the silken valley, charted the fluttering flesh, circled the swollen tip of her, earning me another moan.

"Was this just bare on my bike?" I slid my middle finger into her heat.

A gasp, this one joined with a flex of that tightened her thighs and straightened her back when she pushed her body into my hand to get me deeper.

"*Yes,*" she hissed—as an answer or a plea, I didn't know.

"*Fuck,*" I breathed, my eyes on her lips and my mind on what was in my hand.

Her hands moved from their clench in my hair straight to my belt buckle, and I didn't stop her. I didn't stop touching her. Again, I swallowed her moans as she peeled back layers of my clothes until her hand fisted around me. A stroke. Another, my crown in her palm and her core in mine.

I reclaimed my hand, though she didn't, my heart a jackhammer behind my sternum. Shaky hands retrieved my wallet, found a condom, and discarded the rest. She took it, lifting her chin for a kiss, one that I gave, my hands framing her face and hers busy, first rolling it on, then guiding me to the slick center of her.

The kiss broke with a thrust of my hips. Broken breaths and another thrust, and I came to a stop, the two of us panting and hot, eyes hungry. The city stretched up behind her in shades of blue and squares of light, and she was pale against it. Flaxen hair and skin like cream. Eyes like midnight, and she was sparkling starlight.

With a roll of my hips, I pulled out, only to fill her again slowly. Deliberately.

She sighed, her lashes fluttering closed, head lolling, giving me another advantageous stretch of her long neck. Though one hand was busy bracing her by way of her thigh, the other was free to trail fingertips down the line of her neck, the line of her collarbone, the swell of her breast, the rosy curve of her nipple spilling from her corset as I drove into her. I grabbed the bottom hem of the corset and pulled, freeing them.

I wanted to slow down, to take my time, to savor the sight of her breasts, round and snowy and tipped with dusky rose as they jostled from the force of my hips. But that glorious sight drove me on instead. There would be time to go slow.

That time was not now.

My free hand left its place on her breast and headed south, my thumb seeking the place I knew she wanted me. And when I stroked her, she sucked in a breath, her eyes clamping shut as a flush rose from her breasts to her neck to her cheek. Breath shallow. Body tight.

An uncontrollable draw of pleasure pulled from deep in me.

There was no stopping the pump of my hips or my thundering heart, spurred by desire and the promise of release. My circling thumb begged her to catch up, the point of no return far behind me. A flick. A press. She gasped.

"Come," I growled. Because if she didn't, I was going to.

Her eyes opened slowly, her pant from parted lips matching the rhythm of my hips. A purposeful stroke of my thumb, and they slammed shut again.

A slow tightening around me, a painful squeeze, her body pressing into mine in opposite force, a rising whimper that burst with her pleasure in a pulse that pulled me in, pulled me deep.

"Thank fuck," I breathed, leaning in, arching over her, slapping a palm on the window as I slammed into her, my eyes on her as she rode the end of her high.

She looked up at me, eyes lust-drunk and smoldering.

And that was all it took.

Blinded by sensation, stripped of everything but this, of my body and hers, I drove into her until I was spent, still holding her against the window with my body, her legs trembling around my waist and mine shuddering with pleasure.

My heart hadn't slowed, but the rest of me caught up. And her lips were waiting to occupy mine with a languid, luxurious kiss.

With a growl, I swept her up, keeping her around my waist where my pants hung open, half off my ass as I moved to the hallway where I figured the bedrooms were. She leaned back, laughing, her chin tipped and eyes closed. The picture of freedom. The epitome of joy.

I padded down the hall, knowing the image would stay with me for a long, long time.

"Which one of these is yours? Because I'm gonna fuck you in a bed tonight, or so help me."

"End of the hall," she said on another laugh. "And do you promise?" She tightened her arms, bringing her close enough to kiss.

"Guarantee."

And I closed that gap between us without stopping, kicking the door at the end of the hall shut behind me.

PLUS-ONE

STELLA

FLOPPED ONTO THE BED, SLICK WITH SWEAT AND panting at my ceiling.

Light filtered in through my sheer curtains, the summer sun high and bright. It was morning for us—afternoon for the rest of the world—an unsurprising late rise. I smiled over at Levi as I tried to catch my breath, taking a moment to appreciate the perfection of the male specimen I'd shared the last twelve hours with. His profile a line of strength from brow to the bridge of his nose. The plane and swell of his lips and the cut of his jaw. The rapid rise and fall of his broad, glistening chest moved in opposition to his abs, and my eyes followed the line of him down, charting his nakedness with the appreciation of an art curator.

He lifted a large hand to drag his fingers through shaggy, dark hair before he felt me staring and glanced over with that crooked smile and a flash of teeth.

I rolled over and into his side, wrapping myself around him. "Morning."

He curled his massive arm around me, his hand cupping my shoulder. "Morning."

"Sleep well?"

"Woke up better." He smirked down at me.

"Did I mention I'm glad you came to the party last night?"

"You might have. Where was it … in the shower?"

I pretended to think about it. "Or was it when you had me tied up with your belt?"

"Oh, you definitely mentioned it then. And when I woke you up—when was it? Three?"

"Three thirty," I said on a laugh.

Levi pressed a kiss to my damp forehead, his hand moving to tangle his fingers in my wavy, air-dried hair. "When will I see you again?"

"You're not coming to the next party?" I asked with my first frown since I'd met him.

"Gonna have Cecelia put me on the guest list?" he joked.

Through a pause, I thought about it. "Oh, I think you can scrounge you up a date somewhere."

He leaned back so he could see me, his face colored with amusement. "You offering?"

"Maybe I am. Somebody's got to convince you we're not just a bunch of spoiled rich kids."

"And that somebody's you?"

"Got any other offers?"

He angled for my lips. "If I did, I wouldn't take them."

Before I could laugh, he kissed me. And for a long, lazy moment, that was the sum total of my universe. "Consider the invitation open."

The self-assured expression on his face made my stomach do a back handspring.

"Stella Spencer's plus-one to indefinite Bright Young Things parties? How could I refuse?"

"Guess you can't," I said with a smirk to cover the skipping of my heart.

"No, I guess I can't." He kissed the tip of my nose and rolled away with a sigh. "The last thing I want to do is leave, but the deadline waits for no Bright Young Thing."

I tucked my hands under my head and shamelessly cataloged every glorious inch of him as he stood. "On a Saturday?"

He bent to pick up his pants and stepped into them. "Weekends don't mean a thing when you're working against the clock."

"Pity, that."

With a sigh, I rolled in the other direction and padded to my closet in search of clothes. My limbs and muscles groaned in protest, tired and aching pleasantly from a night in Levi's company. I smiled to myself, stepping into a pair of cheeky panties and pulling on my Blondie T-shirt. Regrettably, by the time I made it back into my room, he was dressed, his vest hanging open and his muscular chest disappearing with every fastened button.

I walked over with the objective of another kiss, and at my approach, he glanced up. His fingers froze, but his smile rose, and when I threaded my arms around his neck, he granted my wish.

Levi was something I could get used to.

Something I couldn't have.

Typical, Stella. You really know how to pick them.

When he'd told me he was leaving, I'd been disappointed, no doubt. But the truth was, I *needed* something temporary. The situation was ideal, one that met both our expectations, and though he really had tried to be a gentleman about it, that wasn't what I wanted from him. And I'd made damn sure he knew it.

"Coffee before you go?" I asked when we parted.

"I think I can make a little time for that."

He popped me on the ass, and with a yelp, I led us from my room and into the empty apartment. As Levi gathered his discarded wallet from the living room floor, I got the espresso machine going.

When he met me in the kitchen, it was with a frown on his face and a dubious look in the direction of the machine. "Got any regular old coffee?"

I smirked. "Don't worry—I won't make you drink it out of a tiny cup or anything. I'll make you an Americano." He still looked wary, so I clarified, "Espresso and hot water. Tastes just like filtered coffee, but better."

He relaxed a hair and sat at the island bar just as the door burst open.

Betty and Z walked in, arm in arm and still drunk, swerving and leaning on each other as they laughed hysterically at an unheard joke.

They looked a glorious mess.

"I see you two made it out okay," I teased, and they turned to me in unison.

"*Stellaaaaaaa*," they cried like Marlon Brando in *A Streetcar Named Desire*, a joke that I'd never found particularly funny. But a wasted Z and Betty howling it in rumpled circus attire left me laughing.

And then they saw Levi and skidded to a stop.

Z appraised Levi shrewdly. "I'd ask what you did last night, but it looks like he's sitting in your kitchen."

Levi lifted a square hand.

"Tell me you've got a friend who isn't Ash," Z said with a twisted smile.

Levi laughed, and I poured his coffee, setting it in front of him with a smile. "One or two. I'll see what I can do."

"I knew I liked him," Z said. "Aren't many gentlemen left in the world, and one who stays all night *and* for a cup of morning coffee is a keeper."

"No pressure," Betty said on a laugh as her shoes hit the ground with a thump.

Levi and I glanced at each other and flushed.

I mouthed, *I'm sorry.*

"Hard not to be with a girl like her," Levi said, his smile tilted and eyes smoldering.

"Tell me he's coming to the next party." Z addressed me rather than Levi.

"A girl can hope," I answered.

Z's smile was sinful. "Yes, she can."

Levi drained his cup and stood. "On that note, I really do have to go."

I tried not to pout.

Z didn't—her lip poked out pitifully. "But I just got here."

Levi chuckled as he made his way around the island to slide his hand into my waist. "Don't worry—I'll see you soon," he said to Z before pressing a kiss to my hair. "Sooner, if you're interested." The promise was hot against my ear.

"I'm interested." I turned around in his arms, our open mouths meeting for a searing kiss that didn't stop.

Until Z hosed us with the sink sprayer.

I squealed, holding up my hands. Levi put himself in front of me to bear the worst of it.

"Cool off—some of us just got dumped," Z said without stopping the sprayer.

"All right, all right," Levi said. "I'm going." With a kiss too swift for Z to interrupt, he headed for the door with everyone calling their goodbyes. And with a final look in my direction, he was gone.

I sighed, smiling into my coffee as I leaned a hip on the counter.

Z and Betty turned piqued, amused faces in my direction.

"What?" I asked innocently and took a sip of my coffee.

"Would you look at that?" Z said with a smirk. "Stella's back."

Betty clapped and cheered. "Dex who?"

My heart flinched, but the rest of me shrugged. "Never heard of him."

"So what have we learned about our favorite hammer

swinger?" Z asked, unhooking his corset, letting loose a long, relieved breath at the freedom of his rib cage.

"He drives a motorcycle—"

Betty sighed wistfully. "Be still my heart."

"He's a photographer—"

"Be still mine." Zeke pulled off his boots. "I need new headshots."

I chuckled. "He has the stamina of a bull, and he makes me laugh. I like him."

Zeke rolled his hand to get me to hurry up. "But is he packing?"

"What do you think?"

He raised his eyes to the ceiling and crossed himself. "There is a God."

"Think you'll see him on the regular?" Betty asked, starting the espresso machine for herself.

"If I'm lucky. But …" My smile faded. "He's leaving for Syria. War correspondent."

"Ew, no!" Zeke shot. "So did he tell you he just wants to fuck around or what?"

"No. I mean, not exactly. I think it's pretty clear he's not looking to get attached."

"Hate that," he said.

"Either way," Betty started, "enjoy it while you can. I've got a feeling he's a good one. Trusting eyes or something." She raised her bagel in salute. "Proud of you, Stella. First step in getting over assholes is to get under somebody else. Especially some *body* like the body he's got."

"Amen." Zeke raised a praise hand. "Did you see him last night?"

"I did," I answered with saccharine cheer. "And I met Elsie."

Zeke's brow rose. "How was she?"

"Fucking adorable, and I got, like, *nice* vibes from her. Made her impossible to hate."

"Ugh, it's just not fair." Betty's nose wrinkled up.

"Tell me you had your hammerhead motorcycle stud on your arm," Z said.

"That I did. I can't pretend I didn't love the expression on Dex's face when he looked up at Levi. And he had to look *way* up."

The keypad on the door beeped, and the three of us turned to the sound. But as I moved for the door, it swung open, and Joss floated in, looking fresh as a daisy after what I imagined was a miserable flight in from Italy.

Just like that, the three of us beamed, bum-rushing her for a tacklehug that only remained upright thanks to Zeke.

Joss laughed between kissing our cheeks.

"You're home!" Betty cheered, squeezing us tighter.

"I'm home!" Joss echoed, her arms slackening, breaking up the knot.

Really, it wasn't fair how naturally beautiful Joss was, from her auburn hair to her electric-blue eyes. Her skin was dewy and luminous, her eyes bright and fresh despite what was likely to be killer jet lag. Perks of being a leading lady with daily access to facials and dermatology treatments.

She abandoned her bags with a hopeful look into the kitchen. "Do I smell coffee?"

"Here, you can have mine," Betty said, bounding into the kitchen.

"Oh, thank God. I'm exhausted." She dropped into a barstool and yawned.

"Could have fooled me." Zeke shook his head at her. "You've got to tell me where to order the virgin blood you bathe in to keep yourself immortal."

She laughed, sweeping her hair off her neck to tie it into a loose bun. "Looks like the party was a hit. Circus theme? Damn, I wish I'd made it home yesterday instead."

"It was a hit, all right." Betty snorted a laugh. "I heard at least a dozen people were arrested when Warren sent his thugs down to bust us."

Joss rolled her eyes. "That guy has got to get some real problems."

Zeke's face was drawn as he stared at his phone, thumb working as he scrolled. "He was there. Warren was actually there, and so was the press."

"What?" I asked, reaching for his phone, which he turned around in display.

A photo of Warren looking pleased with himself graced the top of the article, titled: Delinquent Youths Arrested at Famed Bright Young Things Party.

Zeke flipped his phone back around and read aloud, "*Several underage drinkers, partygoers, and an event planner were taken in for questioning in regard to the unsanctioned party and the Bright Young Things' notorious leader, Cecelia Beaton. For months, the social group has violated city laws and ordinances, and Police Commissioner Warren has vowed to find and prosecute the frivolous rulebreakers. 'For too long, the young and the rich have flagrantly ignored this city's laws, and I'm here to make sure those responsible are brought to justice regardless of the size of their trust funds.'*"

"Fucking asshole," I hissed. "Unsanctioned my ass. We had all of our permits, though I had a feeling we were going to get nabbed on a noise violation. And they got Genie too. *Shit.*"

"Don't worry," Betty assured me. "She'll come by when it's all clear."

"Do you think she needs help? Think she got arrested?" I worried my bottom lip between my teeth.

Zeke shook his head. "You pay her a mil a year to get arrested. Try not to sweat it."

"What a mess." Joss took a sip of her coffee. "And what's with the reporter sneaking into the parties?"

The room went still.

"What?" I breathed.

Joss's eyes bounced from face to face. "You ... you didn't know?"

"Know what?" Betty asked.

Joss set her mug down and reached for her phone, her fingers flying as she pulled something up. She handed over her phone with an apology written all over her face. "Somebody texted this to me when I was on my way over."

The blood in my veins ran cold as I read the article. It was on the front page of *Vagabond*'s website along with an illustration of a '20s art deco party.

Blinded by the Bright Young Things. Writer's credit went to *Vagabond Staff*.

My brain fired too quickly to actually read the article, only able to skip and skim the long piece about the party at the speakeasy. Nothing about it was derogatory that I could glean. Rather, it was a beautiful article about the decadence and spectacle of the night. It felt more like an homage than an exposé, but I couldn't seem to find even an ounce of approval for the thing.

Because someone had infiltrated my party with the intent to pull back the curtain. Betrayal nearly split me open, the cut so deep that no amount of flattery from this anonymous writer could ease the shock or erase the disloyalty that had bred such an invasion.

And with Warren up our asses, this was a dangerous development. Because if a reporter could sneak their way in, so could an undercover cop.

"I feel violated." Zeke stepped back, though his eyes were still on my phone.

"Jesus Christ," Betty said from my elbow, taking my phone from my hand. "Who the fuck wrote this?"

"I don't know," I said distantly, staring out the windows at nothing. "But there's got to be a way to find out."

"Oh, we'll find out," Zeke assured me. "And then we'll ruin the motherfucker *and* the slob who plus-oned the asshole into our party. If they think they can win us over with some pretty words, they're gonna find out how wrong they are."

I drew a long, fortifying breath. "Yes, they will."

"Don't worry, Stell," Betty said, gently bumping my hip.

"I'm not worried. I'm fucking pissed."

"Let's get a plan together," Zeke said. "But first, Betty and I are in desperate need of a shower and a nap."

"Me too," Joss said through a yawn. "Just a little one, or I'll never sleep tonight."

"Please," Zeke started as he stood, "I've got a benzo for you that would beg to differ."

She laughed, but her smile fell. "Wait—what are you doing here? Are you living here now? What happened to—"

"*Ah-ah-ah,*" Zeke warned. "His name has been stricken from memory."

"Oh," she said softly. "That bad?"

"Much worse."

"I'm sorry, Zeke." She stroked his arm.

But Zeke shrugged. "Bigger and better things are coming. Preferably in or around my mouth."

With a collective laugh, we parted ways with hugs and kisses for Joss. And a few minutes later, I was alone with myself in the kitchen, quietly packing away my rage into an air-tight compartment. I turned my thoughts to the rest of the day, making a list of all the things I would do to pretend like some motherfucker hadn't slithered into my space to wait in the grass so they could strike.

Yoga. I would do yoga. Maybe go for a jog. Wait for Genie to text me and let me know she was okay. Plan some more of *Breakfast at Tiffany's.* Ask Levi what he was having for dinner and hope he said me. I could kill a few hours until my friends woke up to distract me. Or organize a lynch mob. Maybe I'd make a few Molotov cocktails in case I needed to firebomb an asshole.

Either way, I'd find a way to occupy myself, or so help me.

My eyes landed on Levi's coffee cup, and I moved it to the sink, replaying the highlight reel from last night. I wondered how many reels I'd have before he was gone.

A frown tugged at my lips. Levi was new, but surely Ash wouldn't be so fucking stupid as to bring a reporter to the party. I scooped up my phone and opened a search for Levi's name, the knot in my throat dry and sticky.

But immediately I was rewarded with a handful of resources, including his website and some places his photos had been featured. And I sighed my relief.

I couldn't imagine what would be worse than sleeping with the enemy.

Instead, I was sleeping with a dreamboat, even if it was only temporary.

Putting my sads away, I chose to be happy with what I had. *It's perfectly fine that he's leaving the country*, I thought as I crossed the room to the windows, coffee in hand. It was good that he'd told me—it gave me a chance to frame up my expectations before it was too late. And it wasn't a bullshit excuse or some tired, patriarchal rationalization for being a dick. He was leaving the country for work, not avoiding commitment.

The city bustled far below, and I thought I caught sight of a motorcycle just like Levi's flying up Hudson.

It was for the best. Because Levi was the kind of guy a girl could fall in love with.

And I'd always had terrible luck with that.

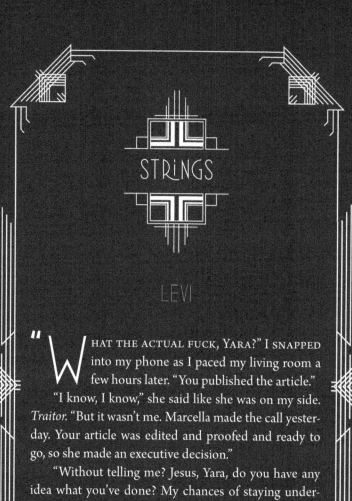

STRINGS

LEVI

"**W**HAT THE ACTUAL FUCK, YARA?" I SNAPPED into my phone as I paced my living room a few hours later. "You published the article."

"I know, I know," she said like she was on my side. *Traitor.* "But it wasn't me. Marcella made the call yesterday. Your article was edited and proofed and ready to go, so she made an executive decision."

"Without telling me? Jesus, Yara, do you have any idea what you've done? My chances of staying undercover just went up in flames."

"Oh, don't be dramatic, Levi."

"Easy for you to say. You're not the one lying to these people."

She ignored the point. "Marcella wants to publish a piece for every party to get the hype up for the big article where we'll reveal it was you, then the feature for the magazine. Assuming you can still get in?"

Suddenly, being Stella's plus-one had new and morally gray meaning. At least before, I'd had an out. I could choose not to publish or rework to Stella's standards, if it came to that. But now … now, I was fucked. Any choices I might have had were gone. I'd officially exposed the Bright Young Things, and I wouldn't be able to explain it away.

But my future depended on keeping up the deception.

"Yeah, I can still get in," I ground out.

"Good. Then keep on going. Give me a write-up about every party you attend—we were thinking eight parties, a wrap up, and a feature for the magazine. And if you can figure out who Cecelia Beaton is, Marcella will pay you triple."

My lungs collapsed. "Triple?"

"Triple. Think you can swing it?"

I dragged my hand through my hair and stared at my shoes for a beat. "I'll see what I can do."

"Attaboy. I really am sorry—I barely had any warning, and since you'd already signed off on the piece, it's hers to do with what she will."

"She should have given me a heads-up."

"Yeah, she should have. But Levi—we've already had four million hits on the article. Nearly crashed the site. You're going to be a household name by the time this is said and done, so be annoyed now, but you'll thank her later."

I blinked at my rug. "Four million? Are you fucking kidding me?"

"Nope. I'd tell you to call the tech department and ask them, but they've got all hands on deck just trying to keep the website online."

I sighed. "I'll get to work on the next one."

"Excellent. Now go get some rest so you can write."

"Sure thing, boss," I said, disconnecting the call.

I ran a hand over my weary face as if it could erase the last ten minutes from memory. It dawned on me, the contrast of my guilt, and I pushed away the wretchedness of it the moment it arose. I shouldn't have stayed the night, but I wasn't sorry I had. Because already, I cared about Stella. I'd only just discovered her, and I didn't want to lose that, not yet.

But I didn't want to lose the story either. And now I was in danger of losing both.

I'd figure something out. And in the meantime, I'd cover my tracks and hope to God she didn't find out.

If she did, she'd blow me to hell, and my story would be the gunpowder.

I rubbed my lips as I strode to my desk, opening my laptop once I was sitting, wishing for a cigarette but stuffing a piece of gum in my mouth instead. I'd been thinking about last night, my brain chewing on scraps of what I'd seen, tugging the strings of fleeting feelings it'd evoked. And then the thrill of getting busted, of running from the cops, of Stella's legs around me, on my bike and off.

There was heady magic in the Bright Young Things, and I wanted to learn how to bottle it up.

I had a feeling Stella was the one who could teach me.

And hour and a thousand words passed before I even realized it, the night unfolding word by word on the page. When I picked up my phone, which I'd absently left upside down on my desk, I found a text from Stella.

Tell me when I'll see you again.

I smiled down at my phone. *How's your Wednesday looking?*

Going to a small house party. Want to come?

Count me in. Dinner first?

If by dinner you mean fucking, absolutely.

A laugh eased out of me as I typed back. *Anything you want. When's the next party?*

We'll know when Cecelia tells us. I'll keep you posted.

Tell me when and where, and I'll be there. Anytime.

Good.

With a sigh both heavy and sated, I set my phone down and turned back to my screen, the words licking at my brain, shivering in my fingertips, anxious to escape.

And I hoped I'd find a way out of the box I'd been so carelessly stuffed into.

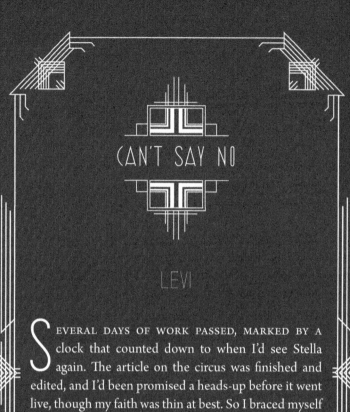

CAN'T SAY NO

LEVI

S EVERAL DAYS OF WORK PASSED, MARKED BY A clock that counted down to when I'd see Stella again. The article on the circus was finished and edited, and I'd been promised a heads-up before it went live, though my faith was thin at best. So I braced myself for impact, just in case.

My editors were even happier with the circus piece than the speakeasy, which was phenomenal for my career.

For my morals, not so much.

I'd been chewing on a game plan for telling Stella, made more complicated by my boss. But the second I turned in the last piece, I had to tell her. I'd explain my duplicity and hope she could see the gray area as a plus rather than a minus. My plan for the articles wasn't an exposé but an applaud, and if she found appreciation for that, there was a chance she wouldn't be mad at all.

If I gained her trust, she might believe my intentions were good. But deep down, I knew better. She was going to feel betrayed no matter what I did. If it hadn't been for Yara and Marcella taking matters into their own hands, things would have been simpler. Maybe not easier, but definitely simpler.

And here I'd thought I knew what I was doing.

When I killed the engine of my bike, the sound was replaced by muffled music that flowed from the brownstone in front of me.

Though the sun had been down for hours, it was still hot, but I'd opted for jeans and combats, not certain of much, but definitely certain shorts weren't going to be up to snuff for an unofficial Bright Young Things party.

I pulled off my helmet and raked a hand through my hair, assessing the house in front of me. Every window was lit, the curtains open and casings framing clusters of the young and beautiful. It was the residence of one of the core members of the group, but Stella hadn't told me whose, just sent me the address and told me to walk right in. So I locked up my bike with the intent to do just that.

I trotted up the cement steps and opened the massive black door, instantly hit with the sounds of a party already well under way.

The foyer was somehow both grand and understated, with white wood paneling and dark wood floors and a ceiling so high, scaffolding would have been required to work on the plaster detailing around the modest chandelier.

I hadn't even known a chandelier could be modest until just then.

Rooms spoked off from the entry, connected through wide casings in what seemed to be a horseshoe around the foyer and staircase. Smoke hung in the air alongside laughter and music as I made my way through the first room, then the second, looking for Stella. But I only found groups of people—longtime friends, judging by their ease and comfort—clustered on couches and standing near windows with crystal glasses in their hands. This was not a crowd for beer, but one for martinis and scotch, and though no one was in cocktail attire, they somehow made even jeans and sundresses feel opulent.

A few eyes followed me as I passed, but no one stopped me. And around I went in search of the girl I'd come to see, the girl I wanted to see off the record and without any objective but her lips and her laughter.

"Well, would you look at that?" someone said in my direction, and I turned to find Ash smirking at me. He extended a hand for a bro slap. "What the hell are you doing here?"

"Stella."

He shook his head, still smiling. "Fucking dog." He leaned in. "If you get me in trouble for this, I'm gonna burn your house down."

I chuckled. "Don't worry. You had no idea what I was doing, did you?"

"Not a clue, and I'll stand by that, even when your head's in the guillotine." He took a sip of his drink. "So you and Stella?"

"Me and Stella."

Ash watched me for a second. "Don't fuck her up, Levi."

"I'm doing my best not to."

One of his brows rose. "Coulda fooled me."

"I didn't know they were going to publish it," I said so no one else could hear. "They were supposed to wait."

"Well, it's done now. Hope you've got a plan."

"I've always got a plan," I assured him with a cavalier smile. "I need to find Stella. You seen her?"

His eyes flicked behind me, his smile tilting higher. "Sure have."

He pointed his drink in the direction of his eyeline, and I turned to find her striding toward me.

I wondered if there was ever a moment where she didn't shine, where the light didn't catch and cling to her. Tonight, she wore a dress of white, covered in small pearly sequins, with spaghetti straps and a short hem, giving me a view of her legs I thanked my lucky stars for. Nothing about the dress was formal other than the shimmer of sequins—the waist was cinched and the fabric loose and draping and Grecian in design. It gave only a hint of her curves, the slightness of her waist and gentle swells of her breasts only whispered.

But her smile was the brightest of all.

She slid into me, arms first, then lips. And I took a long moment to reacquaint myself with them.

Stella broke the kiss to smile up at me but didn't unwind her arms from my waist. "You made it."

"I did." My eyes shifted to assess the room. "Whose house is this?"

"Farrah Rashad."

I hummed my understanding. Her father was Malik Rashad, first a hip-hop artist in the '90s, then a beatmaker, now the head of one of the biggest music labels in the business.

"How do you know her?" I asked.

"We went to high school together. Most of us did, or we met in college, and the ring rippled out from there. Other friends. Significant others. You know how it is."

"Sure," I said, having no idea how it was. I could count my close friends on one hand, and I'd never had a crew, or at least not like this. I didn't call them when I needed something. Hell, I didn't even call Billy—I just handled it. But Stella seemed to collect friends and people, and what an odd and beautiful thing that was.

"How long have you and Ash been friends?"

I glanced over at where he'd been standing to find him gone. I huffed a laugh. "Ten years."

"High school?"

"College." My smile tugged higher on one side. "We went to Columbia together."

She squeezed me tighter. "Oh, you're one of *those* people."

"Now who's the snob?" I teased.

With a laugh, she said, "Come on, smartypants. Let's get you a drink."

Stella took my hand and led me away, affording me a view of the back of her, which was bare all the way down to the small of her back other than the tiny strings that kept her dress on. The thread ran over her shoulders and down her back, through loops at her waist to tie in a bow, the ends swaying with the weight of little tassels.

One tug, and she'd come undone.

I made it an objective to do just that.

We wound our way through the house, greeting people along the way, and when we made it to the kitchen, she poured me a scotch. Once the glass was in my hand, she guided me into another room I hadn't seen, one colored in navy and emerald and gold. People lingered and lounged, and we found a blue velvet love seat and sank into it. Into each other.

Her head rested in the crook of my neck, my arm around her waist and hand high on her thigh.

"How was work?" she asked.

"Long, but I'm glad it's over. How was your day?"

"Well, I spent most of it bitching about that fucking article *Vagabond* published. Did you hear about it?"

My heart tripped. "I caught a little something about it, yeah."

"Can you believe the nerve? God, whoever did this better hope I never figure out who they are."

I frowned. "It wasn't a bad article."

"No, which is why I might spare their life. But someone infiltrated us. They snuck in and wrote up a piece that went viral. And sure, they might love us now, but what about later? Are they going to turn on us? Villainize us like Warren does? Worse—if a reporter can get in, who's to say a cop can't?"

"You just jumped conclusions so fast, I'm dizzy."

She huffed, sitting up and turning to face me. She brought a knee up to rest on the couch back, her hands in her lap to keep her dress down, but her leg was exposed completely. I tried not to stare. It wasn't easy.

"I mean it. The implications are huge. It means someone in the group betrayed us. We have a mole. I don't feel like I'm crazy to be upset about that."

"Nobody said you were crazy. Maybe a little paranoid, but not crazy." When she gave me a look, I chuckled. "What I read of that article was a salute, not a teardown. Nothing about it felt aggressive or predatory. Did it?"

She nearly pouted. "No, it didn't. I actually thought it was beautiful when I finally calmed down enough to read it. But you have to understand, Levi—our walls were breached. And with Warren sniffing around, it's not insane to think he'll put in a mole of his own."

"I get it. I do."

A dramatic sigh. "Did you read all the bullshit about Warren yesterday and today? They searched everyone on their way out, even had drug dogs, for God's sake. They collected everyone's spare joints and coke and whatever, arrested everyone they could for whatever they could. But no one even had over an ounce on them. There weren't any dealers there. I mean, walk into any bar in New York, and *somebody* has an eighth on them. It's ridiculous."

"What's his problem?"

"The million-dollar question. It's got to be political. Or personal. Or for money."

"You've got it narrowed down then," I joked.

But she sighed. "I wish somebody knew. I'd love to crack that so we could put a stop to it."

"Maybe we can sleuth it out. Any of them know anything?" I jerked my chin at the crowd as a guy got behind the grand piano in the corner and started playing a swingy jazz riff, a cigarette hanging from his lips and his fingers dancing across the keys. Those standing started to wiggle and sway a little to the music.

She turned to them, smiling, and nestled back into my side to watch. "I don't think so, no more than you or me. It adds to the excitement of the parties to think we could get raided by the Morality Police at any moment. Everything feels forbidden. Taboo, you know? Between the exclusivity of it, the secretive nature of the thing, and the threat of prosecution, it's a real rush."

"Figured that out the other night when we were running from the cops."

Stella laughed. "I wasn't ready for the party to end, but I can't pretend like that wasn't fun." She paused. Sighed. "But I don't know if we're going to be safe for long. One little fuckup, and Warren is going to make a serious example out of somebody. Nobody wants that. All we want is to … I don't know. Connect. To be a part of something, like I said before. And what a thing to belong to, isn't it?"

"A very bright thing."

"A very bright thing indeed."

"So who are all these people? I recognize some of them, but others …"

"Well," she started, "over there are the Cooke sisters, Juno and Nixie. Their father manages hedge funds and has more money than God. When Jared Leto dumped Juno, she piled up a bunch of his ugly old man sweaters in the sidewalk in front of his house and set it on fire. Barely got away before the cops came. I heard Jared wouldn't come down, just screamed *What the fuck?* at her and pinged her with ice cubes from a second-story window until they heard sirens."

"Charming," I said around a laugh.

"Over there is Tuesday Morrison. Her dad is—"

"The bronze sculptor. He just had a huge exhibit at The MoMA."

"The very one. I swear, she got suspended every couple of weeks for something. Vandalism mostly. But she'd always get back in after her dad appealed to the dean, citing artistic expression. I don't know how spray painting the lockers with *Dean Hensley is a bag of dicks*—surrounded by a dozen illustrations of phalluces with hairy balls—could be considered art, but there it is. You've got Poe Nelson and Scout Neil—kid actors from Nickelodeon. Atticus Abrams, behind the piano. His dad is—"

"Remy Abrams. His coverage of Desert Storm is one of the reasons I picked up photography."

"Some of them are famous on their own merit. But mostly, we're trust-fund kids." She paused. "Does that offend you?"

"That everyone here has more money than I'll make in my entire life?"

"That we're not ... I don't know. Normal."

I looked around the room at their version of normal, considering my original angle to this article—a puff piece about disparaging socialites and the vanity of youth, but I'd realized it was more than what it seemed, as most things were. There was a sense of family about them, the root of Stella's betrayal. And I felt that tingling, that sense of belonging, even though I was the traitor who'd betrayed them.

I shrugged the thought away. "What the fuck is normal anyway?"

She offered a small laugh. "If you figure it out, let me know."

"Deal."

We listened to Atticus play for a minute, and I marveled at his skill in ashing his smoke without interrupting the song.

"What about you?" she asked. "You fit in just as well as anyone—you're an artist, same as Atticus and half the people here."

"I dunno—I don't really think of it as art. Just another medium for transferring a feeling. A moment. To share that moment with someone else."

"How is that not art?"

"Art implies intent. It suggests some preparation or a message. A plan. But I never have a plan. I just shoot what I see and hope whoever sees it understands what I felt when I took it."

"Will you show me?"

"You want to see?"

"I want to know if I understand what you felt. I want to feel it too," she said simply.

"I'll show you with one condition."

"What's that?"

"You'll let me photograph you."

She chuckled. "Me? Why would you want to photograph me?"

I leaned back so I could lay a sober look on her. "Aside from you being the most beautiful thing I've ever seen? I want to show you what I see, and I want to know if you understand that too."

Her cheeks flushed, her eyes both bright and heavy. "How could I say no to that?" she answered quietly, tossing the phrase back at me.

"Guess you can't," I said. And I kissed her to sign the deal.

NOTHING BUT YOU

STELLA

IT WAS SOMETIME AFTER MIDNIGHT WHEN WE SAID our goodbyes and hopped on Levi's bike to speed toward Hell's Kitchen. He was warm and solid in the circle of my arms, my body latched to his from my chin to my knees. Every move he made, I made with him. Every muscle that shifted, I felt contract and release—his abs when we turned, his thighs when he switched gears. When his hand was free, it hooked my thigh, strong and hot against the chill of the rushing air. And I wished I didn't have on his helmet, if only to nestle my cheek in the valley between his shoulder blades.

For as much as I'd experienced in my life, for as many opportunities that I'd had, precious few new men made it so close to me. It was a little incestuous, the group I belonged to, the people I called my friends. We'd known each other forever and insulated ourselves, partly because there were so many of us, but mostly because inside our circle, we were safe. Until now, at least.

I'd combed through the guest list from the speakeasy, trying to figure out who could have brought a goddamn reporter to our party. It had to have been an outsider, I'd determined. One of those not in the original crew, one of the other assholes I'd apparently not vetted well enough. As an experiment, I'd decided to invite our core group to the next party and excluded anyone else. If the mole wrote about it, I'd know someone on the inside snuck the bastard in.

And then we'd really have a problem.

Levi took off from a stoplight, and my arms tightened to hang on. A thrill zipped through me, not just for the speed. For the man himself.

Everything about him was new and fresh, a man from a world very different from mine. His quick wit and sharp tongue kept me happily on my toes, and I lapped up every minute with him like a dog after a 5K. It felt like he'd been dropped into my lap by divinity, a gift with a catch—a gift I couldn't keep. But I did my level best to ignore that particular part of the deal, favoring the present over the future. Moments like this one were worth far more to me than bellyaching over a future I couldn't know. Now was good, pushing perfect. And that freedom was liberating after two years of pretending I wasn't in love with Dex.

I stuffed the thought down, putting everything out of my head but the way Levi felt in my arms.

The turns came one after another, indicating we were nearly to his place, confirmed when he stopped in front of what looked to be an old warehouse and killed the engine.

I pulled off the helmet and shook out my hair, getting off the bike, my eyes upturned to the massive red brick building.

When Levi locked up, he grabbed my hand and towed me toward the entrance.

"It's beautiful," I said. "How long have you lived here?"

"Since right after college. It's lucky, really. I'd never be able to afford this place if I had to lease it on my own, but my buddy Cooper owns a bunch of properties—including this building—and rents it to me for nothing. Even let me convert part of the space to a studio and dark room."

"Cooper Moore?" I guessed.

He smiled down at me. "Should have figured you knew him."

"He used to run with us until he went and got himself all domesticated."

"Well," Levi said as he unlocked the door and held it open for me, "I guess Coop's dad bought the building in the '90s when Hell's Kitchen started gentrifying, gave it to him as a birthday present or something bananas like that. I don't even know that I could afford to live in the neighborhood without the hook up."

"Why Hell's Kitchen?"

He shrugged as we climbed the stairs. "My dad lives around the corner. I help him out around the house, groceries and stuff. Keep him company."

My heart warmed up and turned to goop. "What happened to your mom?"

He paused. Drew a breath. "My biological mom and dad took off when I was a kid. Junkies. Billy was one of the cops who found me. Took me in to foster, ended up adopting me."

For a beat, we climbed the stairs with nothing but our footfalls to fill the silence.

"I'm sorry, Levi," was all I could think to say, too overwhelmed by feelings and questions for anything else.

But he smiled again as if it were no big deal. "Don't be. Billy gave me the home I never woulda gotten otherwise." We turned the corner of a landing and took the next flight. "I mean, not that it was the Upper East or anything, but it was a step up."

"God forbid someone be from the Upper East," I teased, and he gave me a little smirk.

"It's alien sometimes, your world. Even in college, when I was running with Cooper and Ash, I couldn't get used to it. There's something so …" He sighed. "There's no way to say it without being shitty."

"Then be shitty. I won't get mad."

He assessed me for a second before deciding I was telling the truth. "It feels wasteful. You've gotta understand—I've had to scrape and save for everything I've ever had, even Billy. When I think about how he gave his life to the city and barely has enough to live on, then go with Ash to a club where he spends Billy's monthly income on booze? It's hard to be objective."

It stung, I couldn't lie about that. Mostly because he wasn't wrong. "It is wasteful. There's no real excuse for it."

"I get it—you don't know any different. You've all lived your entire lives like this, and I've got a chip on my shoulder about it. I've been working on it."

"Oh, have you?" I said on a chuckle.

"I have. Billy's always telling me not to be a snob."

"Sounds wise."

"That's one word for it," he joked. "Anyway, he has an old injury that makes it hard for him to get around, so I need to be close by."

"He's lucky to have you."

"I say the same thing about him. I'm right down here," he said, leading me to the end of the hall. The massive metal sliding door groaned when he rolled it open.

The room itself was dark, the furniture silhouetted against twenty-foot paned windows that framed a view of Hell's Kitchen and Chelsea, downtown rising up beyond. We weren't very high up—just the fourth floor—but with the low-profile buildings around us, it was just high enough to afford a bit of view and ample charm.

Levi flipped on the lights and headed for the kitchen as I milled around, admiring the space. "Drink?"

"Please. Whatever you've got."

The kitchen was a good size and modern, built under the open loft space that housed his bedroom. Polished concrete made up the bottom floor, and opposite the wall of windows was an equally epic wall of red brick that wrapped around both sides to meet the windows.

"It's beautiful," I said, stopping by the window to look down at the street.

"Like I said, I'm a lucky guy." He jerked his chin and extended what looked to be a glass of whiskey. "Come on. I'll show you the studio."

I followed him up the stairs, curious as to where we were going, seeing as how the entire apartment was visible from the door. But once in his bedroom—a simple and utterly masculine affair—I noted two doors and the slider for his closet. One had to be the bathroom. The other, as anticipated, opened into pitch-dark.

He closed the door behind me and walked away. "This space was used for storage and custodial services—it was too small to make an apartment, plus there were no windows. So Coop split it off for me, keeping the bottom floor for storage like before but giving me the space for this."

A click, and the far wall illuminated, the light soft and diffused. He was a void against it, his features indefinable, a black shape against white light. Broad shoulders, the curves of his arms, his narrow waist. The cut of his profile when he turned his head and reached for a stool, placing it in front of the wall.

"Come here."

Two words, a command that had everything and nothing to do with the stool he'd just set down.

I did as he'd bidden, taking a sip of my drink before setting it at my feet. "I'm ready for my close-up, Mr. DeMille."

A chuckle from the near dark, and I caught movement, just ghostly golden highlights of an arm or his hand or his cheekbones and jaw. And then he came into full view, camera on a tripod pointed at me.

I crossed my legs and straightened my back out of instinct.

His eyes flicked from his camera to me, then back again. "You're not posing for a portrait, you know," he teased. "Take a drink. I'm just checking the lighting."

With a chuckle, I hinged to pick up the glass and take a sip. The click of the camera startled me.

"I thought you weren't shooting yet."

He shrugged, but I couldn't see his face. "Whoops."

At that, I laughed. "What do you want me to do?"

"Just be."

"Just be what?"

"Be nothing but you."

I exhaled, wondering how exactly to do that while on display. *Click.*

"Dammit," I said on a chuckle.

"Take another drink and close your eyes."

I hesitated for a second before downing what was left in my glass. Once I set it down, I closed my eyes and folded my hands in my lap, my body turned three-quarters. My heart fluttered, shaken by nerves. Not because I didn't trust him.

I wanted to be beautiful for him, and I didn't know how.

"Have you been photographed before?"

I cracked a lid to give him a look. "Picked up an *Us Weekly* lately?"

"Close your eyes," he directed, amused. "Not like that. Not a bastardized, unwanted invasion. I mean like this."

"I've done a little modeling, but I've never been good at it."

"No, not like that either. Not a sell, not a gimmick. A truth."

"Then no."

Click.

I resisted the urge to open my eyes.

"Truth can't be staged, can't be forced. It happens when it thinks no one's looking." *Click.* "You can't command something to be truthful, to be real. You can't even ask it of yourself, because thinking about it sends it burrowing deeper."

"Why is that, do you think?" My head bowed.

"It's different for everyone. But mostly, it's because we're afraid. Truth requires trust, and trust has to be earned. But that's the problem—trust is also the space where we're most vulnerable. So how do you give someone that power? How do you give them your truth, knowing they could exploit it?"

Click.

"I don't know," I answered quietly.

"I do—they take it without you knowing, and you won't realize it until it's theirs."

The streak of emotion in my chest was an amalgamation of feeling, of shock and of recognition, of hope that I could find someone worthy of my trust and fear of what would happen when they stole it.

"Open your eyes."

The shutter rapid-fired when I did.

He rose, stepping around the camera, holding my gaze as he approached. Silently, he smoothed my hair, exposing my shoulder as his eyes charted my face. I wondered what he saw, what he wanted behind torn eyes, his face cut in two. One side planes and angles, the other darkness, shrouded but for the catch of light in his eyes and a glint on his cheekbone. Just a glimpse, a glimmer of his truth. What he showed the world cast in light, what he kept to himself left unseen.

A breath, and the moment was gone, wiped away by his cavalier smile. "Come with me."

I stood on shaky knees, all the blood in my body seeming to have rushed to my chest in a hot bloom of warmth so fast, it left my hands chilled. And I followed.

He stopped at his camera and fiddled with it before heading away. The darkness swallowed him up, and I hesitated, too unfamiliar with my surroundings to risk breaking an ankle tripping over anything. But with another click, and a slice of crimson appeared before me with Levi's silhouette cut from it.

A smile rose on my face, my eyes wide as I stepped into his dark room.

The room was shades of red and shadows of black cast over the large table in the middle, topped with tubs of developer, and the counters around the walls housed a number of tools I didn't know the names of. Levi bustled around preparing what I could only figure was a roll of film, and while he was occupied, I came to a stop in front of a wall of black-and-white photos.

They told a story I couldn't put into words, a tale of shadows and light. Faces more darkness than highlight, people in places I'd never been, though none of them were foreign. Children with sunken eyes and lips touched with smiles. A den of smoke and pillows and closed eyes. A silhouette of a prostitute smoking a cigarette, a plume of smoke curling toward the sky, leaning against a wall while she waited.

I felt him behind me before he spoke. "I'm not sure why I've never wanted to photograph happy things. It feels … I don't know. Easy, somehow. But this? This is honest. Even though it hurts, it's the truth, and there's something beautiful about that."

"But it doesn't only hurt," I said. "It's too beautiful to hurt, but there's something … something else." I stared at a shot of a woman, looking into her eyes to find her truth, like he'd said. "It's longing. Searching. Every one of these people is looking for something they lost, and I don't know anything more human than that. The desire to find what's missing. The wish to be whole."

I turned to him, finding him once again cast in shadows. And all I wanted to do was ask him what he'd lost, what he was searching for. But instead, I smiled and said, "How'd I do?"

He pulled me into him by the waist, and I could hear the smile on his lips when he spoke. "You're something else. Anybody ever tell you that?"

"Once or twice."

His lips brushed mine too briefly for my liking. "Want to see your pictures?"

"Would it make me a baby if I said not really?"

"A little," he answered on a laugh, moving for a projector-looking machine. "Come on, I know you at least trust me for that."

After looking at his work, I couldn't disagree. "You didn't take very many pictures."

He shrugged, messing with the machine's dials to lower it a little. "Didn't need very many. I got what I wanted."

That warmth slipped over me again. "Do you always shoot film?"

With a click, the red light went out and the machine lit up, projecting the negative. My brain tried to flip it around and couldn't.

"No. I usually bring two cameras. I have a little pocket-sized SLR—it was Billy's once upon a time—but film is a novelty. A hobby more than a reliable practice."

"So tell me—do you bring all the girls here?" I teased, not really wanting to know the answer.

With a brow up, he smirked. "Only the ones that count."

"And how many are nudes?"

"Why, you offering?"

The machine light clicked off. "Only if I get to keep the negatives."

"That is a deal I'm willing to make." He kissed me swiftly on his way to the tubs of chemicals, and I followed. When the paper was submerged, he handed me a pair of rubber-tipped tongs and gestured for me to poke at it.

"Do you leave the baths out all the time?"

"No, but I was developing before I came to meet you. They're good for a few hours." He reached for one of the photos hanging from the string above the table. It was of a homeless shelter in a church, a slash of sunlight beaming in through stained glass to bathe the transients in divinity.

"They're beautiful, Levi. All of them."

"I'm glad you think so," he said quietly, earnestly, though his lips slanted. He grabbed the photo with tongs of his own and moved it into the next tub.

"How do you find these places, these people?"

"A lot of them are around the East Side, though it's been so fully gentrified, there aren't many more slums. But I've never had a hard time finding trouble."

"I bet you haven't. Ever gotten hurt? Been in the wrong place at the wrong time?"

He moved it to the last tub and had me nudge it around. "Plenty. Pimps don't appreciate you following their girls around with a camera. Drug dealers don't see the artistic value of me taking photos of their corner boys."

"Why do you do it? Put yourself in danger like that?"

"Because they can't speak for themselves, and I want the world to know what they have to say."

My heart twisted, but before I could speak, he pulled the photo out of the stop bath and clipped it up. And we stepped back to look in heavy silence.

I was lit from behind by the wall of diffused light, my body little more than a shadow peppered with glimmers of my dress. There were no lines, only curves—shoulder and arms, a long neck I didn't recognize. Chin and nose and lips, my face angled away from the camera, its features brushed with light.

But it was my eyes that told the story, veiled by darkness, my irises swallowed up by my pupils. Those eyes were bottomless, hungry for something. It was the longing that lived in every one of his photographs.

It lived in me too.

"Levi ..." I breathed. "How did you ..."

"I stole the truth for a moment—that's all."

I turned to him. "What if I want it back?"

With a step, our bodies were flush, his face darkness but for the scarlet light.

He cupped my jaw, lifting it. "You can have the negatives, but you already gave me the moment. Nothing can erase that."

And there was nothing left to say.

His lips captured mine and kept them, stole them like the truth he'd swallowed for safekeeping.

But he could have them. I didn't want any of it back.

You can't keep him, my mind whispered, but my body didn't listen, didn't care. All it cared about was the press of his lips, the sweep of his tongue. The strength of his hands as he lifted me up only to set me on the low counter and fit his hips between my thighs.

With a tug, he untied the strap of my dress, and the top slid down to the curve of my waist as I clawed at his shirt to get it off of him. With a solid yank, he pulled it off and dropped it, his hands moving for my body as mine fumbled with his belt. He hissed when I had my hands around him, and I hissed back when he stroked me in return.

"Fuck, don't you ever wear panties?" he growled, sliding a long, thick finger into my heat.

"Why, want me to start?"

"Never," he said before kissing me long and deep and hard, long enough to leave me panting when he broke away on a new mission.

Red and black, heat and heartbeats, he moved down my body, flipping the scrap of fabric that constituted my skirt. Without preamble, he latched on to me for a bruising kiss, punishing suck, a dangerously delicious brush of teeth against the aching tip of me. My lungs emptied, fingers in his hair like reins, the tendons in my thighs contracting and releasing with every sweep of his tongue. Seconds, and I was on the edge, my awareness shrinking and dimming and receding to the place his lips fastened to my body.

The second he knew, he backed off.

I whimpered, pulling him back to me with his hair knotted

in my fingers, but he only closed his lips for a kiss that sent a shock down my thighs.

"Not yet," he whispered, breathless as I was as he stood.

I reached for his shoulders but couldn't grasp them as he rolled on a condom. And then he leaned in, gave me what I wanted with his salty lips against mine, one hand on my hip and the other on his base as he slid into me.

Hot and hard, he drove into me, the table banging the wall with every pump of his hips, alternating kisses for air. My arms locked around his neck, my back arching to tilt my hips. A gasp when I got the connection I sought, and my body flexed, neck to toes. He picked up the pace, driving my heart to run too fast, my breath to fail, my vision to dim.

A flash behind closed lids, and I came with a breathy call to a higher power, hanging on to Levi, who didn't stop. He leaned in, moaning sweet sounds of satisfaction to the sound of skin against skin. A hard thrust, pinning me still for a beat before he came with a satisfied grunt that sparked a pulse through me and around him, drawing him deeper. He took the invitation, riding it down until we were nothing but the slightest shift of hips, the length of him buried in me.

I didn't want him to go. And I knew instantly just how dangerous that was.

The thought shook me with a resounding no, my arms tightening as if to keep us right there. As if I could hold us in the moment, letting him go only with the promise of collecting more moments just like this.

The feeling was a sign, one I should have heeded.

It was just that I didn't care. I'd collect every moment before I had to let go for good.

His face was buried in my neck, cradled in my arms, and when he caught his breath, he bowed his head and pressed a kiss to the curve of my shoulder. Then my jaw. Then my lips. And then he was smiling down at me.

"We always gonna start off this way?" he asked, smoothing my hair.

"I'm not complaining."

With a laugh and a retreat of his hips, he picked me up and turned us around, setting me on the ground. I held up the strings of my straps and eyed them, too lust-drunk to make any sense of it. Levi took the strings from me, but rather than tie me back up, he dropped them, hooked his fingers in my dress hanging around my waist, and pushed it down my thighs. It landed with a whisper in a sparkling pool at my feet.

"Problem solved," he said, popping my bare rump with his hand. "Now go get that ass in my bed. I'm not done with it yet."

For a second, we smiled at each other playfully, not knowing what the other was going to do. But when I took off running for his room, he chased me the whole way.

Just like I'd hoped.

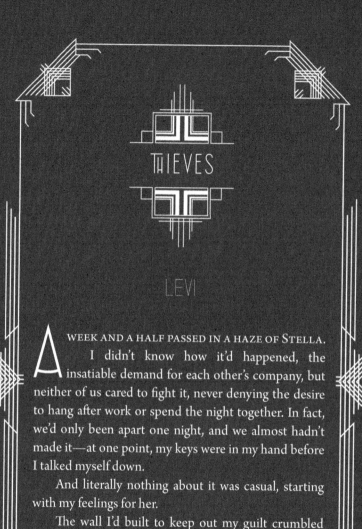

THIEVES

LEVI

A WEEK AND A HALF PASSED IN A HAZE OF STELLA. I didn't know how it'd happened, the insatiable demand for each other's company, but neither of us cared to fight it, never denying the desire to hang after work or spend the night together. In fact, we'd only been apart one night, and we almost hadn't made it—at one point, my keys were in my hand before I talked myself down.

And literally nothing about it was casual, starting with my feelings for her.

The wall I'd built to keep out my guilt crumbled with every day until it was barely standing, and behind it was the truth. A truth I had to tell her—and soon.

It might already be too late.

Last weekend, we'd attended the French Revolution party, where I wore a powdered wig and breeches and stockings and everything, even stupid heeled shoes with a garish buckle. Begrudgingly. But I wore it. I looked ridiculous next to the vision that was Stella in her wig and corset in a dress of silver and white. She'd put a beauty mark on one of her breasts, which spilled from the top of her corset in a most approving way, just another reason I couldn't take my eyes off of her.

Admittance to the party was obtained not only with costume and invitation, but with a donation to Together We Rise. Invitations for the party instructed us as to what to bring and how to donate cash, and in the end, we'd collectively filled up a U-haul trailer with duffel bags and suitcases, toiletries and clothes, comfort items like teddy bears and blankets. A couple of people even brought bikes. But the biggest contribution was the money, which was announced as just shy of a million dollars. Betty informed me half of that was Stella.

As if I didn't have enough reasons to want her.

The next morning, the circus article was published, and the gang went postal again while I listened silently, the voice in my head urging me to tell her turning up its volume by the day. The article on the Revolution party was finished—the rich giving back at a French Revolution party an ironic twist that practically wrote itself—but I hadn't turned it in. Because hurting her had become unbearable.

I had to tell her.

I just had to figure out how.

"You know, this costume thing is way easier for us than it is for you." I tugged the hem of Stella's tuxedo shirt as we walked toward Tiffany's.

"Lucky you." She took a bite of her Danish, and I took the opportunity to admire her.

She was dressed as Holly Golightly when Paul Varjak woke her up—Tiffany-blue eyelash mask pushed into her hair, tasseled earplugs, and a tuxedo shirt. That was it. I, on the other hand, only had to wear a suit to be considered in costume. If it wasn't a thousand degrees out, I might not have minded so much.

Should have just worn a sheet around my waist. Bedroom-eyes

Varjak would have been a better option for the weather, even if it meant a sunburn and lack of places to stash my wallet.

I pulled Billy's old camera out of my pocket and snapped a picture, earning an amused look of warning.

Just ahead of us, a cluster of people in costume stood in front of one of the Tiffany's windows. A couple of the guys were in suits like me, and a couple more were dressed as Holly Golightly. The girls wore some of the less iconic outfits from the movie, from the dress and gigantic hat she wore to meet Sally Tomato to the sweatshirt, jeans, and hair scarf she wore when she sang "Moon River." One even had a guitar slung behind her back.

"*Stella*," one of them called, and the rest turned, smiling as we approached.

"Hey, guys," she said, making her way through the group greeting them all.

Some split off right away, heading to the next point on the treasure hunt. The others milled around for a few minutes, eating Danishes and sipping coffee while we all peered into the window at a necklace that had to cost a cool mil, judging by the number and size of the diamonds involved.

In the bottom corner of the small window was a little window cling with our next stop.

Place: New York Public Library, Bryant Park
Thing: Breakfast at Tiffany's by Truman Capote
Task: Vandalism in the form of your initials inside the front cover
Next clue: In the book

Stella was still talking to everyone as I smirked at the clue. I wondered what the rest of the day would hold. With the sun beating down on me like a baseball bat, I also wondered if my suit would survive.

The last of the group left, and Stella pulled up next to me and leaned in to read our instructions.

"Ooh, the library. God, I wish they had a card catalog room like they used to. Of course, it's easier to find the book this way. Less suspicious."

"Wonder how long it will take the librarians to get wise?"

"I don't know, but we'd better get there before they do." She smiled mischievously, one brow arched as she turned to head down Fifth.

"Are these things always this elaborate?" I asked.

"What do you think?"

"Fair enough. It's just hard to imagine one person doing all this, and this often."

"So long as we keep getting invitations, none of us are asking any questions. You'd be wise to follow the lead." She gave me a look, touched with amusement. "Don't blow it, Jepsen."

I schooled a flinch at the use of my fake name and pulled her into my side so she couldn't see my face. How I was supposed to lie to her for the rest of the parties for the articles was beyond me. And the icy cool I'd once prided myself on melted just from proximity to her.

You can't have the story and the girl, I reminded myself with a slash of pain through my chest.

I pressed a kiss into her hair, wishing I knew what she would say if I told her. *When* I told her. The longer this went on, the worse it would be. Even though I was leaving, even though I couldn't keep her, I cared too much about her, and I knew she cared about me too, more than either of us wanted to admit.

Maybe Yara would understand. Maybe I could hold out for a little while. Collect my experiences and write them up without turning them in, stall until it was through. It would buy me some time. Time to break it to Stella. Let her read what I wrote. Try to convince her I was on her side, like I'd been advocating for my anonymous other self.

Maybe she'd even believe me.

Either that or she'd never want to see me again.

"God, you should see Z," Stella said, pulling off a chunk of Danish and handing it to me. "She went full-blown Givenchy. Black dress, updo, tiara, an opera-length cigarette holder."

"None of that surprises me." I popped the bite in my mouth. "Did she bring a plus-one?"

"Nah. Z and Betty have an arrangement—no plus-ones for a year, but I suspect it'll only last until Z's over Roman."

"Fuck that guy."

"Amen." She let me go in order to veer toward a trash can, dumping the rest of her breakfast and dusting off her hands.

"How long were they together?"

"About a year," she answered quietly. "Roman's always been ... well, he's Roman. Shiny and spectacular and a conniving bitch. I'm not surprised he fucked around and lied to Zeke. I've never liked him. But I'd really hoped he'd rise to the occasion. I'm not always the best judge of character, but I could smell Roman a mile away."

Another flinch of my heart. "What do you mean, not the best judge of character?"

"Well, Dex, for example. I feel like that's pretty self-explanatory," she said on a laugh. "I've trusted a few friends I shouldn't have. One in particular was one of our best friends. But ... it's hard to explain without sounding shitty."

"Then be shitty," I said, giving her the allowance she'd given me once before.

"So you know how we have those moments ... Betty and I call it *forty-five seconds of petty*. Everyone's allowed forty-five seconds of petty every once in a while, in a safe space. Things you'd never say to anyone else, things you get mad about for no reason. Well, she got my forty-five seconds of petty often enough and remembered every word I'd said. Then went around and talked about me like that was who I was, some bitter, petty slag."

"Who?" I asked, instantly angry. "She's not in the group, is she?"

"No, not anymore. She showed her spots and alienated herself. I also have a terrible track record with men, dating back to sophomore year in high school. In fact, you're the first nice guy I've dated."

My throat clamped shut. "And you're sure about me?"

She smiled up at me and bumped my hip. "Dead certain."

You're a fucking charlatan, Levi Hunt. I swallowed the stone in my throat and only managed to sink it an inch.

She sighed. "Anyway, good riddance to all of them, especially Roman. I think Z and Betty are ahead of us somewhere. Joss is with them. All three of them went the black dress route, but nobody looks as good as Z, guaranteed. Maybe on the planet."

"I'd do her."

"Don't let her hear you say that or she'll take you up on it."

I laughed, peeling off my suit coat before I sweat through it. I slung it over my forearm, wishing with quiet desperation that I could roll up my sleeves and get my neck free of this tie. "How'd you meet Z?"

"We have a friend in costume design who was working with drag show, and Z was the headliner. I think it took all of five seconds for the three of us to become best friends. Betty and I have basically lived together since we were ten, but the addition of Z went down in history as the day we went from being a line to a triangle."

I paused, processing what she'd just said. "You lived with Betty when you were a kid?"

"Sort of. Our parents were always gone, so I spent most of my time over at her place. That way we weren't alone."

I thought back to my childhood, to long days spent with nothing but the television to keep me company. To nights spent listening to the noise of the city and listening for the sound of my parents. "I wish I'd had a friend like that. A place to go."

She was quiet for a moment. "I wish you'd had a place to go too."

"Billy was enough. All I really wanted was somebody who gave a shit if I'd eaten. But Billy gave me more than that. He gave me a home, taught me how to live. How to love. Plenty of kids have it worse—I was one of the lucky ones. But I was real happy the last party funded foster support." A smile tugged at my lips. "Betty told me about your donation."

Her cheeks flushed. "Ugh, damn her."

"Why curse Betty? It might have been the hottest thing you've ever done."

"Hotter than riding on the back of your bike without panties on?"

"All right, maybe not that. But it's up there."

She chuckled. "Well, I have plenty of disposable income to work with—I live on the interest from my trust."

I blinked. "Jesus. Must be some trust."

"Pretty sure it had more to do with my dad screwing over my mother than his desire to be a stand-up guy. But anyway, I have a good chunk per year allocated to charity, so it was no big deal."

"I think the kids it'll help would beg to differ."

She threaded her arm through mine and leaned into me, smiling at the sidewalk.

"So the library's next. What's after that?" I asked.

"Nobody knows until we get there. Old Cecelia loves to string us along."

A pause. "You really don't know who she is?"

"I really don't," she answered. "It seems like a hard thing for you to believe."

"I guess I just figure *somebody* has to know."

"I'm sure. But I'm not one of those somebodies. Bet they'd like to know too." She jerked her chin at the cops standing against a wrought iron fence bordering a park.

Their eyes found us and tracked our approach. Silently, we stared back. Four faces swiveled to keep track, and as we passed, they pushed themselves off the fence and followed us. One tilted his head to say something into the radio on his shoulder.

Stella stiffened dramatically, making a show of looking "normal." We picked up our pace, and they picked up theirs.

"Excuse me," one of the cops said. "You there."

We jumped, glancing behind us to find they were, in fact, speaking to us. I noted they were neither young nor fit—their paunches had just enough overhang to cover their belt buckles. My eyes met Stella's, striking a silent accord.

"Run!" she called, grinning.

We took off through the park, hand in hand and laughing like mad as we burst through to the next block and crossed the street.

"*Hey!*" one of the cops called, but we'd ducked into an alley by the time they made it out.

Panting, I held Stella behind me, but her hands were on my arm so she could peek around the brick corner.

They looked around, and one of them pointed the opposite direction. They split up and took off as quick as they could, which wasn't very.

When they were out of eyesight, we sagged against the brick wall, laughing.

Goddamn, she was a thrill, and I loved a good thrill. Free and open and giving of every bit of her. What I saw of her was exactly what I got. And I was the thief, stealing what by right shouldn't be mine and hiding all that I was.

"Jesus, since when is it a crime to walk around New York?" she asked. "Warren must have caught wind of the party. Maybe they really do have a mole. Maybe it's the same person writing the articles. Is it wrong that I hope they are? Because the thought of *two* people sneaking in makes me feel sick."

I avoided answering, saying instead, "I'll bet it's on Instagram. There's no way people haven't posted pictures of themselves in costume. All he'd have to do is follow the hashtag and he'd know enough to warn the beat cops to look out."

"We're not even drinking!" she huffed. "God, what a bunch of assholes. They must hate fun. I bet they sit around all night

and read *Mein Kampf* and take notes in a Lisa Frank notebook."
A scoff. "At least no new articles have come out. Maybe the reporter couldn't get back in. We can hope, right?" she said on a little laugh.

"I think the coast is clear," I dodged, not wanting to lie any more than I already had. "Come on, let's get back on Fifth and hope they don't get wise."

"All right," she said, smiling as she took my hand. "Let's go."

So we did.

Over the next few hours, we ran around Midtown following clues to each location. We walked through the library, wandered around the Rose Room, found one of their many copies of the book, and opened it to initial the inside with a tiny, eraserless pencil we'd snagged from the front desk. There were at least twenty initials on the page, and for a moment, I marveled over the movement itself. With any normal group of young people, there was always at least one who didn't follow or respect the rules. There was always the one who would steal the book so no one else could sign or get the next clue. The one who would pull the cling off the window just to fuck everybody's good time. But not the Bright Young Things. They seemed to have a silent pact to uphold the virtue of the thing and to do all they did in the spirit of fun and companionship. They wouldn't break the rules—they *wanted* everyone to share their good time.

It was remarkable, really. The purest form of camaraderie I'd witnessed firsthand.

The clue in the book read: *Cat is lost! Head to 32nd and 6th and check the alleys for your next clue.*

So down Fifth we went, past the Empire State Building and into Koreatown, searching the alleys for Cat until we finally found it. On one of the brick walls, a life-size mural of the final scene of the movie had been painted—Audrey Hepburn and George Peppard kissing in the rain with Cat smushed between them. It was a perfect rendition, even down to the angle of her body as she leaned into him with rivers of rain on their coats, so perfect that I hated that it was hidden back in this alley where no one could admire it but us. Painted next to them was the next clue.

Things we've never done: steal the cheapest thing you can find from a tourist shop.

"Are you sure this is smart, what with the cops out to get us and all?" I asked as we approached a string of tourist shops.

She shrugged. "Can they take us to jail for stealing something that small?"

"Normally I'd say no, but after the cops chasing us, I wouldn't be surprised if they arrested us and slapped us with misdemeanors."

With a laugh, she pulled me toward one of the open stalls. "Come on. Unless you're chicken?"

One of my brows rose.

"Ever steal anything before?" she asked.

"Sure, when I was a kid, mostly just for kicks."

"I haven't," she said, her eyes bright. "Not gonna lie, I'm a little scared."

"Good. That'll make it that much more fun."

Then it was me pulling her into the bedlam of the shop. Really, this place must have gotten ripped off daily—there was barely any room to walk between racks and shelves of snow globes and bottle openers and *I heart New York* tees. Shot glasses and magnets abounded, the goods practically spilling off the shelves. Behind the counter sat a kid who I was pretty sure wasn't old enough to work, flipping through a comic book and looking remarkably bored. He didn't even glance up when we entered.

We wandered around the shop picking things up and putting them down. She couldn't decide, her face quirked in determination before finding a foam Statue of Liberty crown. When she checked the price, she smiled before handing me one.

She gestured for me to put it on, moving her eye mask so it

hung around her neck. With a quick look over her shoulder, she confirmed the kid gave no shits and was paying zero attention, so she put hers on too and took my arm. We strolled toward the exit just like Holly and Paul did, though we weren't anywhere near as conspicuous in green foam hats as they were in their cat and dog masks, and with a final look to make sure we were clear, we took off running.

We stopped in the mouth of an alley down the street, ducking behind the corner just in case the kid had chased us out. I couldn't stop laughing, not only from the adrenaline but the sight of Stella in that stupid hat. I probably looked the dumbest, which might have been why she couldn't stop laughing either.

I didn't know what caught us in the moment—the rush, the breathlessness, or just the nature of her and me—but before either of us decided to, we were kissing, my hand on her face and hers resting on my chest. I wanted to kiss her like this forever.

I wanted to feel this way forever.

She broke away to smile up at me, but her smile opened up into laughter when she saw me. "That hat."

"You're one to talk." I pulled her closer, wanting to kiss her again. Wanting to stop the clock so we could just be here, right now, when things were simple. When we were the people we'd have been if I wasn't lying.

"What's the matter?" she asked, her smile fading and brows drawing with worry.

"I ... I need to tell you something."

She stilled, though her face didn't change. "All right, then. Tell me," she said gently.

My mouth was dry as sun-bleached bone. I forced a sticky swallow.

Looked into her eyes.

Took a heavy breath.

And lied.

"I think my grandma is a better thief than you," I said with a lordly smile that I didn't feel, unable to do it here, now, wishing I didn't have to do it ever.

But Stella laughed before stretching up onto her tiptoes to kiss me.

"Where to next?" I asked when my lying lips were free.

"Oh!" She took a step back and held out her hand. "Phone, please."

I retrieved her phone from my pocket and waited while she opened it up to her camera.

"Come here." She stepped in front of me and slanted into my chest, holding out her phone for a selfie. At the last moment, I kissed her cheek, wanting to surprise her.

And I did. The photo was candid, her eyes closed and smiling as she leaned into my lips. And while she messed around on her phone for a second, her cheeks were flushed and high.

I rested against the wall, a crook and a liar, wishing for a smoke.

Might as well disavow all my integrity while I'm at it.

I had to tell her, and I had to tell her soon, just as soon as I figured out what I could get away with at work. Because I couldn't keep this up.

She didn't deserve this.

"Aha! There we go," she said. "Just had to text a picture to the number on the invite, and here's the address. You ready?"

"Probably not," I answered her and me both.

And with one more kiss, we were off again.

The address was in Chelsea, and by the time we got there, the sun had begun to dip toward the horizon. The building had an uncanny resemblance to the one in the movie, and up we went to the second floor, following the sounds of pandemonium. She knocked. The door opened. And a chorus of people cheered when they saw her.

It was wall-to-wall bodies, the furniture and decor decidedly mid-century and with the quirks one would expect. They'd even found a couch made out of a clawfoot tub, and just outside the window was a fire escape that'd be just perfect for a cigarette and a song. The record was playing jazz, and the tempo slowed.

Stella pulled me into the throng and looped her arms around my neck, looking up at me with trust and confidence I didn't deserve.

And I kissed her so she wouldn't see her mistake.

SINCE YOU ASKED

STELLA

THE THRESHOLD OF MY FRONT DOOR BIT AT MY BACK, but I didn't care. Because Levi was kissing me, and when Levi kissed me, it was hard to consider anything else.

He broke the kiss by a millimeter. "I'm gonna be late." The words bounced off my lips.

"Then go."

Instead of answering, he closed the gap to kiss me again. But when he closed his lips and stepped back, that was that.

He watched me with dark eyes and that ever-present sidelong smile. "I've got some things to handle today, but can I see you tonight? I need to talk to you about something."

"Sounds ominous," I teased, belying the shock of fear in me.

Levi huffed a little laugh through his nose and moved on. "I'll text you when I'm free, and we'll play it by ear."

"Deal."

He paused, his smile falling as a crease in his brow appeared. Something in his eyes kept that fear afloat, bobbing along the surface like a buoy. A warning.

But then it was gone.

"See you tonight," he said, leaving me with one last kiss before turning to go.

I watched him until he was in the elevator, waving once more as he disappeared. And with a sigh, I closed my door and wandered into the kitchen without purpose.

He's leaving. It's probably about that. Checking in to make sure we haven't caught feelings. Wonder if he'd lie about it.

Because I would.

Pretending I didn't like him was a fool's game, one I wasn't even good at. But I maintained my expectations without faltering—he was leaving, and I knew it. Why not lean into it? Feel what I feel and then let him go? Have a great story for my grandkids about a summer fling that ended with a *what if*?

So I made plans to tell him that tonight and hoped I wouldn't scare him off. My phone buzzed on the granite surface of the island, and I snatched it up, already prepared to carry on a new conversation with Levi. But it wasn't Levi.

It was Dex.

I frowned at my screen, partly because the wrong guy had texted me and partly because there was zero possibility that Dex didn't have an angle. He'd been texting me ever since we'd seen each other at the circus party but nothing inappropriate, nothing forward. Just stupid stuff like we used to send each other when we were friends. Memes or funny things that had made us think of the other. Random gossip.

But it wasn't innocent. He'd seen me with Levi, which couldn't have felt good to anyone but me. Dex was spoiled, a man who got what he wanted and wanted what he couldn't have. And though we had once been friends, that ship had sailed. If you showed me ex-lovers who were friends, I'd show you one fool and one lovesick hopeful. It just didn't work. You couldn't erase those feelings, not with all the years and friendzoning in the world.

I wondered with more disdain whether or not his girlfriend knew he was texting me.

My nose wrinkled up, and I set my phone back down as Zeke and Betty wandered in.

"Look who it is. The Bobbsey twins," I joked.

Zeke's kimono—which I loved so much, I'd tried to steal it half a dozen times to no avail—fluttered behind him, his boxer briefs tight and closer to the brief than the boxer. His platinum hair was perfectly in place.

He mumbled something that at least rhymed with *coffee* and sat on a stool, yawning. Betty pulled up next to him, sleepy-faced and hair a dark, wild snarl. She had on matching white eyelet pajamas in a tank and bloomer set, and her eye mask served as a headband as she scrubbed her face with her hand.

"Morning, sunshine." I made moves for the espresso machine.

"What are you so chipper about?" Zeke asked, then groaned. "It's your steady D that's got you all Disney princess. I'd appreciate it if you didn't rub it in."

"I'm not rubbing anything in," I said archly. "Out, maybe. But not in."

"You're the worst," Betty said from the cave of her arms where she'd buried her head.

"Hey, don't blame me because you made a celibacy pact with Zeke. We all have to deal with the consequences of our choices, Roberta."

She lifted her head enough to give me the deadliest of looks. "There are too many knives within reach to risk calling me that name."

My phone buzzed again. Zeke's brow rose when I didn't answer it.

"Dex."

The other brow met its twin. Betty's head rose.

"What does he want?" Betty asked.

"Who knows, but it can't be good. Don't worry—I'm not encouraging him."

"Good, then you won't mine me looking." Zeke snatched up my phone, but before he could read, he thought better of himself and smiled wickedly. "Today must be my lucky day."

I snorted a laugh. "I don't think Dex would sleep with you, Z."

He waved a hand. "Oh, trust me, I know. But it's not Dex. It's Tag."

Betty and I groaned—my stepbrother was a notorious asshole—but Zeke looked pleased as punch.

"What the fuck does he want?" I swiped my phone from his hands and skimmed his message. "Ugh, he wants to crash."

Zeke rolled his eyes. "Don't act like you don't like a full house. Are you even capable of saying no?"

"Shoulda said no to you."

He stuck his tongue out.

Betty groaned again with her eyes glued to the ceiling. "Where is he?"

"Downstairs," Zeke and I answered at the same time but with very different tones.

"Go put on some pants," I told Zeke.

"Don't tell me what to do, Stella Marie."

"You know that's not my middle name." I shot off a text telling Tag to come up.

"Well, I hate your middle name and refuse to say it."

I made a face at him before putting down my phone to sulk while I still could.

Tag's dad and my mom had been married for two years when I was in high school and he was in college. We barely knew each other, but somehow we'd ended up in the same social group, and since he'd just gotten back from Cambodia, he had nowhere to crash. It wasn't uncommon for him to come here. It was just unwelcome.

A knock rapped at the door, and Zeke was off his stool in a flash and a billow of silk. He draped himself on an armchair.

"Subtle," I said, heading for the door.

And leaning his forearm on the doorjamb was Tag St. James.

His smile was straight out of a toothpaste commercial, his eyes a striking shade of blue against tanned skin. Sandy-blond hair, broad shoulders, the whole nine. If I hadn't been legally related to him for a period of time, and if I didn't think he was a spectacular douchebag, I'd hit that.

Problem was, he knew how hot he was. Which didn't help his cause.

"Hey, sis," he said with a crooked smile.

"Don't call me that." I turned around and let go of the door, hoping it hit him in the nose.

But he just laughed, grabbing his Louis Vuitton duffel bag and striding in. "Ooh, lookin' good, Betty."

"Fuck you, Tag," she said, sliding off her stool to walk away.

"Wait—your coffee!" I called after her.

"I'd rather go coffeeless than talk to Tag."

"*Missed you too*," he sang, taking her seat, then her coffee.

Zeke huffed from the armchair and stood with a whoosh. "God, what's a girl gotta do to get some attention around here?"

Tag's laugh was the sort of sound only made by men without responsibility. "Come here, Freaky Zeke. Come give Daddy a hug."

"There we go," Zeke said as he approached, hugging Tag from behind and smushing his cheek against the back of Tag's head, giving it a conspicuous sniff. "See? That wasn't so hard."

"I could make a dick joke, but I'll let it slide," Tag snarked.

"And I could make one back, but I'll let you have your coffee first." Zeke sat on his stool again. "So you're back. Cambodia as boring as everyone says?"

Tag shrugged. "Been gone three months. At some point, you just want a real hamburger and to order coffee in English." He jerked his chin at me. "Hey, thanks for letting me crash."

"You're welcome. Zeke took your room though."

Zeke smiled. "We can bunk together. Top or bottom?"

I shook my head at him. "You can have one of the others."

"Generous," Tag said. "Since you've got six."

Joss wandered in, yawning. "What's he doing here?" she asked in Tag's general direction.

"Came to crash for a while," he answered. "So what's new? Where's the next party, Cecelia?"

"You're not invited," I said, wishing I were that savage.

"Aww, come on, Stell. Make an exception for your favorite stepbrother."

"*Ex*-stepbrother."

"You can be my plus-one, Taggy," Zeke said. "But you have to let me dress you up."

"Sorry, buddy—gotta draw the line somewhere. Don't want to get arrested for public indecency."

Zeke pouted.

"So party on Saturday. Remy's having people over tonight, but I'm too wiped to even think about it. What else is new?"

"Stella has a *boyfriend*." Zeke sang the word like a second-grader.

Tag's brow rose with his smile. "I heard Dex is shacking with Elsie Richmond, so who's the new guy?"

I opened my mouth to speak, but Zeke beat me to it. "He's a photographer. With a motorcycle."

Tag nodded his approval. "Nice catch."

"I thought so," I said.

"But he's leaving," Zeke added. "Syria, to cover the war."

"Heavy," Tag noted studiously.

"Very deep," Zeke added with a brow waggle. "You'll meet him soon enough. He practically lives here."

"Look at you, Stell. You show old Dex."

"That's not why I—"

Zeke looped his arm in Tag's. "What are we gonna do today, Taggy? Feed you hamburgers?"

Tag patted Zeke's hand on his sizable bicep. "I'd love to, but I've got to sleep. It's been thirty-six hours since I've seen a bed and a shower. But tomorrow, we'll eat the meat."

Zeke laid his head on Tag's shoulder and pouted at me. "Can I have him?"

"I don't think he's up for auction," I said on a laugh. "Now, will you please go put some pants on? Brunch awaits, and I need a new dress."

"What for?" Tag asked.

"Does a girl need a reason to buy a new dress?" I challenged.

"No, she doesn't," Zeke answered. "Brunch and Bloomie's. Who could ask for more?"

"No one," I said with a smile, grateful for the distraction.

Because killing time until I saw Levi had become a sport.

And I was the champ.

LEVI

I paced the length of Yara's office, raking my hand through my hair.

"I'm sorry, Levi. My hands are tied." She leaned back in her chair. "Marcella is thirsty for this piece, and she's not going to let any of us wait to publish. Maybe if the first one hadn't gone viral. But that was chum in the water, and now she's not gonna let it go. She wants the second article. Like, three days ago."

"Give me one more day."

"Levi ..."

"Come on. One day won't matter. I'm never late, and I never ask for anything. You've got to give me this."

"No one has to give you anything," she said firmly but not without compassion. "You've been putting me off, and Marcella isn't happy. She made it very clear that you were to turn the piece in today, and we're to have it edited immediately."

I stopped in front of her desk and planted my hands on the surface. "I just need one more day."

She huffed and crossed her arms. "For what?"

"I have something I need to take care of first."

"Does this something have anything to do with Stella Spencer?"

I drew a long breath through my nose, my teeth clenching and releasing. We'd been spotted all over social media together, though nobody'd had the balls to bring it up until now. "I can't keep lying to her."

"Since when?" she snapped. "If you think you can get the rest of your articles to Marcella without Stella Spencer, then be my guest. But if you can't, you should think long and hard about what you're willing to do. Because Marcella threatened Syria if you don't see the Bright Young Things through."

I stilled, all the way down to my heart.

"I didn't want to tell you, but I don't think you realize the severity of the situation."

"Somebody's going to get hurt."

"And it's time for you to decide if that someone is you or her. This is journalism, not Match.com. Nobody gives a shit about your love life, and it's certainly not a priority to this magazine. You know what is?" She leaned in. "Sales. And you know what gets sales?"

"Stories."

"So are you going to get the story? Or are you going to lose your shot at leveling up over a girl?"

For a moment, I just stared at a nick on the surface of her desk, weighing it all out. But in the end, there was only one answer, and I'd always known it.

"Promise me the article won't break until tomorrow."

Yara surveyed me with an unreadable expression on her face. "I'll talk to her. Send me the article, Levi. Now. I'll have edits back by lunch."

I nodded and turned for the door.

"You'd better be real sure about this," she warned.

"Never been so sure," I said, pushing her door open and storming out.

Because I was telling Stella the truth tonight.

And all I could do was hope it wouldn't bury me.

SHAKE ON IT

STELLA

"**A**RE YOU FUCKING KIDDING ME?" I SAID THE
words to nothing and no one as I stared at the
article on my phone that afternoon.

On *Vagabond*.

About the Revolution party.

Betty, Joss, and Zeke exchanged glances across the
café table. Zeke took a sip of his whiskey with an eyebrow
jacked, but Betty set hers down with a clink.

"This is bullshit," she said, fuming. "Total bullshit."

"It's one of us." I shook my head at my phone, once
again unable to comprehend more than partial sentences
of the article. My brain was too preoccupied with murder.

Joss's brows drew together. "Did you keep track of
the plus-ones?"

"No, there's no real way. Someone would've had to
take names—there were too many of them to casually
remember."

"Maybe it was Tuesday Morrison. That guy she's been bringing is greasy," Zeke said.

"It could have been anyone." My chest ached, my mind skipping. "This is driving me crazy. Like, *actually* crazy. Do you guys realize just how bad this is? Because we have no control. What if they're working with Warren?"

At that, Zeke gave me a look. "If Warren was in on it, the articles wouldn't be this big, gooey congratulatory thing. It sounds like one of us. I mean, it's borderline masturbation—whoever wrote this is all in. No way did Warren have anything to do with it."

I shook my head and didn't stop. "He's going to get ideas. He's going to send someone in to find a chink in the armor and take us down. What if he plants someone? Someone who will do something that gets us in real trouble? We can't go through any more bad press, not after Sable."

Heavy silence fell over us.

A few months ago, Sable—one of ours—had come to a party with her junkie boyfriend, track marks in her arm and eyes ringed in red. When Betty, Zeke, and I tried to get her out of the building, away from that asshole, and into a cab, Sable lost it. She took a swing at me, told us all to fuck off, and left.

We never saw her alive again. She'd overdosed that night.

It was the start of the shitstorm even though she hadn't been with us when she died. But instead of blaming the drug-dealing jackhole who had shot her up, everyone blamed the Bright Young Things. The firestorm had died down—other than goddamn Warren, but I didn't think his crusade had anything to do with Sable. From what I'd gathered, he was just a dick.

I pinched the bridge of my nose. "We have to figure out who this is. How can we flush them out?"

When I opened my eyes, Zeke was on his phone, his fingers flying. He had *that look*, the one that suggested we were about to get in trouble.

"Zeke," I warned. "What are you doing?"

He lifted the phone to his ear and winked at me.

"Here we go," Betty said with a smile.

Joss just watched us, her eyes curious and smiling and the rest of her leaning in with anticipation.

"Hello," Zeke said in his deepest voice. "I have a tip to report. No, I can't give it on the phone. It's about the Bright Young Things. Yes, I'll hold."

"*Oh my God,*" I whisperscreamed, resisting the impulse to jump over the table and throttle him. "*What the fuck are you doing?*"

He held up his finger to silence me. "Yes, hi. That's right. No, I need to meet with the reporter in person. I understand they're anonymous, but this isn't the kind of information I can just hand out. The nature?" He paused, his eyes flicking to me. "I know who Cecelia Beaton is."

At that, I flew out of my seat, nearly knocking it over. But before I could get my hands around his neck, he stopped me with one hand, followed by Betty's and Joss's arms. Betty put herself between me and Zeke and forced eye contact.

Calm down, she mouthed, and I stilled—there weren't many people on the patio with us, but the ones who were there were staring.

"Proof? I have her notebook. Yes, it's a woman. I assume there's compensation for the exchange? *Excellent.*"

Betty clapped her hand on my mouth and looked over her shoulder at Zeke.

"Okay, sure. Have them meet me at Half Moon diner on Fifth. Seven tonight. Thanks." He disconnected and set his phone down, smirking at me.

"*What the fuck, Zeke? What in the actual fuck?*" I whisper-hissed. "Are you crazy? If you tell them who I am—"

"I'm not telling them anything. *You* are."

My face quirked. "What?"

Zeke stood, still smiling. "You're going to Half Moon, and the asshole who wrote the articles is going to show up, thinking they're getting the scoop. And instead, they'll get busted."

I stilled, gaping for a heartbeat before a smile of my own brushed my lips. "You're a fucking genius."

He curtsied. "You're welcome."

"But won't they know I'm in charge if I'm the one there?"

"Just because you're there doesn't mean anyone will assume you're her. Claim you're just nosy. Tie back your hair. Wear a hat and sunglasses. Sit somewhere you can hide. And don't say a fucking word. Just watch."

"What if I go ape and Krav Maga the fucker to the ground?"

"First of all, you couldn't Krav anybody's Maga with those puny arms. And secondly, you have more willpower than that. Look for somebody to come in alone, wait alone, look nervous, and leave without anyone meeting them. Take some pictures. If we can't figure out who it is, we'll look for them at the next party. But we can't confront anybody, not without raising suspicions. Okay?"

I drew a long, steady breath and nodded. "Okay."

"Good girl. Tonight, we'll unmask the motherfucker and take them to the mat," Zeke assured me.

"And we're here when it's over," Joss said.

"Can't you guys just come with me?"

Betty shook her head. "Too much of a chance we'll be recognized. Especially Zeke."

"I'm taking that as a compliment whether you mean it as one or not," Zeke said flatly.

"You've got this, Stell," Joss started. "We'll have booze and pizza when you get home, okay?"

A flash of excitement and vengeance zipped through me. "All right. Tonight, we'll know." The thought was a comfort, as nervous as I was.

Because somebody was going to pay for fucking with us.

Tonight.

LEVI

I flew toward Half Moon diner like a fucking hurricane.

She's the boss for a reason, I heard Yara say when I raged into her office upon finding out they'd pushed the article live on the website within a half hour of my turning the approved edits in.

And nobody had told me. But they wouldn't have, knowing I'd push back. So they'd just gone ahead and fucked me, and with that, my chances. And just hours ago, without any time for Stella to process it. Without any time to calm down before I told her it was *me.*

Fucked. Well and truly fucked.

Part of me wondered if Yara and Marcella had planned this, pushed it live knowing it would complicate things for me in the hopes that I'd fold, keep up the ruse so I wouldn't Chernobyl the whole operation. They'd succeeded in complicating things. But there was no way I would fold. Forcing me to do something I was morally opposed to only had one outcome: defiance. And I was so fucking mad, I'd blast it all to hell before I'd bend, not after they'd disregarded my requests and gone around me to publish.

Stella was pissed. We'd been texting all day, but when the article broke, she lost it. I'd let her talk, didn't say much, and ultimately promised her we'd talk about it tonight. Which we would. She just had no idea that I was about to throw a grenade at her.

As soon as this interview was over, I was onto the next hard thing. And the only way to cope was to stuff it into a box to be dealt with when we were face-to-face.

The tip had come in a few hours ago, answering the question I'd asked in the article—the identity of Cecelia Beaton. Inside the diner I approached was an informer with a condemning notebook and a real name, and once I got them, I had to figure out what the fuck to do with them. Yara had suggested sending an intern first to scope it out in an effort to protect my identity with the intent to plan a second meeting. But hiding had been her idea, not mine. Slinging my work around like it had come to them for free was *them*. I had nothing to hide, not anymore. And I certainly wasn't going to send an intern to do my job. Yara wasn't happy about it.

I couldn't pretend to give a shit what she thought.

The bell over the door rang as I entered, and a waitress somewhere from the back told me to sit anywhere. But I was too busy scanning the diner to hear her. The caller was male, and I noted two males and one female sitting alone. My eyes snagged the woman dressed conspicuously inconspicuous in a baseball hat, Army jacket, and sunglasses that were too big for her face. Her gaze shifted from her phone to me and held it.

A smile spread on her face.

I know that smile.

Oh my fucking God.

I turned to stone, my heart slowing. *Is it her? Is she Cecelia Beaton?*

Stella stood and flew across the room to me.

"What are you doing here?" she asked, still smiling as she hitched up onto her tiptoes to press a kiss to my lips.

I didn't kiss her back. "I'm ... what are *you* doing here?"

She shook her head. "Just this ... thing. It's Zeke's fault, really."

"Zeke," I said to myself as the trap made itself known. "Zeke."

"Can you keep a secret?" she asked, leaning in. "Zeke set up the reporter so we could figure out who it is. Told them we knew who Cecelia Beaton was. Come sit with me—we can wait together. Makes me look less suspicious anyway."

She grabbed my hand and pulled, but I didn't budge. I schooled my face to neutral.

"What's wrong?" she asked, her brain clicking behind her

eyes to piece something together. "Why are you here again? This isn't anywhere near your place."

A storm brewed in my chest. "No, it isn't."

She blinked at me, her frown deepening. "What are you doing here, Levi?"

I drew a deep breath with no idea how to tell her, not caught so off guard. Her face was confusion and suspicion.

I took her arm, looking around the room to make sure we weren't causing a scene, not with Stella being who she was. "Come sit down. I'll explain."

"Explain what?" She removed her arm from my grip.

I dragged my hand through my hair, searching for an approach that would make this easier, but my mind was static. "I should have told you from the start," I muttered. "It wasn't supposed to happen this way."

The truth didn't dawn on her—it cracked like lightning, splitting her in two. "Oh my God," she breathed. "Oh my God, it's *you*."

My chest was too tight, too small for my lungs. "Let me explain—"

"Oh my *God*." Her hand covered her lips.

"Are you Cecelia Beaton?"

"How many fucking times do I have to tell you I'm not? What I am is sick and tired of our circle being infiltrated. We had to know who it was, but I ... I never thought ..." The words broke, and she swallowed hard. "All this time I've been trying to figure out who let the reporter in, and it was me. It was me the whole time," she said half to herself, her voice wavering as she looked up at me like she'd never seen me before. "You lied. You lied to me."

"Please," I begged, reaching for her. "Hear me out."

She dodged me, and my fingers caught air. "Was any of it real? Or did you sleep with me for the sake of your story?"

I opened my mouth to answer, but she waved a hand and looked away.

"No. You know what? I don't want to know." She took a step back. Then another. "I can't believe it was you. That all this was my fault. That you used me this way. But I always do this. I always choose the worst kind of man." Tears rose in her eyes. "Fuck you, Levi, for proving the theory."

She whirled around and shoved the door open, marching down Fifth, and I followed. Because even if she never wanted to see me again, I had to explain. I had to try.

I had to fight, even if it was only for the chance to come clean.

"Stella—" I called.

She picked up her pace, weaving through people.

"Stella, wait. Shit, sorry, ma'am. *Stella!*"

Her eyes were wide and shining as she looked for an escape. A cab, maybe. The subway. If I was lucky, she'd end up stuck on a train with me long enough to hear me out.

I gained on her, called her name, miserable at the sight of her dashing tears from her cheeks.

"Please. *Please, Stell*—" I reached for her. My fingers brushed her arm, but she jerked it away. "Just give me five minutes, and I swear, you'll never see me again."

She slowed. Stopped. Turned to face me, flushed and furious. "You have two minutes."

My brain burst with starting points, rejecting them all on entry. Another rake of my hand through my hair didn't help, and I searched her face with dark desperation for answers.

"A minute forty-five." She folded her arms.

"I'm not out to get you. And I've never used you."

"*Ha.*"

A long exhale. "No, you don't understand."

"Explain it to me. Because the way I see it, you fucked me for information. For a ticket in. Lied about being a reporter. Spied on us, betrayed our trust. My trust."

"That isn't why I've been with you—"

"*Then fucking spell it out.*"

"Jesus, Stella—if you'd stop talking for more than ten seconds, I will."

Her eyes narrowed, but she didn't speak.

"I couldn't tell you who I was"—she started to argue, but I kept going—"not without this happening. And not if I wanted to be able to do my job. I left the speakeasy and wrote down everything I saw, everything I felt. Everything but you. That first piece was just for me, an exercise to produce some material for the big article for the magazine. But my editor took it, and they published it without telling me. I didn't know, Stella. I didn't know they were going to publish it or I would have told you. Warned you. But once they put it out, it was too late." I pleaded with my eyes, with my heart. "This article, this piece, is my ticket to my dream job. It's security for my only family. I didn't know I'd meet you."

"Sure, you're a regular fucking hero," she shot. "You kissed me that night knowing you'd have to lie to me. You went home with me *knowing* you were a goddamn liar. And you betrayed everything and everyone."

"Stella, this is my job—"

"A professional liar?"

I laid a hard look on her. "How I feel about you isn't a lie."

"Stop it," she whispered, her voice shaking. "You don't get to do that. You don't get to tell me you have feelings for me like it absolves what you've done."

"I wanted to tell you—"

"But you didn't. You got backed into a corner and *then* regretted not telling me when it should have been the first words out of your mouth."

I stilled, the tension in my shoulders easing, dropping them. "You're right. About all of it. I think you know I'm on your side— you've read what I wrote. I'm not out to get you, Stella. But I lied to you, and I'm sorry."

"You're sorry because you got caught."

"No," I insisted. "I was sorry from the start. After the circus, when we got to your place, I tried to walk away. Do you remember? I should have walked away—you were always going to find out, and when you did, it was going to hurt us both. But I couldn't help myself. I can't, not when it comes to you. So I kept a secret from you, a big secret, because I'm selfish. And I hate that you found out like this."

Something shifted behind her eyes, softening her face. Indecision.

I chanced a step closer. "My job is to tell the truth about what I write, to give people a window to all the things you love about the Bright Young Things. I don't want to ruin them. I'm not here to dismantle what's been built, what you're a part of. All I want is to give people a taste of what I've come to love about these parties, this group." Another step closer. She didn't take a step back. "I'm sorry, Stella. But I'd never turn on you. I would never hurt anything you love. It's on me to preserve it."

I was close enough to smell her perfume, my fingers lifting to trail her jaw, clasp her chin, tilt it to lock our gazes.

"Tell me you know that," I begged softly.

"I do," she admitted. "But ... I ..." She shook her head.

"How can I make it up to you? How can I earn your trust again? Tell me. Tell me, and I'll do it."

"Why do you care?" she asked without heat, only curiosity. "You're leaving. This? You and me? It's temporary. How am I supposed to believe that you're doing this for me and not your story?"

"I don't have an answer for that," I admitted. "Only my word. I know it doesn't mean much. But the truth is, I don't want to walk away from this. From you. Even if it's temporary."

Her eyes cast down, her lashes long and feathery against flushed cheeks.

I lifted her chin again. "What if I give you every article to edit before anyone else sees it?"

The offer brightened her eyes.

"You can be my partner. Make sure it lands just where you want it."

"Absolute power?"

I smiled. "Absolute power. And I might not be able to stop them from publishing on time without risking my job, but they can't publish anything I haven't signed off on. No chance for it to get twisted."

"Why would you do that?"

I held her face in my hands, fell into the depths of her eyes. "Because you can trust me, just like I trust you, and I'm going to prove it. No more secrets, Stella. I promise."

A shadow passed over her face. "No more secrets," she echoed with an edge to her voice. I didn't know her well enough yet to decipher its meaning.

But I was too relieved to consider it as I pulled her into my chest, my body uncoiling and my ribs free to breathe for the first time in days.

I was the luckiest motherfucker in the world to have dodged the bullet.

And I fucking knew it.

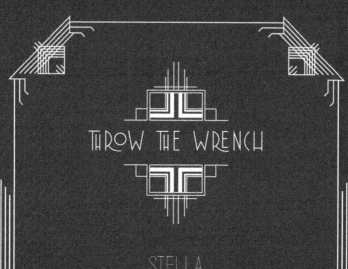

THROW THE WRENCH

STELLA

AM SUCH A SUCKER.

A shaft of early morning light slanted across my bed, illuminating the white comforter with an almost blinding glow. The fluffy down affair lay bunched at Levi's waist, leaving his impressive torso on display. He was a map made of ridges of muscles, discs of his pecs, the fanning of those curious thews high on his ribs and around to his back as he breathed that slow, unbothered rhythm of sleep.

I lay on my side, head propped in my palm, watching him with the promise to get up and make coffee after just one more minute. Just another minute to admire every curve of his stature. Of the strong column of his neck and the knot of his Adam's apple. His dusky jaw, the line made sharper by the shadow of his short beard. The curious planes of his lips, the swell and the flat that beckoned, even in sleep. His utterly masculine nose, the notch above the bridge, the line of his brow.

He was beautiful in a rugged, untamed way, a wild species of man I'd never encountered before. Nothing about him was soft, not at a glance, at least. But I'd seen his eyes shift to molten heat, felt the tender demand of his lips on my body, been privileged to know the sweetness of a caress by hands meant for a forge.

Such a sucker.

And I was. A sucker and a fool, a glutton for punishment for giving myself the luxury of being with him. Because he was a lying liar who'd lied. A lying liar who was leaving.

This is fine, I reminded myself. *Really, it's fine. Better than fine. It's fun and it feels good, and now he's given me an in—I can control the tone and content of his articles. I can protect what I've built and have a goddamn excellent time while I'm doing it.*

With a smile, I sighed. I believed him, and I trusted him—a flaw highlighted by my friends on the regular. I wanted to fight the feeling, and in some ways, I did—there was no way forward without my guard up—but I'd felt the truth of his intention and the relief from the burden of his secret.

Last night, he'd sworn he'd been planning on coming clean, and I didn't doubt him for a second, not after spending the majority of yesterday wondering what he wanted to talk about. His fury at his editors' move to publish yesterday had been plain to see, mostly from the proportion of his use of the word *fuck* to the rest of them. That, and the look in his eyes.

As much as I hated to admit it, he'd been right to keep it from me—if I hadn't gotten into this with him, I would have shut him down from day one. I would have missed all of this, and what a tragedy that would have been.

So we were moving on. He'd told me the truth—including his *actual* last name—and I would get the final say on what he wrote for the magazine. We both won—he got to keep his story, and I got to control it. And we got to hang on to each other for a little while longer.

No more secrets, he'd said.

My stomach twisted at the memory. But there was one secret he couldn't know. If he found out, if anyone discovered he knew, he could ransom my identity for enough money to retire on.

Especially if he took it straight to Warren.

He wouldn't do that, I told myself. But I still wasn't going to tell him.

I might have been a sucker, but I wasn't stupid.

His chest expanded, his breath loud through his nose as he woke, his big hand appearing from the other side of him to rest on his abs. Sleepy eyes blinked open, his lips smiling when he saw me.

"Mornin'," he said with a gravelly voice.

"Morning," I echoed. "Sleep okay?"

He rolled over, sliding his hand over the curve of my hip. "Best night's sleep I've had in weeks." A brief kiss before he mirrored my pose.

"Insomnia?"

"Guiltomnia. I've been trying to figure out how to tell you who I was. I didn't think you'd forgive me."

"Me neither," I said on a laugh. "Has anyone told you you're incredibly convincing?"

"It's been said. And despite my track record, I'm notoriously honest."

"How does that work anyway? Don't you have, like … a code of ethics or something? Am I a conflict of interest?"

"If I were a newspaper journalist, the answer would be yes. But I'm writing a literary opinion piece. Literary journalism is pretty much the Wild West when it comes to the rules. I have my terrible alias, which isn't at all clever, but it gets me where I need to be so I can get the inside look at a forbidden place. If I told you it was the only thing I ever lied about, would you believe me?"

I sighed. "Only because I'm notoriously gullible."

"Wait—I thought I was just *incredibly convincing.*"

"That too. What made you decide to be a journalist?"

For a second, he said nothing, seemingly lost in thought. "A girl I ran with in high school dropped out to start hooking. Safer than living with her dad," he added, noting the upset on my face. "I'd always gone places I wasn't supposed to, hung out with vagrants sometimes, bought them a meal with my allowance and listened to their stories. That sort of thing, maybe out of some curiosity about my parents and the world that swallowed them up. But when she ran off, I made it a point to find her. And when I did, when I saw her truth, I had to write it down. It was too much feeling to speak. It was the only thing I could do for her—there's no saving someone who doesn't want saving. Her story was the first piece I wrote, and I knew. I didn't just give her a voice. I found mine."

My heart twisted in my chest. "It's no wonder your job means so much to you. Why war is a place you'd feel called to be."

"It is. And it's a way for me to help Billy out. I don't know how much longer he'll be able to live alone, and he won't let me move in with him. I've been saving my pennies for a long time in anticipation of that—what he earns from his pension and Social Security won't put a dent in home care or a decent nursing home. He doesn't have anybody else to look after him. So every little bit secures his future, and this gig is going to set us up nicely."

"It's a win for everybody. I just wish you didn't have to go halfway around the world for it." I was thankful that he chuckled rather than it getting weird, and kept talking so it wouldn't start a conversation about him leaving that I didn't want to have. "What are you doing today?"

"I need to swing by work, finish my Tiffany's piece, and send it to you for the first round of slashing. But first, I need to stop by Billy's. Gotta pick up his meds, get him some groceries, that sort of thing. Mostly though, I've got to make sure he hasn't busted a hip or starved to death."

"Want company?"

His brow rose with his smile. "You want to meet my dad?"

I shrugged like it was no big deal. "If it wouldn't be weird, why not? I'm curious where you came from. Who made you such an honest liar."

"Billy would appreciate you saying so." He watched me for a moment. "All right. I'd love your company."

"I only have one request."

"Which is …"

"We go on your bike. I haven't had a ride in days."

He grabbed me, pressed his hips to mine, and twisted to put me on top of him. My hair was a curtain, separating us from the rest of the world. "I can fix that right now."

And with a laugh that he swallowed with a kiss, he fixed that with great skill.

A few hours later, we pulled to a stop in front of what I figured must be Billy's building, a bag of groceries and such on my arm and my shoulders warm from the sun. Fresh air kissed my cheeks when I took off my helmet—Levi had made a habit of bringing a spare for me like a goddamn gentleman—but before I could get off the bike, he took the bag and the helmet, leaving me with nothing but the task of putting my feet on the ground.

I smoothed a hand over my sundress—a gauzy, bohemian affair I'd paired with a bodysuit so all of Manhattan wouldn't see my bare ass—and looked up. It was a beautiful building, if not a little run-down, the front a zigzag of the fire escape over red brick. Levi told me he'd grown up here, that Billy had lived here since the '70s with his wife before she died. This neighborhood had been a lot different then, and I imagined Levi as a little boy, running around these streets causing trouble.

"What are you smiling about?" he asked, stuffing his keys in his pocket before grabbing the grocery bag.

"Oh, just wondering what kind of trouble you got into as a kid."

He shrugged. "I didn't, not really. I'd seen enough to last me by the time I made it to Billy."

"Like what?"

Levi took my hand, glancing both ways before starting across the street. "Well, my parents were junkies, so I bet you could guess."

He said it so casually, his lips in an easy smile and his face untroubled. I, on the other hand, wasn't so blasé—the deep ache in my chest was proof.

"I always assumed growing up hard would … I don't know. Breed resentment against the world. Spark retaliation."

"Probably does. But I was just so thankful to have a safe place to live and with someone who cared, and I didn't want to screw that up. All I ever wanted was stability. Risking that never seemed worth it." He pulled open the door to the building and held it so I could pass.

"You're something else, you know that?"

"Actually, I do," he answered with a smirk.

"And modest too."

"One of my better traits."

I chuckled as we began our climb. "Got an invitation today. A pub crawl. Well, sort of," I amended. "We only know the starting point and time. The bartenders will have clues for us. We have to order a special drink at the bar to get it."

"What's the theme?"

"Disco Chickens."

A laugh shot out of him. "Where the fuck am I gonna get a chicken mask?"

"Nowhere. Cecelia Beaton sent two with the invitations."

"Of course she did. Plastic masks, right?"

"Nope. It was different for everyone, but we got full-blown furry masks."

"How does she figure we'll drink?"

I shrugged. "I *guess* she figures we'll get creative."

"Now that I've met everyone, I'm dying to know who she is. Aren't you?"

"Of course I am. Isn't everyone?"

"We should find out. You and me. You know everybody and can ask around without looking suspicious—"

I stopped and turned, glad for my place a few steps above him so I could look down at him with some authority. "You don't really want to know who it is, and neither do I."

He frowned. "Yes, I really do."

I folded my arms. "No, you really don't. Why do you need to pull back the curtain? Why do you want to see Oz? Look at what we have. This spectacular thing we're a part of. Because the minute you or I or anybody knows, it's over. And if *you* find out, do you really think you could keep it to yourself? That knowledge is dangerous in anyone's hands, but especially yours."

His frown deepened. "I wouldn't betray—"

"Be careful about the next thing that leaves your mouth because you literally just got out of the doghouse for this exact reason."

Wisely, he kept quiet.

"You say you don't want to burn it all down, but uncovering this secret will. So I'm asking you to let it go, Levi. Or you and I aren't gonna be okay. Ice is thin enough as it is—don't do anything stupid, like jump."

His face smoothed, his smile returning as he climbed the steps until we were eye-level. When his arms were wrapped around my waist, he said, "You're right. And I promise to let it go."

"Good," I answered with a smile, kissing him for a moment.

And then we were on our way again.

Levi didn't knock, just unlocked the door, bracing it with his foot while he pulled the key out. "Billy, put some pants on. I brought a girl."

A voice from somewhere inside said, "If I must."

With a chuckle, Levi gave me a look that told me to get myself ready.

And with wild curiosity and an even wilder smile, I nodded.

The apartment was a relic, an old bachelor's pad if I'd ever seen one. If I had to guess, nothing had been updated since his wife had passed, particularly the couch, which had an ass divot like I'd never seen before. But the space was bright, the light from the big windows setting an undeniable cheer on everything. It was a lot like Levi—the light shining on the darkness, highlighting the good and the bad, casting shadows on what didn't want to be seen.

I instantly loved every dusty corner.

"A girl, huh?" the bodiless voice said from the back of the apartment, and around the corner he came, leaning heavily on his cane.

Though they weren't related, I found similarities between the two men that were indisputable. Their sizable height. The weathered air about them, as if they'd seen unimaginable things, things that had changed them irrevocably. They had the same sideways smile, and the peppering of black in his gray mane told me they'd once had the same color and density of hair.

That crooked smile was pointed right at me. "Well, look at that. I'nt just any girl. This girl's something else."

Billy and Levi shared a look, but I didn't ask. Just stepped forward so I could shake his hand.

"It's so nice to meet you, Mr. Jepsen. I'm—"

"Stella Spencer," he said as he took my hand and gave it a proud and solid shake. "Anybody with two eyes and a brain between their ears knows who you are. Nice to meetcha." His gaze shifted to Levi. "If you didn't bring me my sandwich, you can go. But she's stayin.'"

Levi shook his head, unloading the sandwiches onto the table before putting away the groceries. "You're a dog, Billy."

But Billy just shrugged and took a seat at the table, eyeing his sandwich hungrily. "Come on, sit down with me so it's not weird."

He flagged me over with his hand and pointed to the seat next to him. "Whatdya get?" he asked as I sat.

"Meatball sub," I answered, reaching for the sandwich wrapped in foil.

I was met with an approving look. "Look at that. I like a girl who's not afraid to get her hands dirty."

"Come on, Pop," Levi said, setting a cold beer in front of Billy and snagging a napkin from the stack on the table. "You're gonna scare her off."

"Psh—I'm made of tougher stuff than that," I noted, picking up my sandwich. I lined it up and took an obscene bite.

Both of them gaped at me, and I tried not to be smug as I wiped a slide of sauce from my chin.

"Attagirl," Billy said, taking a rude bite of his own.

"Beer?" Levi asked me, still bustling around the kitchen.

"Yes, please," I answered politely around the last of my impolite mouthful.

A second later, he took the free seat at my other side, setting the bottles between us.

"So what do you want to know?" Billy asked. "Sadly, I don't have any naked baby pictures of the kid, but I got stories galore. Like the boiler."

Levi's face flattened. "Don't."

I leaned in. "Oh, please do."

"Well, ya see, Levi here was afraid of the boiler—"

"Pop."

Billy ignored him. "Way back when, before I got nicked, I helped around here with the maintenance, and Levi used to come with me. Whole building knew him. He'd carry my tools—s' what got those muscles started. Anyhow, so it's the dead of winter and colder than a witch's tit, and the boiler breaks. So me and Levi go down to the basement to see what's what."

"Jesus, Billy, I swear to God if you don't shut up, I'm gonna tell Stella about the fire escape."

"Oh, no you won't, because then I'll tell her about Tiffany Blick."

Levi stilled but for a narrowing of his eyes, marking his defeat.

"So anyhow," Billy continued, "we go down to the basement, and you know how these old buildings are—it's creepy as shit down there, rats and a hundred years of dust and groany, old pipes. Levi here's got my tools, holding 'em in front of him like they'd stop the boogeyman coming to get him, eyes like ping pong balls, all white around the edges. So he's draggin' ass behind me, and I get to the boiler, get down there, and pull off the panel to look inside."

Levi dropped his head to his hand to rub his temple.

"So here I am on the ground, surrounded by rat shit and spiders and who knows what, lookin' into this thing with a flashlight. Stand up, flip the breaker, and that thing started up like a screamin' banshee. I mean it," he said when I laughed. "I never heard a boiler thump and hiss and squeal like that before. I look back for Levi—he's gone, tools and all. And before I can take a step, a battle cry if I ever heard one rips outta the kid, and out he jumps with a two-foot wrench, swings like Mickey Mantle, and hits that boiler hard enough to make a dent the size of my head. Broke the goddamn thing for good."

The two of us laughed, and Levi ignored us, eating his sandwich like he was alone.

"But that was always Levi," Billy said with the smile only a proud father could offer his son. "You got yourself a good one, Stella. Because my boy will take a wrench to whatever needs to be handled, 'specially if it's to protect somebody he loves. You know," he said, his voice softening, "when I took him in, I thought I was saving *him*. But the truth is, he's the one who saved me."

Levi swallowed, his face touched with levity but his eyes bottomless. "Come on, old man. You're gonna ruin your sandwich if you cry all over it."

Billy waved him off. "Feh, he's also nosy as hell and a general pain in my ass, what with all the nagging. *Take your meds, Pop? What'd you eat for lunch, Pop?* So take that into account too, would you?"

"I'll add it to the list," I said on a laugh.

Billy picked up the conversation, launching into another story, but Levi and I shared a look—his coupled with a sheepish shrug and mine soft as stuffing. And part of me regretted coming, not because I wasn't enjoying myself. But because I was enjoying myself too much, especially after his betrayal. It was just that I felt closer to him than ever. Like that argument was superglue, and now that what had been broken was put together again, it was stronger than it had been before. Now that he'd stripped himself down to the bolts, his truth was brighter than ever.

I should have run. Stepped back. Put some space between us, because this? Whatever we were playing at? It wasn't just for fun. And those stakes I'd counted as nominal got a little bit heavier with every day.

Instead, I filled myself up with helium and floated away on the lie that I had it all under control.

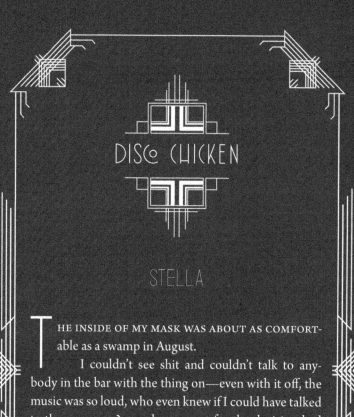

DISCO CHICKEN

STELLA

THE INSIDE OF MY MASK WAS ABOUT AS COMFORT-able as a swamp in August.

I couldn't see shit and couldn't talk to any-body in the bar with the thing on—even with it off, the music was so loud, who even knew if I could have talked to them anyway?—and my regret for the decision had grown with every bar. The only consolation was the photos.

My outfit, aside from the ridiculous mascot mask, was an elaborately jeweled pair of hot pants and a bi-kini top of shining silver and white. An ornate diamond statement necklace was draped around my neck and collarbone, and my shoes were strappy and sparkling and stupid high. I'd have regretted that too had Levi not pushed me from bar to bar in the shopping cart full of disco balls and hot-pink and purple gel lights I'd procured.

We were quite the sight, rolling through the Village in a whooping, clucking brood. The Bright Young Things were all spread out, having started from the first bar whenever they wanted and moving on when they wanted. Our group consisted of all my roommates, including Tag, and Levi. No one had brought a plus-one with pressure from Z, if I was going to guess. Z had refused the mask, dressing instead like a showgirl with a full-blown plume of feathers on her head and her ass and going so far as to install a prosthetic beak on her nose. She'd also attached herself to Tag like a fucking barnacle, who enjoyed any and all sexual attention.

I hadn't been able to convince Levi to dress up like a disco ball with me, so instead, he wore a white leisure suit and black shirt, which he'd unbuttoned to his belly button. I'd found him one of those men's gold necklaces with a horn charm that hung brilliantly in the dusting of dark hair on his broad chest. With his rooster mask on, he looked fucking hysterical. Especially when he threw the *Saturday Night Fever* disco point, hip pop and all.

He pushed his mask head into mine and shouted something, but it was nothing more than a *mwah-mwah-mwah*. So I pulled off my steam trap and shook my hair out, pointing to my ear.

He took his off too, running a hand through his damp hair. "Want another drink, or should we go?" he yelled.

I held up my index finger and mouthed *One more* at him.

With a nod and a kiss, he handed me his mask and headed for the bar.

Unready to put the goddamn thing back on, I set them on the empty table we'd claimed. I turned toward the dance floor, enjoying what felt like cool air on my cheeks. Truth was, it was probably ninety degrees in here, but after the mask, it felt as crisp as fall.

Picking out our crew was easy enough, though the rest of the patrons watched on in wide-eyed wonder when they realized who we were. Cameras were out—snapping pictures for their social, I was sure—and a cluster of people hovered around our disco cart taking pictures. Z and Betty were busy on the dance floor, and Joss cheered for them with a few of our other friends from the sidelines. I caught Tag with his tongue down the throat of a rando, which was super on-brand for him. A pack of Bright Young Things walked into the bar to a chorus of cheers, and more wandered around or danced, waving to each other and chatting.

I always loved the pub crawls—they were a little more intimate, a way for us to all have the same experience but separately. You saw who you saw with stories to swap, and then everyone moved on to the next thing.

A hand slipped into the slick small of my back, and I turned with a smile, expecting Levi.

Instead, I found Dex.

Half of his face was obscured by a masquerade mask covered in white feathers and tipped with a long golden beak. Other than yellow Converse, the only thing he had on was a pair of feathered boxer briefs with a plume of tail feathers on his ass.

I didn't want to invite him, not to anything ever again. But if he was left off the guest list, somebody would put the facts together and find me out, so here he was. The last person I wanted to see.

I stiffened but smiled back, turning to face him so he couldn't touch me so easily. "Hey, Dex."

"Lookin' good, Stell." He paused, seeming uncertain of what to say. "How've you been?"

"Oh, you know, the usual." I gestured to the dance floor.

"It's been …" He glanced down at his drink, then back up at me. When he leaned in, I made myself stay still instead of taking a step back like I wanted to. "Been missing you. Get my texts?"

"I did. Sorry for not answering—I've just been so busy that I see it and forget until three in the morning."

"Three in the morning never stopped you before," he said darkly. "Where's that guy you've been running with?"

"Levi? At the bar. It's too hot in here not to have a drink in hand," I said with a laugh, doing my best to keep it as light as I could, scanning the crowd. "Where's Elsie?"

His lean, muscular chest rose and fell with a sigh, and he looked in the direction of my eyeline. "Bathroom maybe? I don't know."

"Things are going well, then?"

"It's just … different. You know."

I didn't, and I didn't care to. "She seems really sweet, Dex. I'm happy for you."

His face turned to mine, but I kept my eyes in front of me, not wanting to meet his gaze. I could feel the weight, the hot intention, and a wave of revolt rose in me.

Especially when he said, "Are you?"

Two little words that held a deeper question and a darker promise.

"I am," I said with the canned smile I gave when put on the spot.

"So what's up with this guy?" he asked, keeping me pinned to the spot with his eyes. "You guys serious?"

My smile faded with the streak of anger that shot up my spine. "You mean like you and Elsie?"

The asshole didn't even flinch.

"I mean, I didn't move in with him, but I guess there's still time."

"Stella, come on. You can't blame me for asking."

My eyes narrowed with mock scrutiny. "I can't? Because last I heard, we weren't ever committed, monogamous, or even what you would call *together*. It's just a shame I didn't figure out I deserved better before I accidentally fell for you." The second the words left my lips, I wished I could reel them back in—I'd never admitted it to him, and he was too fucking stupid to have seen it for himself. "So the way I see it, it's none of your goddamn business who I'm dating or how serious it is."

He saw what he thought was a window and took another step closer, invading my space. "You weren't the only one who fell."

"Could have fucking fooled me."

Before he could answer, I felt another hand—the *right* hand—on my hip.

I leaned into Levi, breathing a silent *Thank God* into the humid air.

"Hey, Dex," Levi said, somehow with both levity and warning, as he handed me my drink. "I think I just saw Elsie looking for you. Probably oughta go find her."

Dex stepped back two paces as Levi spoke, his face a mask under a mask with a painted-on smile. "Thanks for the heads-up. See you around," he said only to me, his eyes alive with meaning.

And mercifully, he gave us his back.

I sighed my relief and turned to Levi, reaching up on my tiptoes to lay a bruising kiss on him.

When our lips parted, he smiled down at me, but his eyes were guarded. "What was that for?"

"Do I need a reason?" I teased.

"I'm not complaining. You can use me to piss him off any day of the week."

I frowned. "That's not why I kissed you. I wanted to thank you for saving me from the biggest chicken in the joint."

"But you know he saw it too. Can't hurt, right?" His voice was light. The rest of him was pitch-black.

I took a step back, eyeing him. "I don't feel the need to hurt him, Levi. In fact, I haven't thought of him like that since the second I met *you*. I know we're temporary and not serious and what-the-hell-ever else you want to call us, but the least you can do is trust that I'm here *with you*. Because unlike *you*, I've given no reason to mistrust me. I mean, Jesus, Levi."

His face softened to regret. "I'm sorry, Stella." I let him step closer. "It's …" He looked into the crowd as if he'd find the words there. "I don't know that I'll ever feel like I belong here. Or believe you belong with a guy like me instead of a guy like Dex."

"A self-centered asshole?"

"A trust-fund kid from your world. So it's easier to make how I feel about you less than it is. Knowing I'm leaving. Knowing where we are. What we are." He turned those dark eyes on me. "I believe you. I trust you. And if he puts his hands on you again, I'll break his wing."

I laughed, relaxing into him. "First of all, you belong here just as much as anyone. Have you ever stopped to consider it's *you* who keeps drawing the line in the sand?"

He paused. "Once or twice."

"So wipe it away. You're the only one who can."

Levi's smile flicked up on one side. "And what's the second thing?"

"On inspection, seeing you jealous is pretty hot."

"Glad it makes you happy. I'll punch him in the beak if you want."

Another laugh.

"I'm not kidding. Say the word, and I'll turn his face inside out."

"How about instead, you kiss me and promise not to question my devotion again?"

His arm wound around me, his lips tilting into a smirk. "You're devoted to me?"

"*Desperately*, darling," I said like a Golden Age movie star as he moved in for a kiss.

"Good. Let's keep it that way."

And the kiss he laid on me made certain I would.

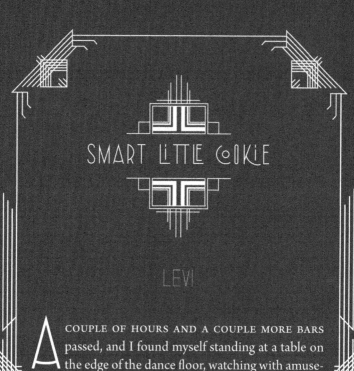

SMART LITTLE COOKIE

LEVI

A COUPLE OF HOURS AND A COUPLE MORE BARS passed, and I found myself standing at a table on the edge of the dance floor, watching with amusement as a flock of chickens bounced around to the music. Funnier still—watching Stella, whose mascot head was flipped around backward and staring at Betty's while Betty slapped her ass.

Honestly, I didn't know how she left the sauna trap on. I'd resigned myself to wearing mine coming and going from bars as well as in transit, which was its own spectacle. A whole other flock followed ours, one with cameras and questions shouted over the rattling of the shopping cart as I pushed Stella toward our next destination. And she'd smiled and waved down at them all from her throne of disco balls like the queen she was.

I was lucky as fuck and not afraid to admit it.

How I'd managed to convince her to forgive my lie

was beyond me. Truth be told, I didn't quite believe I deserved it, but I sure as hell wasn't going to talk her out of it. And as such, I'd set out to make the most of the second chance and ensure she didn't regret giving it to me.

The second I'd seen her in the diner, my first thought had been that she was Cecelia Beaton. But the more I thought about it, the less I believed it. Stella was free in a way I'd never known, never believed existed. And her untethered nature made her being the mastermind of the whole thing almost impossible to believe. Although, I still had a suspicion that she knew who Cecelia Beaton was. But I told her I'd let it go, and I kept my promises.

I respected the group and Stella too much to break that trust.

Zelda pulled up next to me with her eyes on the crowd. "If Ash grinds his hips any harder, he's gonna get Joss pregnant."

I snorted a laugh and took a sip of my whiskey. "Probably wouldn't be the first time. He might be the king of immaculate conception."

"Nothing immaculate about *that*." Z wore a little smile but didn't laugh back. "So you're the reporter."

"I'm the reporter," I echoed.

"You were wise to lie, even though you're a fucker for doing it. You're lucky Stella likes you. It's probably the only reason Ash still has a pulse."

"I'm not gonna hurt any of you."

"I know. That's the only reason why *you* still have a pulse." She took a long pull of whatever she was drinking. "She likes you. A little too much, if I'm being honest."

"Is there ever a time when you're not honest?"

"Not one. It's just who I am as a person, Levi."

"Never said I didn't appreciate it."

She smirked over at me before looking over the dance floor again. "Thing is, Stella has a knack for getting involved with two kinds of men: the kind she shouldn't trust and the unavailable ones. And you, my friend, are unavailable. The jury's still out on the trust thing."

I didn't argue, didn't say anything, just watched Stella out there on the dance floor and wished I could have it all.

"The last guy who did this to her wasn't just unavailable—he was an asshole. And one thing you *aren't* is that."

"Even though I lied?"

"Even though you lied, which was shitty and fucked up, by the way. But you never lied about how you felt about her. Did you?"

"Never. I don't think I could if I wanted to."

"Exactly. You're nothing like him."

We fell silent for a beat, our gazes falling on the man in question. His arm was around that sweet, smiling little girl who was too busy chatting with her friend to notice him watching Stella with all the possession I'd been. Except he had no right to her. And the look on his face made me want to separate his jugular from his throat with my bare hands.

As if he'd heard the thought, he looked right at me, and the testosterone-charged rage that zipped between us was almost tangible. I'd tear that scrawny motherfucker limb from limb if he so much as squared his shoulders.

Sadly, he didn't.

I took another drink when he lost the staring contest. "So is this where you tell me not to hurt her?"

"Oh, I don't think I need to tell you that," Z said with the velvety sheen of a black cat. "You're a smart little cookie. You know what's what. But what you may be blind to—she's in deeper than she realizes."

At that, I turned to gauge Z's earnestness and found it was verifiable, even without her looking back at me.

"Stella believes you're telling the truth about the whole reporter thing, and although she can be a pretty shitty judge of character, I'm not. And I believe you too, especially after you gave her veto power on whatever you write. Something about your face."

"I've been told it *is* a nice face."

Z rolled her eyes. "Modest too."

"Said the kettle to the pot."

A little laugh. "But you should know something about Stella—no matter how hard she might try, she doesn't do halfway. Flings aren't in her nature. Stella Spencer was made for love, and not a single man in her acquaintance has ever been able to provide it, not in the way she wants or needs or gives. I won't tell you not to hurt her because I don't believe you would—*on purpose*. But I'll warn you to be careful. Because if you aren't, you'll hurt her whether you want to or not."

I nodded somberly with the weight of a sinking cinder block in my chest. "That's fair advice, Z."

"Well, I'm helpful like that. Stella trusts you, and I trust her implicitly. Plus, I like you. It's a shame you're leaving."

"That it is," I answered with genuine regret.

"Although it's not like you're leaving forever, right?"

"No, not forever. But I don't know how long it will be. Could be a few weeks. Months. A year. Can't exactly ask her to wait for me."

"Oh, I don't know—you seem capable enough." She reached over and grabbed my chin in her thumb and forefinger to open and close it as she sang in a teenybopper voice, "*I just met you, and this is crazy, but while I'm gone, wait for me maybe.*"

I chuckled when she let me go. "You make it sound so simple."

"It is. What's it hurt to ask?"

But my cynicism ran too deep to hope. "We barely know each other, Z. I'll be on the other side of the world in a war zone while she's *here*." I nodded to the dance floor. "She needs somebody who can be here with her."

"I'd like to take a moment to note that she spent two years trying to convince herself what she had with Dex was healthy. If she put up with that, I can almost guarantee she'd at least want to try when it comes to you."

I drew a long breath through my nose and let it out slow. "I'll think about it."

Z shot me a warning look.

"Not because I don't want to," I clarified. "But this wasn't part of the plan. I just want to give it a second, make sure this is what we both want before we make any promises."

"It *wasn't* part of the plan. But take a look around, Levi, because I think it's time to make new plans."

Before I could answer, Stella bounded toward us and flung herself at me in the best way. Thank God I didn't drop her, seeing as how I only had one free hand.

I heard her muffled laughter from inside her mask. "I wanna kiss you, but I can't."

"Then we'd better get this thing off of you. Now."

Her arms relaxed, and I put her down so she could rid herself of the gigantic mask. I set my drink next to it on the table so I could have both hands to smooth her damp, wavy hair and thumb the mascara from under her eyes. Those eyes were bright as starlight, blinding me from everything but her. Her face, so small in my hands, her smiling lips, the whole of her teeming with joy and vibrance that affected me in ways I couldn't have anticipated. It was a contact high, a secondhand buzz, but even diluted, she was made of potent stuff.

And I kissed her salty lips in the hopes of another hit.

It's time to make new plans.

The words echoed in every heartbeat. Because even though I'd thought I had everything I wanted, I was wrong.

And the girl in my arms was proof.

STELLA

We followed Z out of the fourth—fifth?—bar as she pushed the shopping cart out the doors with the rest of us in her wake. We pulled over just outside of the doors to put on our masks, but before I could don mine, Levi propped his on the handle and picked me up.

"Come on, princess. Up you go."

I laughed as he deposited me on the mound of disco balls, which was super uncomfortable but better than the hell I'd pay for walking around in these shoes. And before he handed over my mask, he stole a kiss that had me looking forward to a hot shower with a naked, soapy Levi.

When our masks were on, Z shouted, *"Tallyho!"* and in a train of chaos, we made our way to the next bar.

Everyone we passed stared and laughed and took pictures, and some were even brave enough to follow us like we were the Pied Piper. Levi pushed the cart, and I held on for dear life—it wasn't a smooth ride—while everyone sang and skipped and made an absolute spectacle. People waved, and we waved back. Paparazzi had staked out our route and lit up a path of flashbulbs to mark our way. And it seemed all was well and merry.

We heard the sirens before we saw them, the pack of us slowing, then stopping, looking at each other like we'd find an answer. Were they coming for us? Should we run or just keep on keeping on?

When they turned onto our block and headed straight for us, we knew.

People scattered in every direction, but we stayed together. Levi took off running with the cart bumbling in front of him, and thank God—there was no way I was running in these shoes, which I was already working on unbuckling.

"Come on," he yelled. "If we can get inside the bar, we should be okay."

My ass bounced on one of the disco balls, the little mirrors cutting my back and legs, and my teeth rattled as we barreled toward the bar. Cop cars screeched to a halt at the curb next to us, splayed at all angles in their haste.

"NYPD. Stop where you are!"

I turned to look behind us and found a trio of cops on our trail. Another three flanked us. My heart was a machine gun.

Because this was it.

In six months, no one in our group had been arrested. And tonight, that streak ended.

A cop car pulled onto the sidewalk at an alarming speed, blocking our path. My scream echoed inside my mask at my certainty that I was about to fly ass over tit when the cart hit the car, but Levi threw all his weight backward, stopping me at the very last second.

Just in time for eight pistols to point at a pack of idiots dressed in chicken costumes.

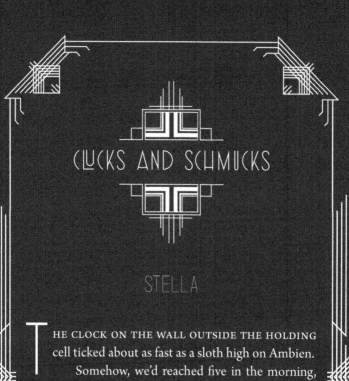

CLUCKS AND SCHMUCKS

STELLA

THE CLOCK ON THE WALL OUTSIDE THE HOLDING cell ticked about as fast as a sloth high on Ambien.

Somehow, we'd reached five in the morning, and I'd felt every single minute. Levi's shoulder might as well have been a Posturepedic for as comforting as it felt under my cheek. But there wasn't much we could do besides lean into each other, seeing as how we were handcuffed.

This made peeing a true challenge. It might have even been funny had a female cop not been staring down her nose at me through the whole ordeal. We'd been denied our phone calls, citing that the pay phones were unavailable, but we'd be able to *Just as soon as they're free.*

The whole thing was bullshit. We weren't being booked, just detained under "protective custody" until we were no longer a menace to society. AKA sober, which we were as of hours ago, but they had the right to hold us for seventy-two hours unless I could get a goddamn lawyer here to bust us all out.

Without a phone call, my odds weren't looking good.

Z was asleep, head against the cinder-block wall, Betty's head in her lap. Joss used Betty's torso like a pillow, and Tag and Ash sat shoulder to shoulder, blinking at a TV screen outside the windows of the cell. Other inhabitants included two bums who smelled like an August dumpster at noon, a guy who'd held up a liquor store, a couple of prostitutes, a drug dealer, and half a dozen other Bright Young Things, all of whom were part of the core group.

This fact hadn't escaped me. If I hadn't known it was a setup, I would have figured it out just on that.

I yawned again, and Levi started with a jerk.

"I'm sorry to wake you," I said with a voice like sandpaper.

But he sighed, angling to kiss the top of my head. "Don't be. You okay?"

"My new bracelets are gonna leave a mark, but yeah. I just want to get home where a hot shower and my bed await."

He hummed his longing. "Mind if I come with you?"

"Please do. After this, I don't think I want to be alone."

"I don't want you to be alone either," he said quietly.

A cop approached, and we all perked up as she unlocked the door with a jangle. Immediately on entering, she made eye contact with me. I had no idea whether that was a good or a bad thing.

"Spencer, come with me."

I stood, heart thundering. My friends' eyes followed me, speaking their support, and I tried to keep my chin up, offering the cop a wan smile. But she was too busy inspecting my ridiculous outfit to see it. I couldn't even blame her—I looked like a disco ball that had rolled down Landfill Mountain and into Toxic Waste River.

When I stepped through the threshold, I chanced a question. "Do I get my phone call now?"

She grabbed my arm and pulled me away. "Not just yet. There's somebody who wants to talk to you. I don't know who you pissed off, kid, but you really must have stepped in some shit."

I frowned, my heart rate ticking higher. I didn't know much about getting arrested, but I knew for a fact that I didn't have to answer a single question without a lawyer. And I didn't plan to, no matter who was so desperate to talk to me.

She led me to an interrogation room and cuffed me to the table in front of a gigantic two-way mirror. And for a while, I sat in that cold room, trying not to look at my bedraggled reflection, trying not to consider that people were on the other side of that mirror, watching me. Talking about me. Deciding what to do with me when I hadn't done anything wrong.

It felt like an hour passed, though in truth, it was maybe ten minutes before the door finally opened.

And in walked the devil himself. Commissioner Warren.

My shock was complete, amplified by the long, degrading night and my lack of sleep. But it made no sense that he was here. Police commissioners didn't question rich girls who disturbed the peace.

Unless that rich girl was associated with the Bright Young Things.

He smiled placidly, cup of coffee in one hand and a folder in the other. "Morning, Miss Spencer. Long night?"

Motherfucker. I smiled back, unperturbed. "I've had longer."

He sat back in the metal chair and assessed me coolly. "Seems you caused quite the scene last night, you and your little friends."

I said nothing, expending all my energy trying to tamp my emotions down.

Warren flipped open the folder. "Says here you were caught riding up Hudson on a shopping cart. Drunk. Making trouble."

"I'm not sure what kind of trouble we caused, but I don't deny the rest."

He flipped the page. "You drew a crowd that stopped traffic. Resisted arrest. Excessive noise with the intent to riot—"

"Wait—what? *Riot*?"

He smiled, and the expression was anything but friendly. "You've got a squeaky-clean record, Miss Spencer. I'd hate to put a grease stain on it unduly. So maybe if you scratch my back, I'll scratch yours."

"What do you suggest?" I asked more out of curiosity than anything. Because there was no way in hell I was scratching his hairy, old back.

"Who's Cecelia Beaton?"

A laugh burst out of me, edged with the hysteria of sleeplessness. "Why do you care?"

"Oh, I'm not the only one who wants to know. That information is a hot commodity. Would you pay for your freedom with it?"

"I want my lawyer," I answered with a shaky voice.

"I'm sure you do. But in the meantime, how's about you and me have a little chat?"

I remained silent, as was my right.

"That's fine too. One of you brats knows who's running all this. We don't want any of you taking up space—we just want the boss."

"How do you know it's not all of us?"

"Because you can't keep that many people quiet. So it's my job to find out who's running the circus, and you, Miss Spencer, are at the top of my list. You're the only one who's had perfect attendance at these parties. I figure if it's not you, you know who it is. And I intend to find out. So name your price."

"Sorry to disappoint, but I know just as much as you do. Aside from how to have a good time, something it seems you're unfamiliar with."

His face shifted to disdain, his eyes flashing with rage in a heartbeat. "I don't care who your daddy is—don't fuck with me, little girl. Your money might get you what you want, but it's not gonna get you out of this. You all think you're so funny, running around town like fucking idiots in chicken costumes. You're a joke, and I'm gonna find out who the ringleader is. And when I do, I'm gonna ruin your whole little operation, top to bottom."

I just stared at him, narrow-eyed and mad as fuck. "Do I get my call now?"

Warren's jaw was so tight, the muscles at the corners were marbles. "We're gonna talk a while longer. And then all your friends are gonna sit right there and tell me what they know. Starting with—"

The door flew open, and in stormed a woman I'd never seen before in a gray suit, her bun a shiny black knot.

"My client won't be answering any further questions, Commissioner, and neither will anyone you arrested with her."

"Like hell. If you don't have a judge's order—"

She pulled a stack of papers out of her bag and slapped them on the table. "Check the signature."

Warren fumed. "How did you—"

But the lawyer just smiled. "You'll find the names of those set to be released in section one-A."

Warren scrubbed his hand over his mouth. But he didn't speak. His hand rose and flicked toward the door, which opened at the gesture like a magic trick. A police officer entered, motioned for me to stand, and walked me out of the room with the lawyer. And we left that bitter son of a bitch seething in the room behind us. I waited for a parting jab as we left, but none came.

He'd been struck speechless in a moment of genuine surprise, and that amused me more than it should have.

"Marissa Alvarez. Your mother sent me," she said, answering my unspoken question. "It'll be a few hours before you're processed, but just try to sit tight. They're probably going to make it as long and painful as possible, but just keep your chin up and your mouth shut. All right?"

I nodded. "Thank you," I said, sounding wearier than I'd ever been.

"Thank your mom. I'll see you on the other side."

The door to the holding cell opened, and the cop deposited me inside to face my worried friends.

But I smiled and delivered the good news with relief I felt to my toes.

"We're out."

RiSE AND FALL

STELLA

EYES CLOSED, I LEANED INTO THE SHOWER STREAM. I hadn't been able to get myself clean. No amount of scrubbing and no quantity of soapy lather could wash the night off of me. So I stood there under the blazing water, hoping I could burn it off instead.

They'd managed to drag processing out for six grueling hours, and by the time I was handed the plastic bag harboring my belongings, we were all over the news. Photos of us being arrested had been splashed across the internet, coupled with headlines like Rich Kid Racket and Busted Young Things. I was too exhausted to do anything about it but sit in the cab and stare at my screen, but Levi sprang into action, calling his contacts to see what he could do. There was no way to head the story off, but he was convinced there might be a way to wrangle a little bit of control, a little bit of leverage.

Mostly, he threw the commissioner under the bus, doing his best to spin the headline in the other direction. Abuse of power. No just cause. That sort of thing.

But I was too tired to even crack open that box.

The lot of us dragged ourselves inside and mumbled our way to our rooms. Levi's phone rang before he could get in the shower with me, so I'd climbed in alone and tried not to think about anything beyond the curling steam and the hissing water and the sting of heat that turned my shoulders and chest pink.

Levi walked in with a sigh, dropping his phone on the counter with a thunk before reaching behind him to pull off his shirt. His worried gaze swept over me.

He grabbed a towel and opened the door. "Come on. I think you're clean. Time to get you in bed."

"I'll never be clean again," I tried to joke, but I was as flat as a slashed tire.

With a chuckle, he turned off the water and opened up the towel, wrapping me up and pulling me into him. My sopping hair sent rivulets of water down his bare chest.

"Any luck?" I asked.

"I think so. Everybody was very interested to hear what the commissioner said to you. There are too many questions. Like why was he even there?" He sighed, a frustrated sound. "The whole thing smells. What the fuck does the police commissioner want with Cecelia Beaton? He acts like she's a fucking drug lord. Hell, maybe she is."

I leaned back to frown at him. "Wouldn't there be substantially more illegal substances at the parties if she were?"

"Maybe. But the truth is, if she were dealing drugs, Warren would have added that to his sandwich board." He paused, his curiosity clicking and whirring behind his eyes, bright despite his lack of sleep. "We've got to figure out what this is really about. Because I have a feeling if we don't, things are going to get much worse."

I sagged. "I can't talk about this until I've had sleep, Levi."

He softened, cupping my neck. His lips brushed my forehead. "You're right. Let's get some sleep, and we'll put together a plan when we're rested. Go on and get in bed. I'll be right behind you."

I nodded and headed to my closet, my hands fully occupied with the herculean task of drying myself off when my phone rang from the other room. Too much had happened to ignore it like I wanted to—the odds of it being important were too high. So with another sigh, I hurried into my room. When I saw the name on my screen, I stopped dead.

I snatched it up, barely answering in time. "Mom?"

"Hi, pumpkin."

Mute, I sank onto my bed.

"I hear you got my lawyer. When the news broke, I had a feeling you'd need her."

"Thank you," I muttered. "They wouldn't give me my phone call."

"I heard that. You're all over the papers and gossip columns. Really, Stella, could you make us any more of a laughingstock?" She sighed but continued on, her tone light. "I'm sending my publicist too, so keep an eye out for her."

"I don't need a publicist, Mom—"

"Oh yes, you do. I can't run damage control from the other side of the world, Stella. Our reputation in New York is at stake, and the stain won't come out. Don't just think about yourself, honey. Think about me too—if you don't cut it out"—her voice lowered to a furtive whisper—"the wedding might be off. Fernando is appalled with your behavior. He's royalty, you know, even if it's in money only."

"Yes, you've mentioned," I said quietly.

Her voice rose back to a normal decibel and shone with a cheer only she felt. "Oh, I'm so happy to help you though. What with the lawyer and publicist and all."

She paused.

I didn't speak.

"Well, *you're welcome*, honey," she sang. "Anyway, I've got to run. I've just had my neck done, and I really can't talk with this much Lortab in my system. Listen to whatever the publicist says, and for God's sake, quit making fools of us all. Okay? Okay. Love you! Talk soon."

With a few kissy noises, she ended the call without waiting for a response.

My hands dropped to my lap, my eyes on the black glass.

I wanted to hate her, but I couldn't seem to muster up the energy. She was too privileged to be graceful. Too entitled to have empathy. My mother had never been cruel, never spoken to me in anger, never hurt me intentionally. She didn't mean to be a selfish asshole—she'd been bred that way.

In fact, I didn't believe she realized she hadn't acted to help *me* at all.

She was helping *herself.*

When the lawyer had informed me that she was a gift from my mother, a foolish, childish hope had flared in me—that she was worried about me. A call from her only fed the flame. But then she'd opened her mouth, and the light had been doused with a hiss.

Levi walked in scrubbing his hair with one towel, another wrapped around his waist. But when he saw me, he slowed.

"What happened?" he asked darkly.

Somehow, I dug up a tired smile. "Nothing." I set my phone on my nightstand.

"Nice try." The bed dipped when he sat next to me. "Who was on the phone?"

"My mother." My towel slipped a little, and I tugged it to keep it in place. "It's fine, really. She just wanted to make sure I got the lawyer."

"I'm glad she checked on you. I didn't expect that."

"That makes two of us. But she didn't want to check on me so much as she wanted to tell me to stop embarrassing her." When his face fell into shadow, I added, "She wasn't ugly. Just …" I sighed. "It's fine."

"How many times do you think you'll have to say it before it's true?"

I looked over at him, and my heart twisted at the care and worry in the corners of his eyes, the brackets on his lips, the line between his brows.

Exhaustion and emotion pushed me closer to the edge. My eyes filled with tears.

In a beat, I was in his arms, crushed against his chest, rocking gently.

"It's okay," he promised. "It's going to be okay. I've got you."

And those words felled the final brace against my emotions.

There was a place in my heart where I put the bad things, the hard things, the things that hurt. I'd buried them all there and planted fields of flowers on top with the intent to turn the rotting pain into fertilizer for something good, something beautiful, something I tended and watered in the hopes that the darkness I'd put in the ground would decompose. But that was just the thing. It was indestructible but not precious like a diamond, not like a gem. It was a smattering of plastic garbage that couldn't decay if it wanted to. It wasn't going anywhere, no matter how badly I wanted to pretend otherwise.

So for a little while, I let it out. Dug around in the earth on my knees and sifted through the trash I'd so desperately tried to forget. There was, of course, my mother—both the woman she was and the mother I wished for. The commissioner and the pressure he'd pinned me with. The escalation to not just my arrest, but the arrest of the people I loved. There was the secret I kept and the corner I found myself painted into. The secret I couldn't share with Levi under any circumstance, no matter how badly I wanted to.

Levi. My leaving, lying Levi.

The thought brought a fresh wave of tears, pulled by a tide of sad surprise.

You do this every time, Stella, always wanting what you can't have. Every goddamn time.

I had to stop crying, or he'd ask questions I couldn't answer. He'd see what I wanted to hide, and then everything would come unraveled. So I thought about anything that made me happy, anything at all. Riding on the back of Levi's bike with the wind whipping my hair and his warm body in my arms. The glorious sights at my parties, the fantasy so rich and lovely. My friends, their laughing faces marching through my mind like trusty soldiers come to ward off what might hurt me.

And after a moment, the tears stopped.

I leaned back and laughed at myself, swiping at my cheeks. "God, I must look like such a brat, crying because my mother is selfish. I'm privileged and I know it, and my life is not that hard. I'm sorry."

"Don't apologize."

I cupped his jaw. "You have been through so much, through things I couldn't imagine—"

"We're not comparing pain. Ever. What hurts, hurts. There's no other metric than that."

For a moment, I looked him over with wonder and longing. "How did you get so wise?"

One corner of his mouth twitched. "I know Billy's a grumpy old sonofabitch, but he happens to be one of the wisest men on the planet."

We chuckled. Fell silent again. Something in his face shifted, tightened with worry or pain or both. I instantly knew I didn't want to hear what he was about to say, not if it meant discussing goodbye. Not yet. Not now.

"Stella, I—"

"I don't want to talk anymore, Levi. Not about anything that means anything. I don't want yesterday or tomorrow. All I want is you and me and now."

His expression settled on resignation, tinged with sadness. "Then that's what you'll get."

Our lips met by his design in a kiss thick with promise and quiet worship. It was a tasting, a savoring of a thing we couldn't keep. I wanted to. I wanted to keep him, whatever that meant. Maybe it was just waiting—waiting I could do. But would he? We had studiously ignored that discussion since the first night we were together, and now we were in too deep to have that conversation without someone getting hurt. And I was pretty sure that someone would be me.

It was easier to pretend that everything was *fine, just fine*. It'd hurt later—there was no doubt about that. But maybe he'd come back and look me up. Maybe we could pick up where we'd left off. Or maybe it would be so much time that I would have moved on. Maybe he would. If there were no rules, no boundaries, it would all be left to fate. Maybe if I wished on the first star I saw tonight, he'd come back to me.

But that was the most dangerous thought of all.

Because all I could count on was this, right now.

So I'd have to make the most of it.

I didn't break the kiss when I climbed into his lap, sliding my legs outside his thighs until our hips locked. My towel came undone, draping at my waist and falling away, but I didn't notice or mind. My thoughts were consumed by his lips, by the humid air between our bodies, by the damp skin of his chest when my breasts brushed those strong, flat planes.

He moaned into my mouth and tightened his arms until there was no space. And the kiss went on and on, hotter by the second, deeper by the minute. The aching center of me found the hard length of him and stroked with a flex of my hips. His towel slipped, and a hot greed bloomed low in my belly, eliciting another grind of my hips, one that shifted the barrier lower, low enough to expose his crown. A soft, hungry *yes* slithered through me, and I sought his heat with mine, desperate for the fullness the contact promised, gasping when the tip of him met that empty space.

A growl and a shift, and I was on my back, caged by his body, pinned by his hips, only not the way I wanted. He knew it too. But his hand on my breast, fingers toying with my peaked nipple, told me I would wait, even if just for a minute.

That hand kept at its task, but his lips moved down my neck, across my collarbone, down my sternum, to my breast. The slick warmth of his mouth was some sort of heaven, his tongue circling my nipple, then flicking, then drawing it deeper. My thighs spread wider, my body squirming and seeking and displeased at the distance between his hips and mine. But he let me squirm despite my mewling, taking a long moment right where he was to pay tribute to my breasts with his lips and his tongue and his eager hands. And when he left his post, I was unsurprised he went down instead of up.

Resigned, I sighed and quit fighting, and unfazed, he threaded an arm under my thigh and lifted it to his shoulder, his hand on a track for my ass. When he found it, he squeezed until flesh spilled between his fingers. The other hand spread my free leg wider, trailing up the inside of my thigh with a zip of electricity in its wake. I could feel his breath against the places that wanted him, even the stroke of his finger secondary to the anticipation of his mouth. I watched him hover there, his gaze charting what lay before him, and I waited, unable to breathe, unable to blink until he took what he wanted.

His lips parted, his fingertips making way for his tongue, and with shuddering pleasure, he tasted my flesh in a decadent, luxurious sweep. I sighed to the stars and sank into the bed, heavy and useless and at his disposal, permission that he took with no small amount of indulgence. As if my pleasure was his, and he would take it in excess.

And so he did.

A tracing, a latching, a delving of tongue and fingertips, around and around in a rhythm that pressed and drove and spurred me toward the edge of the world. The gallop of my heart, the tremble of my thighs, the sweat on my brow as the precipice drew closer, tightening my vision, my awareness, my body, my lungs.

With a flash of heat, I burst free, my lungs shooting open as I came beneath his touch, the pleasure-pain of every lick and suck cracking like lightning down my thighs, up my spine. Until finally, sadly, it faded until it was gone.

Only then did he close his lips and climb up my body, settling his hips between my thighs where I'd wanted him all along. The length of him nestled in that tender space that already ached for him again, his arms bracketing my shoulders and hands on my face, fingers tangled in my damp hair.

But he didn't kiss me. And for that long moment, I didn't want him to.

There was something about his eyes, something that stopped my heart and breath and time as he looked down at me. It was that part of him that lived in shadows, what didn't want to be seen, illuminated by a moment of sheer honesty and truth. They were the things he wished for, things he didn't want to say.

In his eyes was infinite longing, and I sank into them until I might have drowned.

But he saved me with a kiss, breathing into me, breathing me. A shift of his hips, and he breached me. A flex, and he filled me. A sigh, and he stayed right there, our bodies as close as we could get. If we could get any closer, we would, but for a luxuriant stretch of unknowable time, that was more than enough.

It was everything.

My mind was a haze, our bodies a pulsing beat, a tempo we both knew without thought, a drum pounding faster, harder, deeper until we felt it tremble in our bones and marrow.

The heartbeat of silence when we came held a truth, one that stretched like a horizon, where the sea met the sky, delineating an unattainable destination.

What we felt for each other was bigger than we would admit, more than we could afford.

And we both knew it.

He fell asleep before I did, marked by that long, gentle breath and the occasional twitch of his fingers in my hair. But I lay awake, wrapped up in him, my head tucked under his chest and the scent of his skin a lullaby.

In a moment of bare honesty, he'd shown me his longing—the longing to belong. And I wanted him to belong to me. When I searched my ribs, my heart was gone—he'd stolen it when I wasn't looking.

And when I finally fell asleep, it was wondering how in the world I'd ever get it back.

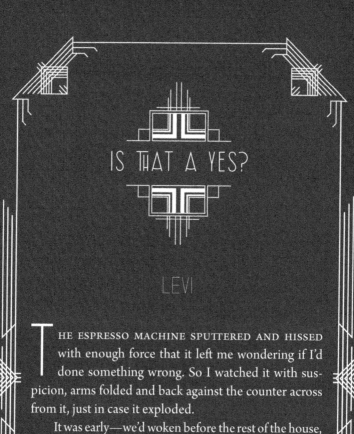

IS THAT A YES?

LEVI

THE ESPRESSO MACHINE SPUTTERED AND HISSED with enough force that it left me wondering if I'd done something wrong. So I watched it with suspicion, arms folded and back against the counter across from it, just in case it exploded.

It was early—we'd woken before the rest of the house, our sleep cycle out of whack from being up for over twenty-four hours, thanks to Warren. We'd slept most of yesterday afternoon, waking around dinnertime. The rest of the night had been spent in her bed, eating takeout and half-watching movies, half-making out in what had to be the laziest Sunday ever.

I figured we'd earned it.

We were up with the sun this morning and currently on our second cup of coffee. My eyes shifted to the patio, where Stella sat, eyes closed and face upturned, and warmth spread over me just like the sun illuminating her face.

If the last forty-eight hours had taught me anything, it was that I was a goner for Stella Spencer.

The knowledge wasn't a shock, but an understanding of fact. I didn't know when it had happened. Maybe the first time I laid eyes on her. The first time I made her laugh. Some mundane moment like this. A breath between nothings that meant everything. Or that each moment was just another reason to love her. We weren't there yet, but I could see the path laid out in front of me, straight as an arrow to the horizon.

And now that I knew I couldn't be without her, I had to figure out what to do about it.

All I'd ever wanted was a gig like I was about to land. And then I met her, and the blessing of my job became a curse.

I sighed, wishing things were simpler. That we'd met long ago or even after Syria, as much as I hated the thought of waiting any length of time for what she'd given me. Now that I had found her, waiting for her seemed like the only thing I *could* do. Whether we talked about it or not, whether she agreed or didn't, I couldn't see myself getting involved with anyone else. I couldn't see any outcome beyond me returning, clutching my hope in my fist that she'd want to pick things back up. Even if we parted ways, even if she was dating, I would still hang on to that hope. Of that, I had no doubt.

In that context, it seemed stupid not to tell her. I just had to figure out how.

But first, more coffee.

I added hot water from the little spout like she'd shown me before heading back outside, putting my thoughts away so we could get back to our bigger problem.

Warren.

She smiled up at me when I appeared, extending her hands for her cup. "Thank you."

"Don't thank me until you've tasted it."

I took the seat next to her on the loveseat, and she twisted to put her feet in my lap.

"So what about Warren's ex-wife?" she asked, picking up the conversation where we'd left off. "Think she knows anything?"

"Maybe, but I can't imagine her talking to me about it."

"No, me neither. But somebody has to know something. Did you ask Billy?"

"I tried, but he didn't have much to add, just that there's likely more to it than we knew. There have been watercooler whispers about Warren's more unsavory ties for years, but nothing's ever come of it. He's got enough friends in the force to leave him bulletproof."

"Yeah, because he's using those friends as human shields." She took a delicate sip of her coffee, testing the heat.

"I was thinking about the process he went through to become the commissioner. The mayor appoints him, but a committee vets the candidates. I wonder if one of them knows something."

"Probably the president, or whatever title they have. The one on top *always* knows something."

I set down my mug in exchange for my phone, and with a little bit of digging, I found a name. "His name's Jameson, Ed Jameson. I know that name—must be from Billy. I wonder if he'd meet with me."

"I wonder if he'd be honest with you."

"Probably not. But it's worth a shot, right? I'll set up an appointment, and in the meantime, I'll see if I can uncover any substantial leads. It doesn't make any sense, what he's doing, and we can't be the only ones who think so."

"I just thought he was a fun-hating old grump until the other night. Now I'm not just annoyed. I'm mad and a little scared, if I'm honest."

I stroked her calf, gave it a squeeze. "Don't worry. I'm gonna figure this out before I leave—I promise you that."

When she smiled, it was touched with sadness. "What am I going to do without you?"

"Same thing as me, I suppose."

"Doubtful since you'll be in a war zone and I'll be in a party zone."

One of my brows rose. "So you won't miss me?"

That lifted her smile along with the color in her cheeks. "Oh, I will. Terribly, I'm afraid."

We were silent through a pause I spent drawing up my courage. "What if I told you I didn't plan on seeing anybody while I'm gone?"

"Do a lot of relationships start covering war-torn countries?" she deflected, smirking to disguise the longing in her eyes.

"You'd be surprised." Another pause. "What would you say if I asked you to wait for me?"

Her expression didn't change, but her eyes sparked. She didn't answer.

"I know. It's crazy." I tracked my hand as it charted the shape of her leg. "I can think of twenty reasons for you to say no. I don't know how long I'll be gone. You barely know me, I lied to you. And I can't think of any reason why you'd say yes. But I want you to. It doesn't have to be all big and official, and I don't want you to feel pressured to stick it out. If you meet somebody, just tell me. I won't be mad, won't blame you. I might put his picture on a dartboard and hope you dump him before I get back, but I won't hold it against you, Stella. I'm coming back single either way."

She chuckled but still said nothing.

"Tell me you'll think about it."

For a breath, she said nothing. And then she set her coffee down, rose up on her knees, and climbed silently into my lap, hooking her arms around my neck.

"I don't need to think about it," she said. "Ever since you told me you were leaving, I've been wondering how I was going to get over you. Now I don't have to."

I pulled her closer, my heart thumping against my chest and into hers. "Is that a yes?"

With a smile, she said, "That's a yes."

The slightest of shifts, and our lips met, the air crackling with effervescent happiness, that joyous relief that came with getting a thing you wanted but couldn't have. It was a kiss from lips that couldn't smooth their smiles, not until it slowed, mouths stretching, tongues delving deeper. A twist at my waist had her pinned beneath me. A handful of heartbeats and a flurry of hands had me a literal inch away from fucking her right there on her patio.

I broke the kiss to glance around, peeking over the back of the couch for her roommates. But she shifted her hips to close the small gap between us, and there was nothing to do but sigh and give in.

Because I was already gone.

GOOD BOY

STELLA

ASH'S PLACE WAS HOPPING A FEW NIGHTS LATER, an impromptu celebration for none of us getting booked over the weekend. He lived in the ultimate bachelor pad—tall ceilings and paned windows, industrial touches and textures set off by unaffectedly cool furniture. The guy had style, no doubt about it, and it didn't go unnoticed, as evidenced by the three girls following him around like puppy dogs. In turn, he magnanimously held their leashes.

I glanced around the space with a wistful sort of gladness to have all my favorite people in one place. Levi's arm around me while he talked to Cooper Moore, who had come out of domestic retirement for the night with his wife, Maggie. Betty had on the hottest black dress, the hem short enough that it garnered the attention of every single straight man on the premises. Which was funny if only for her pact with Zeke, who stood shoulder to shoulder with her, absorbing the male attention Betty so studiously ignored. For a tall drink of water, he looked thirsty as fuck, his blond hair neatly combed and his suit touched with a deliciously '20s flair, as was his custom. Tag had some poor doe-eyed girl pinned against a brick wall, smiling at her like a wolf. Joss, by all appearances, looked perfectly attentive to the group she was chatting with, but I knew better—her mind was a thousand miles away, her distant expression reminding me to talk to her, *really* talk to her. I'd been so busy, so wrapped up with the Bright Young Things and Levi that I felt like I hadn't seen any of them in a month, and we lived together.

But in the last few days, since Levi had told me he'd wait for me—an admission that filled up my brain with exclamation points—I'd felt myself *settle*. It was a strange feeling to be still and content. To get the sense that everything would work out just fine, even though I was under Warren's gun. Zeke and Betty had convinced me to stop the parties for a little while, though pulling the plug on parties I'd worked so hard on made my insides monkey screech. I hated the thought of Warren winning this round, but we hoped if we took a little breather, maybe he'd calm the fuck down.

It was worth a shot, even if it was a long shot.

"You know Joseph Bastian?" Levi asked Cooper in wonder. "The photographer? Like, you *know* him?"

Cooper laughed. "Since kindergarten. He's less intimidating once you've seen him get an atomic wedgie on the playground. Come on—I'll introduce you."

Levi looked down at me with hopeful eyes, and I cupped his cheek with a smile. "Go. Tell Joey I said hi."

At that, he huffed a laugh, rolled his eyes, and kissed me in the same breath.

I watched them walk away until I realized I was alone, and I began to make plans. My drink could use a refresh, that was item one on the list. Then I thought I should go save Joss, maybe pull her aside, find somewhere we could catch up. It was a good plan, one to deploy immediately, and I took a step toward the kitchen to do just that.

I didn't see Dex coming, a common mistake of mine. He'd come without Elsie tonight, and in her absence, there was nothing to stop him from brooding at me from across the room. Levi and I had only discussed it long enough to agree to ignore him as best we could and to make the pact to stick together.

One it seemed we'd forgotten.

Dex was drunk, that was plain to see. Heavy lids over bloodshot eyes, his hair a little mussed, his shirt rumpled, but the telltale sign was that one shoulder sank a little lower than the other, giving the impression of a permanent tilt.

When he smiled, it was that of a predator. "Where ya goin', Stell?"

On alert, my back stiffened. But my face smiled in what I hoped was amiability and not masked disgust. I held up my drink. "Need a refill."

"Me too. I'll come with you." He laid his hand on the small of my back, but I turned away the second I realized what he was doing.

"Come on, Dex," I said playfully. "You know better than that."

He frowned to the point of sneering. "What, you afraid your guy will be jealous?"

"I know he will, even though there's no reason. You and I are through."

"Says you."

"No, says *you*," I reminded him. "Don't do this. Not to me and not to Elsie. Now, I really need to find Levi, and you should call a cab, okay? Go home to your girlfriend."

When I moved to walk away, he grabbed my arm and pulled me into his chest. The scent of scotch slipped over me like I'd crawled into a barrel. Instantly, I was transported back in time, back when I thought accepting what little he gave me was a means to an end. Back when I thought I loved him.

Stupid old me. I'd had no idea what love was, not if I'd convinced myself that was what he gave me.

I was about to push him when his grip tightened. "What if I don't want Elsie anymore? What if I want you instead?"

"Then I'd say you're a little late for that," I answered, my voice low and shaky. I tried to pull away, but he wouldn't let me.

"I don't know, Stell. I think you're gonna give me another shot."

"And why would I do that?"

He leaned in until his lips were at my ear. "Because I know who you are."

Cold fear trickled down my spine. "You wouldn't, Dex."

"Wouldn't I?"

"You would bring everything down just because you want something you can't have?"

He leaned back so I could see the smile on his face. "Cecelia Beaton says I *can* have what I want."

I tried again to remove my arm from his fist without luck. "Let me go," I ground out.

"Tell me you'll think about it."

"Let me *go*." Hysteria rose when I realized he might not.

"Get your fucking hands off her."

Levi's voice startled Dex enough that his fingers relaxed, and I pulled my arm free. The second I was clear, Levi shoved Dex hard enough that he slammed into a wall, his head rebounding off the brick.

"Fuck, man." Dex gave his head a shake. "Fuck you."

Levi sprang, grabbing him by the shirtfront as a flock of people converged. It took three guys—Ash, Zeke, and Tag—to wrangle Levi away.

Ash jerked his chin at Zeke. "Put Dex in a cab."

With a nod, Zeke turned, smoothing his hair and sliding into a feline smile. "Come on, Sexy Dexy. Party's over."

Zeke reached for Dex, but Dex bucked, pushing him away. "Fuck you too, Zeke."

Zeke's face darkened, but his smile didn't budge. "Don't

make it worse than it already is. Come with me, and I'll make sure you get home to your girlfriend."

Dex's face twisted. "Fucking queer. If you think I'm letting you suck my dick—"

Zeke's fist flew out like a fucking python, connecting with Dex's nose with a crunch and a spurt.

"*Jesus, what the fuck*!" Dex screamed, clutching his nose.

Zeke looked murderous, though he was still smiling, shaking out his right hand. "Now, are you ready to be a good boy and come with me?"

Dex growled but turned for the door, and Zeke followed, hands in his pockets and velvet tongue serving insults all the way.

But I'd already turned for Levi, hurling myself into his arms.

"All right, all right," Ash said with his trademark smile. "Who needs a drink?"

A host of hands rose with a wave of laughter, and just like that, things were back on track.

For everyone but Levi and me.

He pulled back from the hug to look me over. "What did he say? Did he hurt you?" He grabbed my arm and extended it, drawing an audible, furious breath when he saw Dex's finger marks. "I'll fucking kill him," he snarl.

"He's not worth doing time for," I joked, but Levi was too far gone to be amused.

He yanked me into him, and when my cheek rested on his chest, I realized he was shaking. "Tell me not to go after him."

"Don't go after him. I'm here. I'm safe. I'm yours."

His head bowed, his shoulders curling and arms enveloping me like armor. "What did he want?"

"I think you can guess."

An angry sound rumbled in the back of his throat. "Can I admit I'm jealous Zeke got to hit him?"

With a laugh, I shifted so I could look at him. "Can I admit I'm jealous too?"

A smile flickered on his lips. "Tell you what—next time, I'll hit him first, then I'll hold him and you can take a turn."

"Maybe we'll get lucky and there won't be a next time."

But he darkened like a thunderhead. "I have a feeling he's not smart enough to avoid it."

For a moment, I looked up at him, pressing down my fear.

I know who you are.

And Dex did. He knew too much, the man I'd once thought was safe. Even after we parted ways, I never thought he'd expose me, not like this. Of course, I never thought he'd try to get me back, nor did I think I'd refuse.

Guess he didn't either.

One word from Dex, and I was fucked. Especially if Dex told anyone outside the sacred circle, because Warren would find out.

I had to tell Levi—he was the only one who could possibly help me get ahead of Dex. But telling a reporter carried its own risk regardless of how he felt about me.

What would he do with that information? Because everyone had a price.

Looking into his eyes, I wanted to believe he'd never betray me. But I'd thought that about Dex once too, and before all this, Dex had never threatened me.

Levi had deceived me, and in a much more dangerous context.

"Kiss me," I whispered, grateful when he complied.

But not even a kiss from Levi could distract me from my secret.

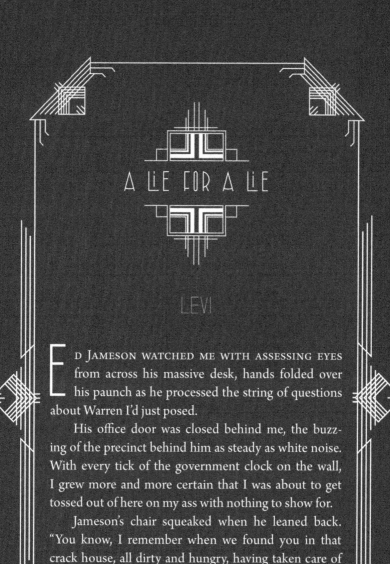

A LIE FOR A LIE

LEVI

Ed Jameson watched me with assessing eyes from across his massive desk, hands folded over his paunch as he processed the string of questions about Warren I'd just posed.

His office door was closed behind me, the buzzing of the precinct behind him as steady as white noise. With every tick of the government clock on the wall, I grew more and more certain that I was about to get tossed out of here on my ass with nothing to show for.

Jameson's chair squeaked when he leaned back. "You know, I remember when we found you in that crack house, all dirty and hungry, having taken care of yourself for weeks. Never seen Billy look at anything like that before, not the way he looked at you. I'll tell you, we all put in a word to do what we could to convince the state to award him custody of you. And I'm glad you made something of yourself, son. I'm not surprised, not with Billy's hand on your shoulder. And I'll tell you, that is the only reason you're sitting in my office today." His expression hardened.

"Thank you, sir."

The noise he made was more of a huff than a sigh. "We're off the record, son. Anything I say here, I will deny to my last fucking breath. Because if you think I'm gonna stick my neck out to save some rich kids, you're mistaken."

"Understood, sir."

He watched me through a beat. "It hasn't gone unnoticed, Warren's obsession with those kids. It seems personal, like you said, and I think it is. But I don't think it's *his* beef."

"Then whose?"

"Couldn't say. But Warren doesn't give a shit about much besides money and power. If I had to guess, one or both of those is what's driving him."

"Which means he's a stooge."

A single nod. "I can't tell you much, son, but you know someone who will."

"Billy."

"Go see him. Ask about the Blaze job, '05. Tug on that string, see what you come up with."

My mind spun with possibilities, and he watched with his brows drawn.

"Be careful, kid. He's one of the most powerful men in the city, so be sure saving these party kids is worth what he might do to the lot of you. All right?"

I nodded. "All right. Thank you, sir."

"Don't thank me yet," he warned, though he wore the slightest of smiles. He stood and extended his hand in dismissal. When I took it, he pulled me a little closer. "If you dig up anything substantial, bring it straight to me. I never wanted Warren where he is but …" A sigh. "Like I said, he's got his finger in every pot, and I'd love nothing more than to cut off every digit."

"I'll see what I can do."

"I don't doubt you will."

With an exchange of niceties, I left his office, heading for the elevator with my heart hammering.

Jameson had confirmed my suspicion that something bigger was at play—the longer it went on, the less sense a personal vendetta made. And as if that wasn't enough, he'd given me a lead.

A lead that I had unadulterated access to.

I'd promised Stella I'd come back by, so I hopped on my bike, started the engine, and sped toward her, my mind running at the same horsepower as my motor. And a few minutes later, I was heading into her building and then her apartment.

She stood behind the island with her hands full of raw chicken and a smile on her face. "Hey! How'd it go?"

She extended her cheek for a kiss that I granted, leaving my lips smiling for more than one reason.

"I've got a lead."

Her eyes widened. "Well, go on. Tell me."

"Jameson doesn't think it's personal … he thinks someone's paying Warren. He told me to talk to Billy. Gave me a topic of discussion—a job they'd worked in '05."

She flipped a chicken breast and sliced into its side, separating it to make a pocket for whatever stuffing was in the bowl next to her. "A lead," she sai, her smile widening. "Well, what are you doing here? Get your ass to Billy's."

I chuckled. "I told you I'd come back. Plus, I needed a second to think." I watched her work for a moment. "Look at you, all domestic. What's this?"

"Dinner for you and me tonight. Everyone's going out, so we'll have the house to ourselves."

A beeping floated toward us from the direction of her bedroom.

"Shit. That's my alarm."

I frowned. "It's two in the afternoon."

"It's the no-babies alarm. For my birth control." She held up her salmonella hands and eyed them.

"Well, let's not fuck around with that. I'll get them. Where are they?"

She giggled as I pushed off the counter. "My phone's plugged in next to my bed, birth control's in the drawer."

"On it."

I headed for her room, spotting her phone on her side of the bed. I killed the aggressive alarm and opened her nightstand, easily finding the pink plastic case that housed her birth control. But when I closed the drawer, I caught sight of a book on the bottom shelf of her nightstand, one I might not have noted if it wasn't for the heavy gold leaf papers sticking out of it.

Curiosity piqued faster than any warning. I knelt to pick up the pink-and-gold book and flipped it open to the page marked by the gilded papers—invitations, I saw on inspection.

You are cordially invited
to dine with the Bright Young Things ...

But it wasn't the invitation's presence that sent a tingling down my spine. It was the date.

Because this invitation was for a party two months from now.

Numb, I flipped back through the pages, stopping when I found her notes from when she'd planned the circus party. *She* had planned the party. All the parties.

Because Stella was Cecelia Beaton.

Abandoning everything but the planner in my hand, I walked on leaden feet back to her.

She smiled up at me, drying her hands over the sink. But everything slowed and sank when she saw what was in my hand.

"What are you doing with that?" she asked like the answer was a bomb. She wasn't wrong.

"What are *you* doing with it?"

"You went through my things." The color rose on her neck, in her cheeks. Her eyes were locked on the book.

I tossed it on the counter, and it slid a few inches in her direction. "It's you. This whole time, it's been you."

"You went through my things," she repeated, her eyes finally breaking from the book to pin me down. "You're still spying on me."

"Spying?" A defensive wind blew through me, kicking up dust in whorls. "Hang on one fucking minute, Stella—"

"So you can explain it away like you did last time? I might be gullible, but I'm not a fucking idiot. That book was not out. It was not open. It wasn't accidentally picked up—you made a choice to pick it up and open it. What the fuck?" Her cheeks blazed, her eyes on fire, sparkling with furious tears. "What the fuck am I supposed to say to that?"

"And how about you?" I shot back. "You're *Cecelia fucking Beaton.* You've been lying to *me* from the start."

"Because I *had* to! Jesus, Levi—this is *nothing* like your lie. Don't you think I wanted to tell you? But too many people already know, and I'm supposed to add a reporter to the list? Especially a reporter who fucking lied about spying on me for weeks. How the fuck am I supposed to believe a word you say right now? Why the *fuck* should I say anything but *get out of my apartment*?"

"Because you respect me, for starters."

"Like you respect me?" She gestured to the book. "Like you respected me when you lied to me about who *you* were?"

My mind emptied of arguments.

"The other night at Ash's, Dex threatened to expose me, and I decided telling you was a *when*, not an *if*. But I didn't know if I could trust you. Seems I was right to question it." She trembled from head to voice to hands. "Did you ever stop digging? Or has all of this, you and me, just been more lies? Am I just collateral damage, a sacrifice for the sake of your story?"

"You can't be serious. You can't honestly think I would play you like that."

"I don't really know what to think, Levi. Now you know who I am—and not because I told you, but because you fucking snooped around in my things. You had no right—*no right*—to open that book. So what are you going to do with the information you stole? You went to all this trouble to mine it out. How much do you think Warren will pay you for it? Enough to set Billy up for life?"

"You think I'd sell you out?"

"You've done it for less."

A long inhale stoked the embers in my chest to fire, and an exhale let it out. "You talk a big game about my lies when you're no better, *Cecelia*. And if you think I'd fucking betray you, you don't know me at all."

Angry tears filled her eyes. "Did I ever? You lied to me from the minute you met me, so why stop now? How could I expect someone like you to keep my secret? You lied to me because of what you could get for it. I lied to you to protect myself. Because if Warren finds out, I could go to jail. So think about that before you tell your fucking editor."

"I'm not going to tell—"

She held up a hand and closed her eyes, forcing a tear down her flushed cheek. "Don't make me a promise you don't know you can keep."

"What if I know I can?"

"Everybody has a price, Levi. Who I am is a commodity—just look at Dex. The second he wanted something from me, he exercised that power. And I want to think you'd never do that, but I never thought Dex would blackmail me, and here we are. I can't trust myself any more than I can trust you." She looked down, shaking her head. "Please go."

The command struck me still, bolted my feet to the ground. "Stella, please. Let's talk about this."

"I don't want to fucking talk!" she shouted, the words break-ing with a hitch of her chest. Angry eyes begged me to listen. "You took something that wasn't yours, and I want you to go. Right now. Because I cannot be reasonable. And no matter how badly I want to believe you wouldn't use this against me, I don't know if I do."

I watched her for a moment, my throat clamped around a knot that wouldn't budge. I wanted to beg her, to convince her, to hold her and kiss her and explain. I wanted to yell, wanted to argue and fight and burn it all down.

But I wasn't able to be reasonable any better than she was.

So all I could do was leave.

"For the record," I started, my voice rough and raw, "I'd never betray you. I wasn't digging. I know I lied to you once, but I promised you no more secrets, and I seem to recall you promis-ing me the same. So before you stone me, take a fucking look in the mirror."

She covered her mouth with her palm, her face wrenched and shoulders sloped, and the pain written on her was etched on my heart, a vision that would haunt me.

Because it was the last I had of her before I walked away.

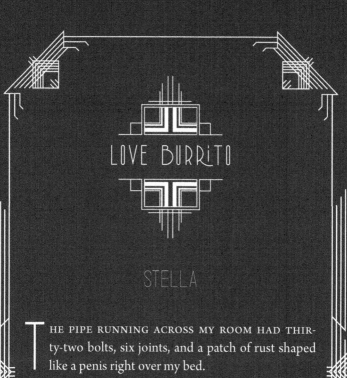

LOVE BURRITO

STELLA

THE PIPE RUNNING ACROSS MY ROOM HAD THIR-
ty-two bolts, six joints, and a patch of rust shaped
like a penis right over my bed.

This data had been gathered in the long hours of
the night while I lay here not sleeping. Exhaustion—or
lack thereof—wasn't a factor, and the bottle of wine I
drank before stumbling to bed didn't put me out like I'd
intended. Instead, I stared at the pipe as it spun slowly,
my body listless and half out of the covers, alternating
between the sweats and a chill.

Never should have had merlot.

My spectacular backfire was indicative of so much
more than my beverage of choice. And I hadn't been
able to distract myself from that mistake, not with
booze or Jane Austen movies—they actually made it
worse—or even K-dramas. The empty apartment didn't
help, but I couldn't bring myself to text anyone. The last

thing I wanted was to ruin their good time with my sad panda moping.

Okay, that was a lie. The last thing I wanted to do was talk about it.

So my phone remained painfully silent, the screen black and depthless. I hadn't texted anyone. And no one had texted me.

Didn't matter where it was—flipped upside down on the coffee table, stuffed in the couch cushions, plugged in the kitchen—I kept on checking. But the text I was looking for never came. Which I shouldn't have been so disappointed about, since I'd told Levi to get out, telling him without saying so that I needed space. And I did.

But I wished he'd fought for me all the same.

I wanted to be wrong so fucking bad, I felt sick. It festered in my stomach like poison, and though it could be the hangover, I was almost positive that wasn't my problem.

My door squeaked as it opened, and my eyes shifted from the penis pipe to the sound, where they found Betty's bodiless head in the sliver of space.

"Oh good. You're up!" she cheered. "Can I cuddle?"

I nodded, my eyes filling up with tears. So I trained my eyes on the blurry penis pipe and started doing math until I reabsorbed the teardrops.

The bed dipped and bounced until she was under the covers with me, lying on her side. I practically felt her worried frown when she figured out something was wrong.

"Babe, are you okay?" she asked gently.

That fatal question was it—there was no holding it back, and I rolled into her arms. What was it about that question that kicked over whatever walls you'd thought you had standing and sturdy? One person asking one harmless question, and that wall was gone with the tide.

I cried for a little while there in Betty's arms, and when I'd finally caught my breath, she grabbed a box of tissues on my nightstand before pulling the comforter over our heads. I took one when she offered and dabbed my nose.

"Okay, now tell me what happened."

"You start—tell me what happened last night. Did you guys have fun?"

She gave me the thickest, most *are you kidding me* look I had ever seen. "I swear to God, Stella."

I groaned. "It's bad. It's so bad that I don't even know if I can say it out loud."

The look melted into genuine fear and concern. "Well, now you really don't have a choice."

"Did I ever?"

"No, not really. What fucking happened? Where's Levi? His bike wasn't outside when we came home, and I wondered if you guys left or what. Do I need to kill him? Did he cheat on you?" Her brain caught on fire at the thought. "Oh my God, if he cheated on you, I swear I will burn his whole building down."

"No, no. He didn't cheat on me—put away your matches."

She visibly relaxed.

"He knows who I am."

Had there been an abundance of air in our little nest, it would have been sucked into her lungs when she gasped. "You're kidding."

I shook my head and rolled onto my back, letting the blanket settle over my face so I could hide. "He found my planner—"

"I can't hear you."

With a huff, I flipped back over. "He found my planner. No, he didn't find it—he fucking picked it up and opened it."

Her jaw came unhinged. "That motherfucking snoop."

"That's what I said."

"I can't believe he read it."

One of my brows arched. "You can't?"

"Ugh, I *can*," she realized. "Fucking fuck, Stella. What's he going to do? Oh God, the magazine." Another gasp, this time coupled with bugged-out eyes. "Oh God. Warren."

I rolled over again, pressing the backs of my hands to my eyes.

Betty flipped the covers back. "Where's my switchblade?"

I couldn't even muster a tiny little bitty smile. "He threw Cecelia Beaton in my face, playing like I was just as bad as him. He had the fucking nerve to act betrayed, Betty."

"You have *got* to be fucking kidding me."

"I wish I were." I stared at the pipe, wondering absently if the joint leaked, would it make the rust weenie look like it was coming? "He said he didn't go looking for it. Like, he didn't have any intention to snoop on me."

"But he did."

"But he did," I echoed.

"Do you believe him?"

I sighed. "I don't know."

Joss's door opened, and she glanced in, frowning when she saw us. She climbed into bed. "Scoot."

We shuffled around until I was comfortably bracketed by my friends. Joss looked like she'd just stepped out of makeup even though she didn't have a smidge on. When she asked what happened, I met Betty's eyes, and she launched into the brief explanation. Color splotched Joss's cheeks, her eyes big and sad and glimmering.

"Goddammit," she whispered. "What are we going to do?"

"Do about what?" Zeke asked from the door, his brows drawn. "Move over." He climbed in, literally on top of me, and shimmied his way between me and Betty.

"Ow! You're on my hand, Zeke!"

"Spoon me," he commanded, ignoring her. "Why are we all nuzzly in your bed, Star Bright?"

"Nosy fucking Levi found her planner," Betty answered.

Zeke stilled. "No. No, he didn't. You're fucking with me."

Our eyes met. His face fell.

"Oh, hell no he didn't. I'll burn his house down."

"Oh good, I was worried I'd have to do it alone," Betty said. "He said he didn't go looking for it, like that excuses him from opening something that was none of his fucking business."

"Right, just like Roman said fucking that bitch was an accident. You don't slip and fall your way into somebody's ass. I'm just saying." He waved a hand, composing himself. "This is not about me. This is about that fucking liar. And you. How are you?"

"I'm ... everything. I feel all the things, and none of them are good."

"What do you think he's going to do?" Joss asked.

"I can't see him telling anyone, I really can't, but what the fuck do I know? I never saw Dex blackmailing me either. In fact, I never see *anything* because I am a gullible fool."

"I wonder if it would have gone down this way if Dex hadn't threatened you," Joss mused, "if he hadn't betrayed you only to have Levi uncover your secret. It doesn't do much to build faith."

"My track record sucks, and the only takeaway is that I am a terrible judge of character, and I can't trust myself. I think I'd buy anything Levi sold me just so I could keep him. And even if he didn't have intent, he still violated my privacy and stole my biggest secret. I forgave him once, but a second time? How many chances do you give someone who's lied to you? Why isn't there a rulebook or something for this?" I took a shaky breath. "I want to believe him. I should. Shouldn't I? Don't all the things he's done since then and now count for something?"

"*When someone shows you who they are, believe them.* Maya Angelou," Zeke said. "I want to believe him too, but trusting his intentions are good after all of this is dangerous."

"Okay, don't get mad when I say this," Betty started, and I gave her a warning look. She made hard eye contact with Zeke. "But Stella, you *were* planning on telling him, just not yet. He was going to find out, and you trusted him enough then."

"But it's not about the knowledge itself, don't you see? It's how he came about it. I was going to tell him when the articles were through and I was sure he wouldn't use the secret against me. But he stole it instead."

"You didn't have control over the situation, and that was your only weapon," Joss said.

The sting of tears nipped the corners of my eyes. "Instead, all I have is my fear and the hope that he won't share the secret he took from me. But without trusting him enough to back it up."

"So what are we going to do now?" Zeke asked.

"Please, no arson," I said, then sighed. "What are my options?"

"Ask him if he plans to tell anyone," Joss said. "Then ask yourself if you believe him."

"If I do feel like I believe him, I won't trust myself."

Joss's eyes softened. "Then it sounds like it's over."

Pain burst from my rib cage when my heart broke.

"I think you should listen to him," Joss continued. "Hear him out."

"And then you've got to protect yourself," Zeke added. "You've got to find out the price for your secret and pay it."

I laid my hand over my eyes, willing myself not to cry.

"Hear me out," he said. "This isn't your first rodeo, Spencer. You know what's at stake. So if you don't think you can take him on his word, you need to secure that information."

"God, that stresses me out," Betty said. "What if it was all a lie? An elaborate game? Like, did he come into this with the intent to use you? Jesus, seriously, where is my switchblade?"

"And what if," Joss added with a frown, "what if you decide to trust him, to believe him, and then he exploits it when he gets mad, like Dex?"

No one had an answer to that.

"You're right, all of you. It's easier this way." I tried to convince myself. "Just call it off, pay him whatever it will take, and walk away. Because it doesn't matter if he did it on purpose or not—that's what I'm realizing. More than my name was exposed, so was the fact that I don't trust him. Even though he apologized for lying, even though he promised me honesty, I didn't have time to get past that lie before this happened." I swallowed hard and lied my face off, pretending like I didn't realize I was doing it. "I mean, whatever, guys. It's no real loss—I barely know him, and he's leaving. We were a total shitshow from the start. It's fine. *C'est la fucking vie* or something."

Zeke's brows came together in a disapproving look. "Don't pull that shit. Don't do that thing where you pretend like it's not a big deal and just skip on. It's not fucking fine—you cared about him, things got fucked, and nothing about that is okay. So let yourself not be fine, for fuck's sake."

A sob broke out of me. Joss was the first to curl into my side and rest her head on my shoulder. Then Zeke. Betty, feeling left out, rolled over Zeke to a chorus of giggles to lie on top of me, putting me smack in the middle of a love burrito.

"It's gonna be okay, Stella," Zeke said with such certainty, I almost believed it.

Almost.

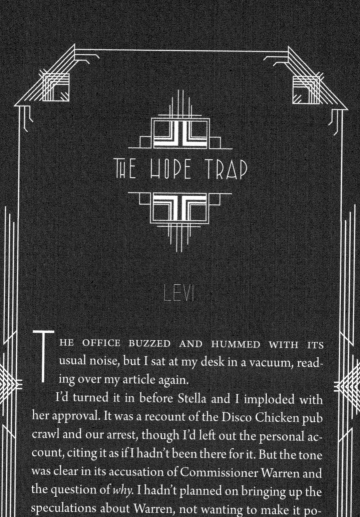

THE HOPE TRAP

LEVI

THE OFFICE BUZZED AND HUMMED WITH ITS usual noise, but I sat at my desk in a vacuum, reading over my article again.

I'd turned it in before Stella and I imploded with her approval. It was a recount of the Disco Chicken pub crawl and our arrest, though I'd left out the personal account, citing it as if I hadn't been there for it. But the tone was clear in its accusation of Commissioner Warren and the question of *why*. I hadn't planned on bringing up the speculations about Warren, not wanting to make it political, not wanting to detract from the group itself, but I was too curious and too fucking pissed to stop myself.

Yara had eaten it up like fresh pastries. Wanted me to slide into that angle, see what I could dig up.

What she didn't know was that I'd lost my in. What she'd never know was that I knew who Cecelia Beaton was.

I'd replayed the fight a hundred times, then a hundred more for good measure, considering every possible potential outcome and thing I could have done differently. I shouldn't have looked. Once I knew, there was no way to keep it to myself—that lie felt so much worse, like I had something to hide when I didn't. I'd told Stella no more secrets, and I wasn't about to start with that one. And while I understood why she didn't trust me with the information, what I couldn't fathom was how she'd sent me away without even trying to talk it through. Without giving me even five minutes to explain.

Of course, I'd asked her for five minutes once before, and she'd granted it. But we were, I supposed, in a *fool me once* situation, one wherein I'd used my extra life and damaged the bridge of trust, weakening it to the point of collapse. And under the first sign of pressure, it crumbled and fell into the ravine.

But in the end, I'd fucked up again. And I owed her an apology for that.

I shouldn't have been surprised that she thought I was lying, but I was, fully and completely. Maybe it was because I was telling the truth that I couldn't fathom her disbelief. It wasn't an unreasonable assumption or too far a conclusion for her to jump to. But the truth of my heart told a different story, one of hurt and loss and no small amount of frustration. Because she'd lied to me too. Sent me away without discussion. Hadn't reached out in the two days we'd been apart, and I was starting to wonder if she ever would.

And that was the hardest part of all.

Never seeing her again wasn't something I could stand for, even if only to have a fucking adult conversation about it and to say goodbye. But being shut out and shut up never did sit well with me. She had a few more days to take her space before I put myself back in it. I only hoped she came around sooner.

And more than anything, I hoped I wouldn't lose her.

I sighed, pushing back from my desk with the day's big task

at hand—tell Yara I'd been permabanned from the Bright Young Things.

When I knocked on the doorjamb, she looked up from her computer and smiled. "Hey, I was just about to call you in and get a plan together. Marcella wants a strategy for uncovering whatever's going on with Warren through the last articles. And her plan for the big article has shifted too—we're going full-on war against Millennials and how the fight has climbed all the way up to the upper echelons of our local government."

I'd taken a seat while she spoke, my frown deepening with every word. "That wasn't the plan."

"Well, plans change. So adapt."

"It's not that simple, Yara. Even if I wanted to write the piece she wants, I can't say it's true. I have a hunch something else is at play here, something bigger than a generational gap."

"Then figure out what it is and write about that. Just keep going to the parties and start leaning in that direction so we can end it all with pyrotechnics."

I shook my head. "The second problem—I lost my in."

Her face flattened. "What the fuck did you do?"

"Stella and I fell out, and I don't know that we'll fall in again." My ribs squeezed my heart like a fist. "Parties are off the table."

"Goddammit, Levi. Do you have any idea how big this story is? Our circulation is up and multiplies exponentially every time a new article posts. You have to figure out how to fix whatever you fucked up and get back in there."

A dark anger swept over me. "I'm not exploiting her, if that's what you're asking. And if that's a problem, Marcella knows where to find me." I stood, not wanting to discuss it any further than that. "I'll write a closing piece, but that's it."

"She's not going to like it," Yara said to my back as I walked out. "She'll pull Syria, and you know it."

I turned to level her with my gaze. "Let me say this one more time—I'm not going to use Stella's feelings against her, not now and not ever. So do me a favor and send out the fucking memo, Yara."

She didn't answer, and I didn't wait for her to before storming out of her office. Once back at my desk, I dropped my head to my palm and leaned in, eyes closed and mind on fire. The weight of her threat bent my shoulders, filling me with dread and inevitability. Because I wasn't going to put any more of this on my relationship with Stella—that was burdened enough as it stood. And if there was one thing I knew, it was that I would never betray her trust again, no matter what she thought. I couldn't stomach even the thought of bullshitting her for an in, never mind doing it. Lying to her wasn't an option, and it never would be.

That undeniable fact could cost me everything. And there was nothing I could do about it but fucking wait to lose what was left.

I only wished I'd have Stella when it was all said and done. But that was looking as inevitable as my ability to hang on to both my job and my morals.

My phone buzzed in my pocket. With a sigh, I leaned back, extending a leg so I could retrieve it. I was so deep in my thoughts that I didn't even consider who might have messaged me.

Stella's name rang like a bell in my mind, my pulse doing double-time.

Hey, can we talk?

I stared at the message like it was written in hieroglyphics. Once past the hopeful shock, I stared at it some more, assessing it for anything that would indicate whether talking was a good or bad thing. I decided to respond as vaguely as I could in return.

Anytime.

Little dots popped up while she typed, then stopped. Then, they popped up again for a second but paused once more. And I sat there, watching the tease with my ribs in a vise.

Come by whenever you're free. Just text when you're on your way.

Without hesitation, I stood, heading for the elevator with my fingers typing out a response.

Heading to you now. Be there in fifteen.

The dots showed up again, but when they stopped, they didn't start up again. No message came through. So I shoved my phone in my pocket and hoped, putting together a speech that— if I was very, very lucky—would absolve me. If nothing else, it would give me the best chance of bringing her back to me.

I didn't want to do without her, not unless I had to.

And she'd be the judge, jury, and executioner of that.

It was as hot as a fucking griddle, so hot that the wind licked at me like flames as I sped to her place, bringing no relief from the temperature. Oppressive was what it was, a hellish heat indicative of my situation. But when I walked into her building, it was to an unnerving chill, the stony cold of a tomb.

I brushed the thought away. *This is it. Maybe she wants to talk it through, set things right. Hear you out, let you apologize. An hour from now, you're going to have her in your arms, and all of this will have been worth it. Manifest it, asshole.*

When I got to the door, I knocked, staring at the keypad while I waited, wondering if I'd ever use it again. Maybe she'd already deactivated my code. God, I hoped she hadn't, just for what it would mean if she had.

I thought I heard her before silence fell. Just when I'd convinced myself I imagined it, the door swung open, and Stella stood on the other side of the threshold.

On a glance, everything about her was soft, from the gentle waves of her golden hair to the freshness of her face. Her sundress was the palest blue, an abundance of fabric printed with a tiny pattern and shot with silver thread, giving her just the slightest bit of shine, just like she always wore. But when our eyes met, they were cold steel, armored for battle.

And my hope seeped out of me like rainwater.

She stepped out of the way. "Thanks for coming."

I walked past her, wishing I could touch her, my brain working on a new strategy. Because this wasn't going to be easy, if it was possible at all. "I'll always come when you call, Stella."

The door closed, and when I caught sight of her again, she was in the process of tamping down her emotion. In a breath, she was stone. I followed her into the living room, my disquiet rising when she chose an armchair, putting an unreachable distance between us.

I sat on the couch, unsure how to start, unsure what to say, the speech I'd carefully composed discarded and useless.

So I landed on keeping it close to the vest. "What did you want to discuss? Because I had a list, but I have a feeling you don't want to hear it."

She didn't react but for a flash of pain behind her eyes. "I'll listen. But it won't change anything."

"You haven't heard my argument yet. I've been told I'm incredibly convincing."

I didn't even get a shadow of a smile.

"Levi, we've been a train wreck from the beginning. We started off on a lie. And even if we tried this again, we can't ever go back. This will hang over us. And then you'll leave. We need to call it before it gets any worse."

I wanted to argue, but I wasn't sure that she was wrong. That knowledge didn't make me hate it any less.

"You want to call it, regardless of how you feel about me?"

"My feelings are the last thing I can listen to when it comes to you."

I swallowed the gravel in my throat. "That's too bad. They're the only thing I can listen to when it comes to you."

Her chin flexed, her color rising. "We have a bigger issue, one that puts too many people at risk, myself more than anyone. The information you have is a commodity that can be bought and sold, and I need to secure its safety."

"I'm not telling anyone who you are, Stella. I won't betray that, not for any price."

"Forgive me for not taking your word on that." Her voice was soft, almost pleading. "I have to protect myself whether I believe you or not. So I'd like to buy my secret back from you. Just name your price."

My eyes narrowed in confusion. Surely I'd imagined what she'd said.

After a pause, she added, "If it's money you want, I can give you whatever you ask for. If it's invitations to parties, that's easy to arrange. But please don't ask me to pretend we're still together. Please … just … I can't."

The room emptied of air, and the world emptied of words. Under my shock and disbelief was simmering rage. "Ask that of you?" I breathed. "*Ask* that? The only thing I wanted to ask was for your fucking forgiveness, Stella. And you … you think I would … you think you could …" I sputtered, unable to complete a thought for my fury. "We haven't even *talked*, Stella, and you're throwing rolls of money at me? This might be how you solve problems, but I cannot fucking believe you'd even *think* to pay me off."

"I don't know what's truth and what's a lie, so it doesn't matter what I ask or what you say. And if you tell me … if you tell me …" Her voice broke. "If you convince me you're telling the truth and you aren't, I might break. I *will* break, and I won't be so easy to put together."

I stood, unable to even look at her, swallowing bile. "I don't want your fucking money. All I ever wanted was you." I flew toward the door, unable to hear anything but a rush of blood in my ears. When my hand rested on the doorknob, I paused, staring at my shoes without seeing through a series of shaky, shallow breaths.

"And to think," I said just loudly enough for her to hear, "I thought I was falling in love with you. But I couldn't have loved you, not if this is who you are." I turned the knob and opened the door. "Send me an NDA, and I'll sign it. Keep the rest."

Without looking back, I walked out the door.

But I left my broken heart at her feet.

STELLA

The door slammed shut so hard, I jumped, knocking the tears barely clinging to my lashes down my cheeks.

There wasn't enough air, the ringing in my ears sharp. A sob ripped from my mouth, and I clapped my hand over my lips to stop another from escaping.

What have I done?

It had seemed foolproof on paper, cut and dry. It wouldn't have been the first time I'd solved a problem in this exact way, a plan that had never failed.

But I'd never loved one of the recipients. In fact, I'd loathed them all.

And that mistake had proven fatal to my heart.

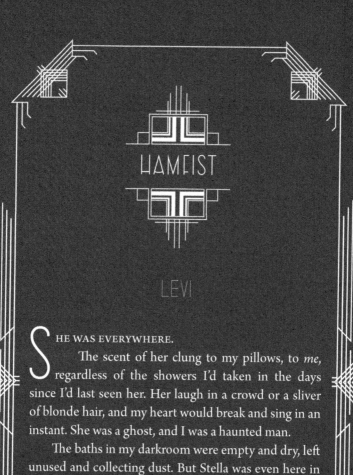

HAMFIST

LEVI

SHE WAS EVERYWHERE.

The scent of her clung to my pillows, to *me*, regardless of the showers I'd taken in the days since I'd last seen her. Her laugh in a crowd or a sliver of blonde hair, and my heart would break and sing in an instant. She was a ghost, and I was a haunted man.

The baths in my darkroom were empty and dry, left unused and collecting dust. But Stella was even here in my sacred space, photographs of her that I hadn't collected hanging from cables.

I yanked one off with a snap of the clip and added it to the stack in my hand.

The only word I knew to explain how I felt was *dark*, as if the light had been shut off, the sun doused. It was an amalgamation of innumerable feelings—betrayal, loss, longing, regret, to name but a few—all mixed together and left to harden to stone. I had yet to find a way to move past it, not when so much of me was left in her hands. Careless, untrusting hands that had slapped me just as easily as they'd once soothed me.

She hadn't been in touch since I'd walked out her door, and for that, I was glad. Glad and glum.

I hated every fucking thing about this, including no small amount of blame to myself—if I hadn't gotten involved, if we'd just been friends, it wouldn't have gone so wrong. But the truth was that we could never be just friends. *I* could never be just friends. The second I first saw her, I knew that as fact. And rather than walk away like I should have, I kissed her and damned us both.

Me leaving, her status versus mine, who I was and who she was, never mattered. Because we'd started off on a lie, and we'd ended on one too. She'd kept me in the dark from the start, and while I didn't blame her from keeping it from me, I was pissed and hurt and shocked that Stella—my Stella—was Cecelia Beaton, and I didn't know it

Even more pissed that she blamed *me*. Accused me of using her.

Again.

But the worst part of it all, worse than the fight or our lies, was that I'd lost her for good, and the pain of missing her had taken up permanent residence in my ribs.

Snap, snap, snap. I pulled pictures off their clips and added them to the stack, trying not to look at them.

I'd shot her a few times after the first time, bringing my camera along with me to a few parties. But the only ones I'd left hanging were of her. The pale curve of her shoulder and waist, the valley of her spine, my sheets pooled around her hips. A series I'd done here in the studio in the dress she wore when I met her, her hair in finger waves, her body backlit, the light catching only the curves of her, marking their shape with glittering sparkles.

Snap. They started in smiles and into dancing, hands over her head and face turned to the side, earrings swinging, body a curve.

Snap. Pensive and quiet, all shadows.

Snap. The strap sliding off one shoulder, then the other.

Snap, snap. And I couldn't look at the rest as I took them down, not that there were many. Hadn't done much shooting after that.

I stopped at the last photo, standing before it with my heart thudding. It was one I hadn't known I'd taken until I developed the film, having forgotten about the timer when I abandoned the camera. We stood in profile, darkness against white light, our foreheads connected. I held her face in one hand and her waist in the other, our bodies curving into each other in a moment of silent exaltation before a kiss.

That picture held everything I felt for her in a single image. It was hope and covetous longing. It was a wish that I'd known would never come true, I'd just been too bewitched to acknowledge it.

Snap.

I turned with the stack of photos, tossing it into a drawer rather than the trash, unready for that final a motion. But I couldn't come in here with them mocking my thoughtlessness, whispering that I should have seen it coming.

They weren't wrong.

I exited the darkroom, my disquiet seeping away when I was safely in my apartment. With every step toward the door, I left her behind me but for that ghost that had become my companion.

There were more important things in front of me.

Like Warren.

I'd spent the last few days writing in my notebook, bits and slivers of the final story I'd promised. Not that the issue of shorting them on promised pieces was settled. Yara had my feet to the fire, and I knew it was only a matter of time before I'd have to duke it out with Marcella.

It was one thing to tell Yara to fuck off. It was another thing entirely to face the editor in chief of the magazine with the visceral *no* I had in store for her.

I could have laughed at the irony—not only did I not get the story *or* the girl, but I might not have my job when it was all said and done. Because regardless of what had gone down between Stella and me, I'd lose my job ten times over before I'd betray her.

I had a little money saved. If it came to it, I could move in with Billy. Wouldn't be the worst idea—in fact, it was probably the only way he'd ever let me get close enough to really watch after him. I had enough of a name that I could easily freelance for a while, maybe something bigger once Marcella revealed my identity. Even Syria seemed unattainable now, and I couldn't muster any real anger about it. Everything in my life felt gray and distant except my hurt and regret.

The night I went home with Stella, I'd made a choice, and this was my consequence. As badly as it hurt, I couldn't say that I regretted that particular choice. Only the circumstance and outcome. Because for a moment, I had been a part of something.

I'd been a part of her.

By the time I walked the few blocks to Billy's, I'd packed it all away as best I could, even digging up a smirk for him as I opened the door.

"Hey, old man."

He looked over from his ancient recliner and smirked right back. "Look at that—he's alive. I was getting ready to call the morgue."

I snorted a laugh and rolled my eyes, taking a seat in an armchair on the far side of the coffee table so I could see him. "Aw, you missed me."

"Psh—I had better company."

One of my brows rose. "That so?"

"Sure is. I have other friends, you know."

"Rufus from the barbershop? Larry from the bar?"

"Peg from the Laundromat."

At that, I genuinely smiled for the first time in what felt like forever. "Oh-ho. Easy there, Casanova."

"She made lasagna, and no, you can't have any."

"Fair enough," I said on a chuckle. "She came yesterday?"

"And the day before. Twice."

I eyed him. "We *are* still talking about her visiting and not something else, right?"

But he only gave me a devilish smile and shrugged.

That earned him a full-blown, bottom-of-my-belly laugh. "You fucking dog."

"We are what we are, son. Where've you been?"

"Just busy," I hedged.

"For three days?"

With a shrug, I changed the subject. "Wanted to talk about Warren."

Billy sat back, his face souring. "I can tell you he's a slimy sonofabitch. I also possess a number of colorful adjectives I'd use to describe him. Grab a pen."

A little laugh left me. "Had a chat with Jameson the other day. Told me to ask you about the Blaze job in '05. Does that mean anything to you?"

His face darkened. "It does." He picked up the remote and muted the TV, spinning his chair to face me. "The Blaze job, huh? I think I can guess what he wants you to know."

"Well, don't leave me hangin', Pop."

He ran a weathered hand over his chin, the scratch of silver stubble against his palm audible. "Warren was a detective then, undercover to infiltrate the Russian Mafia syndicate. A handful of us had a suspicion he'd turned, Jameson included, one solidified after we raided the Blaze warehouse."

Silently, I leaned back in the chair, brows drawn together.

"It was a sting—we were set to bust a shipment of drugs, but it went sideways. Someone tipped them off, because one of the heads of the hydra, Vadim Orlov, was supposed to be there, and the shipment was half of what it should have been. They were waiting for us, opened up on a firefight. Lost a couple of good men that day, and we didn't get Orlov. Blaze was the bust that put me behind the desk." He patted his bad leg. "But the part Warren played that day always stank. Orlov was ready for us—somebody told him. And Ed and I were the lone witnesses to something we couldn't prove, something we couldn't accuse him of, not without putting marks on our backs. Ed has a family, and I had you. Couldn't risk it, not without evidence," he said half to himself.

He paused to take a breath. I held mine.

"Warren shot our guys. He opened fire on *us*, not them."

Shock ripped down my spine. "Did he ... was he the one who ..."

"Shot me? I don't know. Coulda been—he knew Jameson and I were suspicious, might have been trying to take us out. Or it could have been some sort of trial, proof of loyalty Orlov asked of him. But in the end, Warren was commemorated a hero, and from there on out, he made regular Mafia arrests, making headlines for busts I always figured Orlov set up to keep the heat off the both of them. Nobody asked why Orlov didn't have him axed, which is batshit—nobody betrays Orlov and lives to talk about it. The only explanation is that Warren's involved with Orlov. And somehow, that slippery piece of shit has avoided getting nabbed for the last fifteen years."

"Jesus," I breathed. "So money, then? Is that why he does it?"

"That's why he does it, and that's *how* he does it. It's how he's slithered into his office despite Jameson's efforts to stop him. Warren has people everywhere, and now that he's commissioner? He can pretty much do whatever the fuck he wants, so long as it *looks* like it's above board. But he's crooked as fuck, and everybody knows it."

"Anybody tried to take him down?"

"Sure, but nobody's lasted long. If you're lucky, he'll put you back on the beat. If you're unlucky, you get framed for something *he* likely did. So nobody fucks with him. It's hard enough to get cops to turn on each other, but when one wields that kind of power, it gets even stickier. Every board meeting, every committee, he's got stacked in his favor. It's the brotherhood that protects us when we're filing into a sting, the bond that makes certain your crew has your back. But it's the brotherhood they exploit to cover their fuckups too."

"So how do I bust him?"

"You don't." It was a warning.

"What the fuck does he want with the Bright Young Things? He questioned Stella, you know."

Billy shook his head. "*Abuser of power* should be on his business cards. Listen, if I had to guess, I'd say it's nothing personal and everything to do with money. Somebody powerful wants those kids to stop and went to him because of his reputation."

"The Mafia?" My face screwed up.

A snort. "Orlov doesn't want shit to do with a bunch of kids. In fact, he's probably got spawn of his own running around with them. If he wanted it to stop, it'd stop without the pony show. No, I'd guess it was political."

My mind raced for answers. "And important enough he'd stick his neck out for it when he's already got enough irons in the fire to keep him busy." I paused. "He doesn't have a wife or kids, right?"

"No. Was married once but lost her. Probably because he's a useless shitbag."

My thoughts skipped around, wondering where Warren had slipped. Because if he thought himself bulletproof, he'd be careless. It was a long shot, but maybe if I followed him—

"Whatever you're thinking, quit it," Billy said. "This isn't something to fuck with, Levi. This isn't some crack house or sex trafficking ring, dangerous as they are. This is the goddamn

Russian Mafia you're thinking about toying with. And unless you want a bullet in your skull, I suggest you cut it out."

"All right," I lied, already concocting a plan to stake him out.

Billy only looked mildly assuaged, but he relaxed just enough to indicate the topic had been shelved. "So are you ever gonna tell me what you're moping around about?"

"If I say no, will you leave it be?"

"Nope."

I sighed and rested my head on the back of the chair. "Stella and I are through."

He didn't react, just watched me for a second. "Well, are you gonna elaborate, or do I have to badger it out of you?"

And so in the briefest of terms, I explained what'd happened, all the way up to her trying to fucking buy me off, masterfully avoiding anything to do with my feelings on the matter, of which I had many. Buckets worth. Dumptrucks full.

I fell silent, and again, he watched me with that assessing look of his. "So you fucked up?"

My brows fused together. "She offered me money to keep my mouth shut."

"Because you lied to her."

"Once."

"About reporting on her. That's no small thing."

"So you're saying I shouldn't be mad?" I scoffed. "What the fuck, Pop? I figured you'd get it."

"Let me let you in on a little secret, kid. Sometimes, you just gotta let them be mad about you being a meatheaded, ham-fisted dummy. Oh, don't look so offended. It's the curse of our sex, to be meatheaded and ham-fisted. And it's our job to be a man and take our lumps. Stop worrying about what she did when you're the one who cocked it up."

"What am I supposed to do? Apologize again? Because I tried, and she didn't want to hear it."

"First of all, I've heard you apologize, and it's never been what one would call trying. And secondly, you were standin' there with her diary in your hand. What'd you think was gonna happen?"

"Planner."

"Huh?"

"It wasn't her diary—it was her planner."

He laid a look on me. "Same fucking thing. She was in the middle of being mad at you, jellybrain. Shoulda let her yell and kept your temper."

"And then what? Forget it ever happened?" I asked in disbelief.

"No, dumbass—you wait until the storm passes. Then you try again, and you try harder. I mean a real good, on-your-knees groveling, not any of that half-ass crap you like to pull. You need to sit her down and tell her all the ways you're an idiot and hope to God she agrees well enough to forgive you."

I swallowed the knot in my throat. "She doesn't want to talk about it, Billy—I've tried twice and gotten nowhere both times. She doesn't want to see me. Said it didn't matter what I said because she didn't believe me."

Billy sighed and scratched his jaw. "Listen, I didn't say it would work. She might be done once and for all with you, but if you want a shot, that's the best you've got. Give her some more time and then try again, for God's sake. Don't roll over and give up. All right?"

With a long exhale, I said, "All right."

"Good. And in the meantime, keep your nose out of Warren's business. You hear me?" He pointed at me with both his eyes and an index finger.

"Loud and clear," I answered.

But I was pretty sure he knew I was gonna do it anyway.

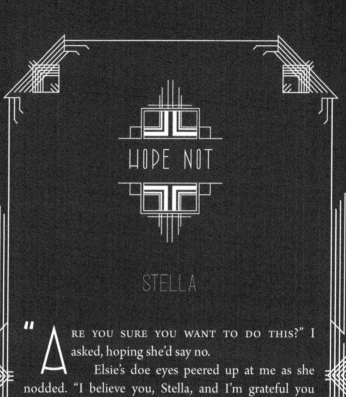

HOPE NOT

STELLA

"**A**RE YOU SURE YOU WANT TO DO THIS?" I
asked, hoping she'd say no.

Elsie's doe eyes peered up at me as she
nodded. "I believe you, Stella, and I'm grateful you
came to tell me about Dex. But if I'm not here, I won't
hear the truth with my own ears. He'll lie. And I'm
afraid I'll believe him."

A heavy sigh slid out of me.

"Are you sure *you* want to do this?" she asked.

"Bust Dex and humiliate him? I'm always in for
that, but I'm more worried about what it'll do to you."

"It was my idea, so try not to think about me. I'll be
okay, especially if there's booze on the premises."

"Plenty for you and me both."

"Thank you for doing this. Especially since … well,
I heard about your breakup. I'm sorry, Stella. I don't
know what happened, but I've seen you two together.

You were … I don't know. You just looked *right* together, does that make sense?"

I did my best to smile. "Well, things aren't always what they seem. Like Dex."

It was her turn to sigh. "Like Dex. Although I hope Levi didn't treat you like Dex did."

"No," I answered with a pang in my chest. "No, he was much better than that. But sometimes things are just too broken to glue back together. And when trust is broken, it's almost impossible to mend. Especially the second time."

She nodded just as the doorbell rang. The two of us jumped at the sound, and Elsie hurried into my bathroom and shut off the light, closing the door but for a crack.

I turned for the door, wiping my damp palms and smoothing my dress in the same motion. The last thing I'd expected when I told Elsie the truth about Dex hitting on me was for her to suggest we set him up. But I couldn't pretend like I wouldn't enjoy it, as nervous as I was.

At least it was a distraction from Levi. And I would take all the distractions I could get, especially if they got me out of my pajamas.

I took a deep breath as I approached the door, telling myself I was prepared for what was on the other side. My hand paused over the doorknob just long enough for me to take another fortifying breath and put on a smile. And when I opened that door, I found exactly what I was looking for.

Dex looked like a dream, a tall, blond, familiar dream. A dream that had turned into a nightmare, wearing a jackal smile, wielding thieving hands.

"You came," I said wistfully, doing my best not to flinch when he leaned in and kissed me.

The connection was unexpected and alien and utterly wrong—noted with an aching heart now that I knew what the *right* lips felt like—but I endured the gentle brush of his mouth with the patience of a hunter.

When he backed away, it was with a smile and a hot look. "I've missed that."

"Me too," I lied. "Come on in."

He slithered past me, surveying the room.

"Want a drink?"

"Sure. Scotch."

With that bullshit smile on my face, I headed to the bar cart and poured him a finger of scotch and another for myself, walking them back to him. He watched me approach like the opportunistic fuck that he was. How had I not noticed it before? How had it taken two full years of neglect, a painful rejection, and Levi for me to realize that Dex was the very last thing I wanted in a man? It baffled me that I could be so dense.

But tonight, I'd pretend like he was the center of the universe so I could settle the score.

He took the crystal glass and held it out for a toast. "To us."

I couldn't repeat him, so I just smiled and said, "Cheers."

A clink of glass, and I took a sip that turned into a searing gulp that burned its way through my chest. I coughed, lips closed, and he laughed.

"You're not fucking around tonight, are you, Stell?"

"Nope," I said, grabbing his hand and pulling him toward my bedroom, depositing my glass on an end table as we passed.

He chuckled like a patronizing shit and followed without argument, just like I knew he would.

My room had been sexified with low lights and quiet music. I'd considered candles, but Dex didn't deserve candles any more than he deserved the kiss he'd stolen. The second we crossed the threshold, he stopped and turned with hungry eyes, leaning in for another kiss, but I backed away playfully, smiling at him as I shut the door. And he watched every step while he kicked back the rest of his drink and set the glass on my dresser.

When I approached again, I laid a hand on his chest and

applied enough pressure that he knew where to go, which was backward toward my bed.

Here we go.

"I'm glad you came," I cooed as I walked him back. "You were right the other night to try to talk me into this."

"Anytime you need somebody to talk sense into you, give me a call."

I laughed like he was *the funniest* and guided him to sit. I found I liked looking down at him very much. "I just didn't know if you were serious until then. You know, because of Elsie. I just"—I tucked my hair behind my ear—"I thought you didn't believe in monogamy. So when you moved in with her so soon, I didn't understand."

Everything about him smacked of starvation, from his greedy hands to his smiling lips to the smoldering heat in his eyes. Those hands traced the curves of my waist and ass as he spoke. "Elsie was just a phase. I thought I could do it, the whole settle-down thing, but I couldn't. Especially not when I saw you with *him*."

I stroked his face, sliding one leg along the outside of his, then the other until I straddled his waist. "Poor thing. When are you going to tell her?"

Hypnotized by my lips, he hummed into a question mark, "Hmm?"

"When are you going to tell her? About this. I assume you haven't."

"You assume right, but I will. I'll tell her soon."

I pouted. "But you're still going to live with her?"

He shrugged. "Dunno. But come on, Stell. You know sharing me is part of the deal. Does it matter that I'm living with Elsie?"

"Not to me, but don't you think maybe she should know?"

"Listen," he soothed, "Elsie isn't like you and me. She has all these … *feelings*, you know? She wouldn't get it. So let me handle her. I'll tell her when the time is right. And in the meantime"—he flipped me over—"I'm gonna fuck you until you can't walk. God, I've missed you."

He descended for a kiss, but I stopped him with both hands on his chest. I hardened to steel, cut by a knife smile. "Heard enough, Elsie?"

His eyes flew open, wide and shocked and snapping to the sound of my bathroom door opening. Sweet Elsie stood in the doorway, her cheeks shining with tears and her face twisted in pain. Even crying, she was heartbreakingly beautiful.

Dex scrambled off of me, sputtering. "Elsie? What … how did you … where …" It didn't dawn on him until he looked back at me and saw sheer retribution in my eyes. A flash of fury shot across his face before he wiped it smooth and turned back to her. "Babe, this isn't what you think. I swear—"

She shook her head and backed away when he reached for her, bumping into my nightstand, the jolt of which knocked the books to the floor. My planner hit the ground with a thump, and the contents spurted out of the top in a brazen display of my secret.

I tore my eyes from that to Elsie and Dex as he tried to mollify her.

"Stop," she whispered.

"Els, you have to believe me. I love you—I'd never hurt you. Especially not with *her*." He spat the pronoun like his mouth was full of sour milk.

"Stop," she said again, a little louder.

"What happened to fucking me until I couldn't walk?" I asked smartly. "Don't listen to him, Elsie. He's a fucking liar and a cheat. I wasted two years on him. Don't make my mistake."

"I … I didn't want to believe her," Elsie said, her breath hitching and eyes searching his face. "I couldn't believe it was true. But Stella has no reason to lie—"

"Are you fucking kidding me?" he shot. "She has every reason to lie. She's jealous that I love *you* when I never loved her. I never chose her like I chose you, and it kills her."

The hot slice of pain in my heart stole my breath. "Maybe once, but not anymore. Now I know better."

His face swiveled, bent in fury. "Shut the fuck up, Stella. You've done enough."

"The way I see it, *you've* done enough."

Ignoring me, he turned back to Elsie, pinned against the wall with nothing more than his presence. "Elsie, let's go home and talk about this," he soothed. "You know I love you."

"Please, Dex. Please stop." She tried to slide away, but he stopped her with his hand on the wall.

"Don't do this."

My hackles rose at the sight of her trapped and searching for escape like a baby deer in front of a wolf. The tone of his voice, the strength of his stance.

He's going to hit her.

Danger sparked, alive and electric in the room. I moved to intervene, prepared for a blow and ready for a fight, if that was what it took to get her away from him.

But before I could get there, her face wrenched up, her eyes full of anger and betrayal.

"I said, *stop!*" she yelled, shoving him hard enough to knock him back in surprise.

She slipped away, but he snagged her arm. And when she whirled around, it was with an open palm.

The smack of flesh rang in the room. Elsie was fury, and Dex was defeat.

"Don't do this?" she asked. "I didn't do anything. It was *you*, you asshole. *You.*"

Again, he reached for her, and again, she spun away, hurrying to my side where we stood to face him.

"You need to leave, Dex," I said.

He stank of spite. "You have really fucked with the wrong guy, Stella. If you think I'm keeping quiet about your little secret, you're fucking wrong."

"You know, I remembered something the other day, something I think your father would be very interested in. Your step-mom too. It'd be a shame if your dad got so angry you fucked his wife that he tampered with your trust, wouldn't it?"

He growled. "You wouldn't."

"I won't if you won't. Food for thought. Now get the fuck out of my apartment."

"And don't show up at mine," Elsie added.

Dex's raging eyes bounced between the two of us a few times before he finally accepted his position. "Fuck you, Stella," he said as he passed.

I ignored him, not wanting to goad him any more than I already had as I followed him to the door, giving him a wide berth, just in case. Just in case of what, I wasn't sure, but I wasn't taking any chances.

"This isn't over," he said from the doorway.

"Pretty sure it is. Don't fuck with me. Don't talk to me. Don't text me or call me. And that goes for Elsie too."

He watched me through a long pause. "I never thought I could hate you. But here we are."

"Here we are," I echoed. "See you around, Dex."

"You'd better hope not."

The door slammed shut, and I sighed my relief, hurrying back to my bedroom where I found Elsie sitting on the edge of my bed, crying.

I sat silently beside her, gathering her up. "I'm sorry. I'm so sorry, Elsie."

But she shook her head. "This was m-m-my idea—don't be s-sorry. I always do this. I always trust the wrong guys."

"You and me both."

We were quiet for a minute, aside from her shuddering breath as she tried to collect herself.

"You're a good friend, Stella. A good person. Don't let anyone ever make you feel any less than that."

"Hey, us suckers have to stick together, right?"

A sad chuckle. "Right." She sighed. "What are the odds of him actually staying away tonight?"

"Slim to none. If you don't want to go home, you're welcome to stay here. I have a spare room."

"Don't, like, ten people live here?"

I laughed. "You'd think. I collect strays."

Another sigh. "Thank you, Stella."

"You're welcome. What do you say to that drink?"

"I'd say fill 'er up."

"Good. There's a bar cart in the kitchen—help yourself. I'll be right behind you."

She smiled at me for a long moment before launching herself at me. "You're magic," she whispered into my hair.

"Blood magic maybe," I joked.

"No. Real live fairy godmother glitter magic. And I'm thankful to get a little stardust on me."

Before I could argue, she bounded off, smiling at me over her shoulder.

Fuck Dex for mistreating her. Fuck him so hard. I found it no surprise that he'd been struck by her and, sadly, no surprise that he'd hurt her.

That happened to be his modus operandi, the spoiled fuck.

With a noisy exhale, I picked myself up and made my way around the bed to clean up the mess. As I knelt, I reached for my planner, stroking the invitations that had spilled out. It was so conspicuous, I wondered if the tables were turned, would I have looked? If I'd found something suspect, would I have fallen prey to my curiosity?

And I knew I'd have been no better than Levi.

I'd told myself a story, made up the mantra that he'd lied too many times to entertain another. But there was a reason under that reason, the truth of my fear.

I'd been fooled before—by him, no less—and the thought of

being fooled again was too much to bear. So I'd pushed him out, sent him away, even though it wasn't what I wanted. Even though it hurt us both. And as if that wasn't enough, I'd offended him so deeply, I didn't know if there would be any coming around.

No, it was too complicated between us to ask for forgiveness. Better to just walk away, even if it was through broken glass.

I slipped the invitations back inside and closed the planner, stacking it on my other books before pulling them into my chest, my fingers stroking the spine, wishing I could tell him how wrong I was.

And my heart was full of regret.

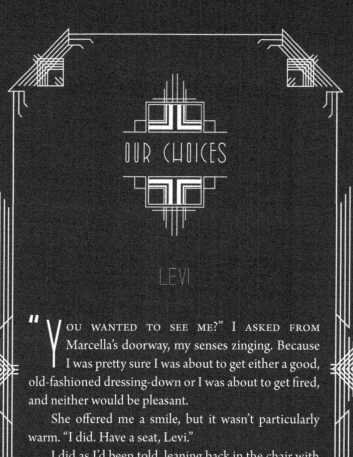

OUR CHOICES

LEVI

"Y OU WANTED TO SEE ME?" I ASKED FROM
Marcella's doorway, my senses zinging. Because
I was pretty sure I was about to get either a good,
old-fashioned dressing-down or I was about to get fired,
and neither would be pleasant.

She offered me a smile, but it wasn't particularly
warm. "I did. Have a seat, Levi."

I did as I'd been told, leaning back in the chair with
an air of equanimity I didn't feel. I didn't speak.

She folded her hands on the desktop. "I hear you've
lost your connection to the Bright Young Things."

"That is true."

"Yara says you can't get it back, but I find that hard
to believe. Getting into places you don't belong has
never been a problem for you before."

"I didn't say I couldn't. I said I wouldn't."

"I see." She sighed and sat back, feigning casualness.

"Well, you promised me an eight-article series, plus a magazine feature, in exchange for a padded bank account and a trip to Syria. So what do you suggest we do from here?"

The words said negotiation, but that wasn't what we were doing. My jaw tightened.

"You knew this was contingent on my ability to get into the parties. What do you suggest I do? Because using Stella isn't an option. I'm a good liar, but I'll never be that good."

"I don't really care how you do it."

I exhaled a focused stream so I didn't snap. "I have a lead on Warren. I could write one more article with what I have, then a big wrap-up, and a big-picture piece for the magazine feature."

"That wasn't our agreement."

My nostrils flared. "I'll still fulfill my commitment with the story itself, but you've gotta cut me some slack, Marcella."

"I might be *your* boss, but I'm not *the boss*. Subscriptions jump with every article. Engagement is higher than it's been in twenty years. They want more, and they've tasked me with delivering. It's not just your neck on the line—it's mine too."

We held eyes for a long, assessing moment before I spoke. "I can promise you two more articles and the big-picture piece. If they want to fire me, that's their prerogative. If you want to take Syria, be my guest. But I'm not going to lie my way back in."

"Not even for your job?"

"There's nothing you could offer me that would change my mind."

"Seems a little shortsighted."

"It does. Short-term gain—my job. L—long-term loss—my self-respect. I'll give you what you want and get a bunch of things that don't really matter, but I'll lose everything that *does*."

"Stella Spencer's good graces?"

"My dignity. My morals. And Stella Spencer's well-being. Her good graces aren't anything I could hope to find my way back into."

"So that's your final word?"

"That's it. Tell whoever you need to tell. Or fire me on the spot. I'm sure I can find somebody to buy the piece, especially when I tell them I know who Cecelia Beaton is."

Her face shot open in a rare moment of surprise. "You what?"

"I know who she is. The last piece in the series will be the exposé."

A smile curled on her lips. "You should have led with that, Levi. I'm pretty sure you can have whatever you want if you write *that* piece."

"I'll settle for my job and the Syria gig."

"Give me that article, and I'll promote you and book your ticket to Syria right now." She was all smiles. "So a lead on Warren?"

"A little one, but a lead nonetheless. In fact," I said, standing, "I need to run if I'm going to follow it."

"Go, go," she urged, waving me out. "Learn all the things and make us famous."

She'd never know how fucking annoyed I was that nobody seemed to give a shit about what'd happened with me and Stella, only how it affected them. Not that I would tell them if they asked, but their blatant disregard hadn't gone unnoticed. And not that they were my friends. It just seemed the decent thing to do, something that would have made me feel more like a human and less like a commodity.

It didn't matter either way, I supposed. Soon, I'd be on my way to the other side of the world where I could make a name for myself on a whole new level. And I'd leave all this behind, Stella included.

If I *could* escape her. I had a feeling even five thousand miles wouldn't do the trick.

Once outside, I hopped on my bike and headed downtown where I'd wait for Warren to leave work. Again. For three days, I'd hung out on a side street for him to exit headquarters and followed him home, where he stayed all night. Nobody came or went that I could tell, and overall, my reconnaissance was starting to feel like a bust. I'd promised myself a full week before abandoning the goose chase for something more tangible, though I wasn't sure what that might be. All that hanging around had given me plenty of time to think. Stella being the lingering topic.

I'd tried to quiet thoughts of her, working instead on writing the next article in my notebook, flipping ahead to make notes, but that only got me so far. She'd creep back in, whispering reminders of my rights and wrongs and what-could-have-beens. I should have been clued in to the depth of my feelings for her by the pervasiveness of my thoughts. I couldn't seem to let it go. Maybe it was because I'd fucked up so royally. Maybe it was because although she'd hurt me, I'd already forgiven her. Maybe it was because I wanted her back.

But I couldn't have her. That I'd ever thought I could was an illusion.

It was after dark when Warren stepped out of the building, greeting people on his way out. I slid on my helmet. He shook hands with an officer before kicking his head back in laughter. I started my engine. He stepped to the curb where a cab idled and climbed inside.

And I followed.

I'd become intimately familiar with the route to his apartment, and within one turn, I knew we were headed somewhere else. I didn't get my hopes up. Honestly, I really hoped he was on his way to a colonoscopy or maybe to have some boils removed, but that was probably too much to ask for too. So staying a reasonable distance behind them with a couple of cars for cover, I wound toward Alphabet City, wondering where he was going, particularly when we reached the older, tumbledown part of the neighborhood, which hadn't yet been gentrified. Rain began to fall, first in fat, scattered droplets, then in a pinging deluge, slicking the street and dotting cab windows.

The cab stopped in front of a bodega, and Warren exited

and stepped inside while I waited, tucked in an alley. When he emerged, it was with empty hands and a glance up and down the street before giving me his back. I locked up my bike and followed as he walked away.

He wound through the streets in a zigzag, deeper into the projects with every block until he came to a dilapidated building next to an alley. A seedy motherfucker greeted him with a jerk of his chin, and the two of them entered together.

The rain let up but didn't stop, fueling a constant stream of rivulets rolling down the arms of my leather jacket. I was soaked otherwise, and Warren had to be too.

What the fuck is he doing here?

I stayed on the opposite side of the street, inspecting the building as best I could without being conspicuous. A couple of girls bracketed the door, leaning against the rail, smoking as they watched me with hungry eyes. It was a flophouse, and I'd been in enough to guess that most of its inhabitants were sex workers. If I was right, the man who'd greeted Warren was a pimp.

But it didn't make any sense. Warren was no millionaire, but he could afford something—some*one*—a little more luxurious. Maybe my gut was wrong. Maybe there was some deal going down, and this was just a meeting point.

One of the girls flicked her cigarette onto the sidewalk as I passed, making hard eye contact as she licked her lips.

Nope, definitely hookers.

I offered her a smile and shook my head. Disappointed, she whacked her friend in the arm to head inside.

When the coast was clear, I trotted across the street and doubled back toward the alley, ducking in before I looked in my urgency to get out of the street.

A drizzle was all that was left of the rain, a collection of infinitesimal drops to form a misty shroud. Everything shone, from the brick walls to the metal of the fire escape to the warped and broken pavement.

Well into the alley, a girl leaned against the wall, ankles crossed in front of her and a cigarette in her hand. Slowly, her head turned, then cocked like a bird when she got a good look.

"Levi?"

Shocked by the sound of my name, I frowned. "Who's asking?"

"It's me, April. You took my picture for your magazine."

The memory struck like flint of a thirteen-year-old girl I'd met investigating a trafficking ring in Queens a couple of years ago. I smiled to cover the cut of a hot knife to the gut.

"Hey," I said. "What are you doing here?"

One of her brows rose with a snarky smile. "Take a wild guess. I'm more interested in what *you're* doing here."

I glanced up the building she was leaning on. "You living here?"

"Living and working, yeah. It's a good place. Better than anything Vlad did for us."

"The bar was pretty low there."

She laughed. "Yeah, it was." She snuffed her cigarette on the wall and immediately took another one out of the pack in her hand. "Want one?" She tilted the pack in my direction.

"What the hell?" I said, resigned. The slim cylinder felt like an old friend in my hand and a lover on my lips.

She sparked her lighter, and I set the end ablaze, taking a drag that rolled my eyes back in my head.

"Goddamn, that's good."

She lit hers, exhaling a plume of smoke. "You quit or something?"

I took another drag with my eyes closed. "Yeah, but it's been a real shitty week, April."

"I know the feeling." She paused. "You never said what you're doing out here. Surely you're not looking for a good time."

I huffed a laugh, breathing smoke out of my nose like a dragon. "Might be looking for trouble. Who runs this place?"

"Petey Milovich. Hard to be scared of a guy named Petey, but he's got a right hook that'll set that straight." She chuckled, though I didn't find anything funny. "Nah, he's good to us. Especially the little ones."

A tingling cold cracked through me. "The little ones?"

She took a long drag, watching me. "Yeah. Russian kids. They get sold by their parents and shipped over here in fucking crates with a shit bucket." She shook her head. "Makes you thankful you had a choice, you know?"

"Yeah," I answered quietly. "You know a cop that comes around here? Just walked through the front door."

"Oh, yeah. That Warren guy. Seen him on TV a bunch." Her face soured. "I hate that fucker."

A stone lodged in my throat at the thought of him fucking April. "He ever hurt you?"

She shrugged. "Sometimes. Always hits where you can't see so Petey doesn't get pissed. Not that he'd do anything about it. How else do you think we stay open?"

"So he uses Petey's services, and in exchange, nobody gets busted?"

"Well, yeah. It's kinda the dream, staying out of jail. Especially since they keep trying to put me back in the system."

"How often does he come here?"

"Once a week or so. Petey calls him when we get new kids, so sometimes twice. Prick always gets first pick."

Bile climbed up my esophagus. I looked up the wall of the building as the rain fell, the droplets clinging to my upturned face. He was in there right now.

The urge to open the metal service door and find him so I could beat the fuck out of him was so strong, I took a step before stopping myself. If I walked through that door, I'd get shot.

"You always were so sweet," April said sadly. When I looked at her, she wore a quiet smile that knew too much for a girl of fifteen. "But there's not anything you can do, Levi. If they bust us here, they'll just send the new girls they get somewhere else, like to Vlad, that son of a bitch."

"Doesn't mean there's nothing I can do."

She sighed. "Don't do anything stupid. Not now, at least."

I took a long drag and let it out slow. "Think you could help me?"

"Depends on how."

"I need proof on Warren. I need proof he's here and what he's doing."

Her brows ticked together. She took a puff of her smoke while she thought. With a sigh, she dropped her cigarette and stepped on it. "Lemme see what I can do. Wait here."

The minutes she was gone were agonizing. Pacing didn't help. I smoked the cigarette down to the filter, which didn't help either. Because my mind chewed and shredded the information I held and the knowledge of what was happening right up there with that fucking waste of flesh.

When she finally came back, she closed the door gently behind her. "He's got Nessa in one of the rooms facing the alley. If you can figure out how to get up the fire escape, you should be able to see in."

"How old is she?"

"Fifteen."

I scrubbed a hand over my mouth to keep my stomach in place. I looked up again. "No blinds?"

"Curtains, but they're never shut. No windows across the alley." She glanced over her shoulder. "I gotta get back inside, but she's on the third floor. Hope you find what you're looking for."

"You still have my number, right? In case you get in any trouble, if you need anything …"

She smiled, turning for the door. "Yeah, I got it. See you around, Levi."

"Take care of yourself, April."

"Take your own advice," she teased, opening the door.

And then she disappeared, leaving me to my task.

The dumpster was the only thing tall enough to reach the fire escape, and even that was going to be a stretch, but it was my only option. It was thankfully empty, its wheels rattling and squeaking as I pushed it under the platform. I closed the lid, hoisting myself up in the dark. Once standing under the ladder, I was thankful for my height—a full-force jump would reach it. My heart hammered painfully as I wound up, eyes on the ladder rung, and with an exhale, I jumped as hard as I could and prayed.

My hands clasped the rung, and my weight lowered it. Up I went, creeping silently as I pulled out my phone and readied it, not wanting to linger any longer than I had to, my pulse quickening as I climbed the final steps to my destination.

I found him at the second window I searched, the curtains parted just like April said they'd be. And there in the bed was Warren, naked and thrusting over a girl who looked much younger than fifteen.

And with trembling hands, I got what I needed to end him once and for all.

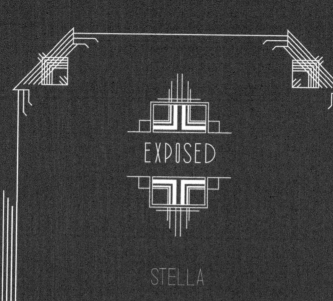

EXPOSED

STELLA

MY BEDROOM DOOR FLEW OPEN LIKE THE POLICE kicked it in, and I shot out of bed, swiping my sleep mask off in alarm.

All of my roommates, with the exception of Tag, spilled into my room like a flock of starving seagulls.

"What the fuck?" I slurred, squinting against the daylight.

Zeke shoved his phone in my face as they descended into my bed. "Warren was arrested."

At that, my eyes flew open, instantly alert. "What?" I asked, swiping his phone from his hand to take in first the photo of Warren being arrested by the FBI, then the headline.

Commissioner Warren Arrested on Sex Crime Allegations

The article was on the *Times*, a short write-up citing what little information they had. Warren had been photographed engaged in sexual activity with a minor, leading to the bust of a prostitution ring in Alphabet City.

"Oh my God," I breathed, exiting out of that article to do a search on Warren himself. The first article listed was, oddly, from *Vagabond*.

"Fucking pig," Betty spat. "Disgusting fucking pig."

"They'll murder him in jail for this," Joss said, shaking her head.

But Zeke shook his head for a different reason altogether. "He won't go to jail. And if he does, he'll have protection. We wouldn't be so lucky for actual justice, not in America."

I waved my hand to hush them. "Did you see Levi's article?"

They frowned in conjunction.

"What article?" Zeke asked.

So I took a breath and read it aloud, the sprawling piece about Warren's corruption. About the girls found at a place like that, their lost innocence and shattered youth. He described the atmosphere like he'd been there — the shadows and the rain, the savage survival, the hopeless cycle.

And I knew it wasn't just his imagination that had painted the picture.

He *had* been there.

My throat squeezed closed, and I paused, swallowing to open it up, pressing my fingers to my lips to stop the words from breaking. His curiosity had led him there, following Warren, no doubt. He'd saved all those girls and taken out a corrupt man in one motion. Because I knew his words and I knew his heart, and reading that piece, I knew without a doubt that he'd somehow managed all of this, from the FBI to the massive press coverage.

"Do you think Warren will resign?" Joss asked.

"I don't see how he'll wiggle his way out of it, slippery or not," Zeke answered. "No city government leaves a pedophile in office."

"And then we'll finally be rid of him, the fucking skeevy perv," Betty added.

"I … I think Levi did this. Found this out. Maybe even took that picture. Saved those girls." I couldn't vent the pressure in my chest, and my friends watched me struggle for words with worried faces. "I need to call him," I said to myself. "I need to talk to him."

In a flash, I flipped back my covers and reached for my phone, but before I could unlock it, the doorbell rang.

"I'll get it," Zeke said, rolling off my bed to head for the door.

"And I'll make coffee," Betty said, following him.

I opened my phone, then Levi's messages, pausing to read our last texts. It felt like a lifetime ago, like the people who'd sent those texts were nothing but dust. Everything had changed.

But that didn't mean it had to be over.

I'd apologize. I'd tell him I believed him. That I trusted him. And I'd beg for another chance, if he'd give it.

If he'd even speak to me.

"Stella," Zeke called from the door, "come sign for this."

Frowning, I slid out of bed, phone clutched absently in my hand as I made my way toward them. The courier handed me her digital pad to sign and traded it back for a legal envelope before turning for the elevator. And I stared down at the name on the return address, struck dumb.

Levi's name was written in the corner in strong, square letters, and without thought, my fingertips swept across them as if they'd bring me closer to him.

My friends stared at me as I drifted to a stool and sank onto it.

"Well," Zeke started without patience, "what is it?"

"It's from Levi," I said distantly, tearing the envelope open to retrieve the contents.

The small stack of papers weighed heavy in my hand, the note on the top stopping my heart at the sight of my name in his resonant writing.

Stella,

In this envelope, you'll find the last article of the series for your approval, as promised. The final say is yours, as it will forever be. Because I keep my promises, always. Especially when it comes to you.

I know it doesn't mean much, but I'm sorry. I'm sorry for the original sin, the lie that first seeded doubt. I'm sorry for what I said, for letting you go so easily, for letting you think the worst for the sake of my pride. I'm sorry for the final lie I threw at you like a weapon—that I thought I was falling in love with you.

The truth is, I fell for you long ago, knowing I would only lose you.

As deep as my hatred is for the fulfillment of that prophecy, it wasn't unexpected. But that didn't make it hurt any less.

With the promise of this article, Marrella promised me a ticket to Syria, and by the time you get this, I'll be on my way. I'm sorry I couldn't say goodbye because there's so much more I'd like to say. But this will have to do until I see you again, if I see you again.

For the record, I hope very much that I do.

Take care of yourself, Stella.

—Levi

My vision was a blur as I read the letter again, and only then did I gather myself, shuffling it to the back so I could read the article. At the title, my heart and stomach swapped places, and at the first line, both charged up my esophagus.

UNCOVERING CECELIA BEATON
Levi Hunt, Senior Staff Writer
I know who Cecelia Beaton really is.

Frantically, I read through the article, which began as his reveal as the anonymous author of the exposé articles, then launched into the regaling of the parties he'd been to and what he'd seen and heard and experienced, all without mentioning a single name. But I slowed down as I approached the end, savoring every word.

So much of the Bright Young Things was a surprise, from their genuine joy to the immersion in fantasy. What we see on social media and the news is only a superficial glimpse into something truly spectacular—a celebration. Not one of debauchery or extravagance, though I'd be a liar if I said those players weren't part of the game.

The Bright Young Things celebrate a singular, spectacular gift we all possess.

That we are alive.

It's a fact we systematically ignore, a thing never celebrated simply for its truth. But from the moment I first walked into the speakeasy, the room sang an axiom that rings in me even now: we are alive, and what a magnificent thing that is.

With every party I attended, with every night spent with the Bright Young Things, I peeled back the layers beneath that shining veneer. One for friendship, one for the collection of minds and spirit. One for the unbound joy we lose too soon in the flash that is our lives.

But the deepest layer, the one curled around the heart of the movement, is connection.

We live in a time of constant stimulation. Of social media and the breakdown of distance and the rapid sharing of knowledge. We live in a time of connectivity, but we're perhaps lonelier than we've ever been, opting for our screens as the emptiest of fulfillments—what we get there doesn't keep us full for long. But the Bright Young Things have found each other and held fast through the shared experience of something so trivial and decadent as a party. But that party wasn't built for entertainment, not really.

Everyone wants to know just what it is about the Bright Young Things that fascinates the world so, its voracious inhabitants devouring everything on the group that it can find. Spurring copycat groups all over the country. Following the movement with the devotion of a pilgrim. The answer is so simple, I don't know how I'm the first to state it so plainly.

What we long for most in this world is a place to belong, and that is what the Bright Young Things gives us.

A secret society. Lavish parties. The young and the beautiful, the idyllic timelessness, the snapshot in time of a moment made of magic. Friends in the arms of friends, frozen in their euphoria in a picture of perfection.

But nothing is perfect. No one is free of problems, nor are they free of flaws.

It's a weakness Commissioner Warren has done his best to exploit, testing the boundaries of his power in search of an easy breach. And the name on his lips along with the rest of the world is Cecelia Beaton.

Part of my task was to quietly seek the identity of the elusive leader of the Bright Young Things. Asking around lent me nothing. Digging only proved to be destructive. But in the end, her identity was clear and crisp and plain to see, if I'd only taken a moment to look.

Cecelia Beaton is all of us.

You might feel tricked as you read that declaration, but I feel that truth in the depths of my heart, as much as you might doubt it.

I am Cecelia Beaton, and so are you, for we are alive and must celebrate it. Cecelia Beaton is those of you who feel the command along with me, living through the photos and recounts of their parties. Her presence alone issues an edict, one none of us should ignore. Because our time in this world is brief, and if we spent more time celebrating *the gift instead of wallowing in all we hate, the world would be a very different place.*

So party on, Cecelia Beaton.

The world needs you now more than ever.

I lowered the papers into my lap, my eyes still on his words and my heart an unfettered tempest.

A feeling arose in me, one that had been bubbling beneath the lies I'd told myself.

I didn't want to be without him.

I didn't want to lose him

I was wrong, so wrong, and careless to have denied myself what I really wanted.

I'd handled all that had passed with clumsy hands, leaving it shattered and sparkling, the pieces too small to put back together.

Because now he was gone.

"What happened?" Betty asked gently, wrapping her arm around my shoulders.

A tear splashed on the back of my hand. I brought my fingertips to my face, unaware I'd started crying.

I didn't know what to say, so I handed Zeke the stack, which he took with greedy hands, and stared at my fingers twined in my lap.

Wretched was the word I landed on. Worse than miserable, not quite distraught, with a waft of disgust and mingling sorrow.

I recounted what I'd learned—could it have only been a few minutes ago? There was Warren's arrest—one Levi had a hand in, no doubt. And then there was the note bearing his apology, echoing his declaration from the article directly to my heart. Then the article, the proof of his loyalty in words, on paper. A declaration that my secret was safe when I shouldn't have needed one at all.

He'd sent all of this to me when he didn't have to. An offering, perhaps. A clearing of conscience.

Or he wanted to tell me in not so many words that he loved me, or could, if given the chance.

My chest hitched, and a sob jolted me in surprise.

I owed him so much, but rather than extending him grace, rather than trusting him, I'd accused and insulted him. And even then, he was the one to apologize.

I didn't deserve him, and I couldn't have him even if I did. There might be a way to beg his forgiveness, but I couldn't fathom a way to get him back.

Zeke lowered the letter, and he and Betty stared at me.

"He loves you," Zeke said.

I shook my head as tears slid down my face. "But I've lost him."

"This doesn't sound like you've lost anything, Stella." He held up the papers and gave me a look.

"He's gone. It says it right there. What am I supposed to do? Text him? Send him an email, for God's sake?" My breath shuddered, and I swiped at my cheeks. "There's too much to say for anything short of a letter, and I don't know how I'd find the words for even that."

They were silent for a moment, Zeke's brain working on an idea and Betty's teeth working on her lip.

"Maybe you can video-chat," she offered.

But something struck Zeke like a lightning bolt, lighting him up and setting him on fire in the same breath. He grabbed my hand and yanked me off the stool.

"I've got a better idea."

Once I regained my balance, I trotted behind him as he dragged me toward my bedroom. "Are you going to tell me, or do I have to guess?"

He shot a wicked smile over his shoulder without breaking his stride. "Try to guess so I can feel superior."

And so I tried.

But I never did get the answer right myself.

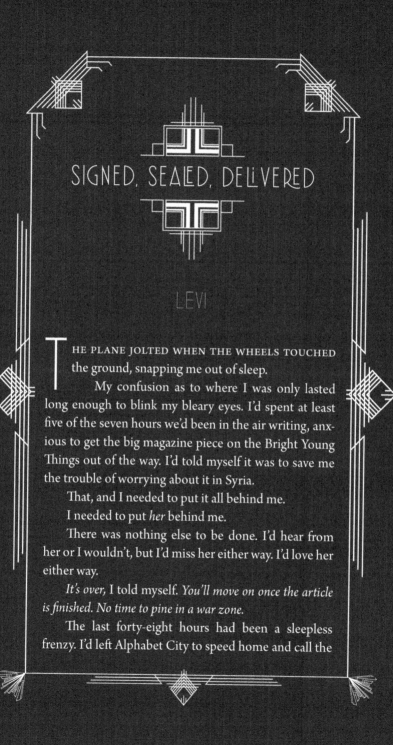

SIGNED, SEALED, DELIVERED

LEVI

THE PLANE JOLTED WHEN THE WHEELS TOUCHED the ground, snapping me out of sleep.

My confusion as to where I was only lasted long enough to blink my bleary eyes. I'd spent at least five of the seven hours we'd been in the air writing, anxious to get the big magazine piece on the Bright Young Things out of the way. I'd told myself it was to save me the trouble of worrying about it in Syria.

That, and I needed to put it all behind me.

I needed to put *her* behind me.

There was nothing else to be done. I'd hear from her or I wouldn't, but I'd miss her either way. I'd love her either way.

It's over, I told myself. *You'll move on once the article is finished. No time to pine in a war zone.*

The last forty-eight hours had been a sleepless frenzy. I'd left Alphabet City to speed home and call the

FBI hotline. After hours on the phone and all I'd seen, there was no chance of sleep. So I wrote.

I wrote about Warren first, the article pouring out of me in a single shot. Once I sent it to Yara, I reached out to my media contacts to tip them off, hoping if we could nail Warren in a blitz-krieg of news breaks, he wouldn't be able to hide. Turned out, I was right.

The flophouse was raided in the middle of the night, the girls all gathered up and saved—or as saved as they could be. The young ones at least would have a chance in the system. The older ones, like April, would run away the second they were placed. All I could do was hope she took care of herself. All I could do was pray she'd stay safe.

I'd sacrificed April's safety for the sake of the little girls in the hopes that the FBI could dig into the Russian fuckers who were trafficking them. And to unseat Warren from the throne of skulls he ruled from.

I should have tried to sleep, but after staring at my ceiling for an hour, I peeled myself out of bed to sit down at my laptop with my notebook. The article on the Bright Young Things had been written in pieces on the pages, waiting to be transcribed. So I wrote until the first sign of morning and printed it out when it was finished. Wrote Stella a note. Packed it up and booked a courier, leaving it outside the door for pickup.

Only then was my brain quiet and my soul tired enough to sleep.

I only got a few hours before my phone rang. Marcella was out of her mind with excitement—Yara had sent copyedits on the Warren piece for my approval, *immediately, please*. My promotion to senior staff writer had been signed off on. And Syria was wait-ing—all I had to do was say when.

So I said when.

She booked me a flight for that night. I spent the day packing and preparing, getting through my edits, setting Billy up with Peg as his caretaker, who generously offered to move in. Billy smiled like a goddamn fox about it, and Peg wasn't any less enthusiastic. The honest truth was that I found myself less worried about him than I'd ever thought I'd be. His insistence that I get the hell out of his apartment didn't hurt.

And I watched Warren's story unfold with a deep satisfaction.

My tip-off had the media waiting for Warren, not imagining they'd catch his arrest by the FBI instead. Articles broke out all over the country throughout the course of the day, citing the anonymous photographic evidence that had been delivered and the girls in custody as all the proof anyone needed. The mayor, who had appointed him, denounced him and removed him from office within hours, promising to put together a force to aid him in selecting a new commissioner within the week.

I successfully dodged my circling thoughts about Stella, putting what little energy I had into the tasks at hand. But then I slid into a cab that afternoon to head to the airport, and there was nothing left to distract me from the fact that I hadn't heard from her. That I'd even thought she might was stupid—not only had I told her I was gone, but she didn't even wake up until after lunch most days. Part of me hoped she'd reach out anyway. Call me at least. Tell me she got the article and that it had her approval. Maybe I'd even be so lucky as to earn her respect and forgiveness. Maybe she'd even ask for mine.

But she didn't reach out, so I boarded my plane, turned off my phone, and vowed to let it go.

I'd done a shit job of it.

I stretched in my seat as we taxied, peering out the window the guy next to me had opened. It was morning in Paris, and I wondered how the hell I was going to head off jet lag with so few hours of sleep in the last two days that I could count them on one hand. Marcella had booked me two days in Paris as a pat on the head for being a good boy, writing it off as an acclimation to the time zone change at a comfortable midway point. So if I could get into my room, I figured I could sleep until after lunch and then do my best to stay up until the evening.

Either that, or I'd just sleep for twenty hours and call it good.

We gathered our things and waited in the aisles to shuffle off the plane like the undead. And while we stood jammed together, I turned on my phone, my heart stopping when my messages rolled in, waiting for her name to appear.

But it never did.

I answered what was urgent, let Billy know I'd landed, and slid my phone in my pocket in the hopes that I could forget. But I felt its presence there as much as I felt her presence in my heart.

It's beyond saving, no matter how badly you want to. Her silence only proves that she's lost to you. So let it go, man.

I scrubbed my face, grateful when the line began to move. It gave me something to do. Something to think about. Forward motion, even if I was running away.

My thoughts were fixed ahead of me as I walked the winding ramps to the gate exit. I was so exhausted, it felt like I was walking in a dream.

Especially when I stepped into the terminal and saw what had to be a mirage.

Because Stella Spencer stood just beyond the flow of people with a carry-on at her side and her face shining with cautious hope.

I stopped dead, and a guy ran into me from behind, nearly knocking me over.

"What the fuck, man?" he shot.

But I didn't even glance at him, muttering, "Sorry," before drifting toward her.

She showed no sign of jet lag, though a tiredness in her eyes told me she was exhausted, and not just from the flight. As always, she shimmered with that radiance powered from within, and I marveled over that beauty as I so often had, not only in wonder, but in utter disbelief.

I didn't know how long we stood there, staring, before she extended her hand, which held the envelope I'd only just sent to her.

"Your edits," she said.

I looked at the envelope stupidly for a second before taking it. "How … how did you …" The question died in my throat as my gaze shifted from the contents of my hand and back to her.

"Find you? Ash. Beat you here? Well," she started, "Ash didn't know much, but he knew you were on the eight thirty to Paris, and Air France was the only flight at eight thirty. Your flight was full, but the four thirty flight on Air France had one seat left. Probably because it was first-class and cost four grand."

"All of that just to bring me this? You could have emailed it, you know," I joked.

She shrugged. "I've always had a flair for the dramatic. As Cecelia Beaton, I think we'd all agree it's on-brand, isn't it?"

At that, I laughed.

"But I didn't just come to bring you these. You must know that, don't you?"

My smile faded. "I hoped."

"Levi, I …" She cast her eyes to the floor. "Open the envelope."

After a moment of curious assessment, I did.

Inside was the article, but on top was a letter, written in her hand.

Levi,

In this envelope, you will find my edits, though there aren't many. Because, as always, your words hold the truth.
For the record, I was wrong.

For the record, I am a fool.

For the record, I'm sorry.

I broke faith, broke your trust and respect the minute I accused you of lying to me, of using me, of betraying me. I was wrong not to trust you, not to listen. I was a fool for letting my fear police my happiness. I am sorry, so sorry, for my lack of loyalty. Because I love you. And rather than believe wholly in that love, I gave in to my fear, and that was the moment I lost you.

I only hope you aren't lost forever.

I'm here to ask for your forgiveness. To promise you that I'll wait for you and to hope against hope that you'll forgive me. Because my life has never been so bright as it's been since you.

Yours,
Stella

I stared at the letter, at a line, at a single word that spurred a flurry of whispers in my heart, saying, *She loves me, she loves me, she loves me.*

When I looked up, our eyes met like the click of a lock.

"I'm sorry," she whispered, the flush in her face splotched with emotion I could see mirrored in her welling tears.

But I took a step closer, reaching to cup her jaw. "For the record, so am I."

Her eyes closed, her hand rising to clasp my wrist. "I owed you this, Levi. To come here and to beg your forgiveness. I needed you to know I'd go to the ends of the earth to prove myself worthy of you after how I treated you. But don't say I'm forgiven just because I'm here. More than anything, I just wanted you to know that I was sorry, and—"

I kissed her to stop her words, to swallow her sadness, to breathe in her apology and exhale my own. I kissed her to tell her without words that she was forgiven and to slip into the sweet relief I found in the warmth of her body against mine.

When I broke the kiss, she blinked up at me with her lips still parted in wait.

My smile tilted. "You don't honestly think I'd refuse after you flew halfway across the world just to apologize, do you?"

"Yes. Yes, I absolutely do," she said with a flat earnestness that made me laugh, thumbing her cheek. "I couldn't sleep the entire flight, thinking of all the ways you'd say no. But I had to see you. I had to tell you face to face that ... that I ... that I love you, Levi. I know this because you took what I thought I knew of the word and smashed it into a thousand pieces. I couldn't walk away from that without a fight. Not for anything."

"For the record, I was wrong," I echoed her words before my lips brushed her cheek. "For the record, I'm a fool," I said on my way to kiss her other cheek. "For the record, I'm sorry." My lips pressed to her forehead. "And for the record, I've loved you since the second I laid eyes on you. It's about time you caught up."

She started to laugh, but I kissed her smiling lips, kissed her until we were wound together and breathless.

"*Eh, y'a des hôtels pour ça!*," a flight attendant said as she passed, inciting a chorus of laughter from her colleagues and Stella too, who broke away, chuckling.

"What did they say?" I asked.

"To get a room," she answered, beaming up at me. "Luckily, I already did."

"Oh?"

"Mmhmm." She smoothed my shirt, watching her hands. "At Shangri La."

"Is that a metaphor? Because I can't pretend like a couple days with you in Paris isn't some sort of heaven."

She laughed, and the sound was its own Shangri La. "No, it's an actual hotel," she said as she took my hand and we began to walk toward baggage. "Napoleon built it for Prince Bonaparte as a private mansion."

"So it's modest, then."

"*So* modest, including the humble views of the Eiffel Tower."

"Sounds approachable."

Stella slid her arm around my waist, meeting my stride. "All I want right now is you and me in a gigantic bed."

"Naked?"

"Definitely naked. I hope you've been to Paris before, because you're not seeing anything but me and the inside of that room until we leave to put you on the plane."

"Shangri La, indeed," I said, kissing the top of her head as I thanked my lucky stars, as bright as they were, that I'd have a chance to love her.

And it was a chance I wouldn't waste.

A-FUCKING-PLUS

STELLA

A T SOME POINT IN THE LAST FORTY-EIGHT HOURS, time had ceased to exist.

Between jet lag and each other, Levi and I had spent the last two days in bed, leaving only to answer the door for room service and to shower. We'd slept a lot, talked much more, and the rest of the time was spent in each other's arms—a place we preferred to stay.

I sighed at the thought, and Levi smiled down at me where I lay splayed on top of him, chin on the back of my hand, which rested over his heart.

"I think you've sighed twenty times in the last five minutes." He tucked a lock of hair behind my ear, grazing my cheek with his knuckles on their retreat.

"I can't help it. I don't want you to leave today."

"I don't want to go either."

Another sigh. "You really don't know how long you'll be gone? Not even a ballpark?"

"It all depends on the work I do and the budget."

"Well, I hope they run out of money."

I bounced with his chest when he chuckled.

"I don't want to go back to New York."

"You won't have to worry about your parties getting busted, at least."

"Yes, there's that. I can't believe what he's done. I knew he was the devil, but I didn't realize just how deep it went. All those girls …"

"Fucking pig," Levi spat. "But Billy's not wrong. I don't think anything he did to the group was personal. He was just one head of the hydra—someone else is pulling the strings."

Dread slithered through me. "Then we'll have to find the other heads and cut them off."

"We will. Just promise me you'll wait until I get back. If you got in trouble while I was gone, or worse—if you got hurt …"

"I'll leave it alone. I promise."

The warmth in his smile sparked a fire in my heart.

"So let's go over the plan," I said, resurrecting my mental checklist.

One of his dark brows rose with his smile. "Again?"

"Yes, again. It makes me feel better to think about when I'll talk to you, so just humor me, Hunt."

"Yes, ma'am."

"So we'll go to the airport together. Make out in front of your gate like a couple of pervs."

A laugh.

"You'll text me when you land in Damascus, and I'll video call you when I land in New York. We'll be seven hours apart, so I'll text you every morning when I wake up."

"At two in the afternoon your time?"

"Psh—I'll wake up before seven if it means I get to see you for a minute."

"That right there is true love."

With a face-splitting smile, I climbed up him to give him a kiss in the hopes that it would ensure hearing that word from those lips a million times between now and when he came home.

When I broke away, he swept my hair over my bare shoulder.

"I already added you on WhatsApp," I noted like he hadn't watched me do it, "so that's all set—no international fees for you. Hopefully, I can catch you at least once a day. And if I can't, you owe me nudes."

That earned me a full-blown laugh. "As soon as I have any idea whether we're looking at days or months, I'll let you know, and we can plan a trip to Dubai."

"Which you can plan to see about as much of as you have Paris."

"I mean, I can see the Eiffel Tower from right here," he said with a nod to the French doors to the patio, where said tower rose from the city to the sky.

"Okay—expect to see less of Dubai, smartass."

He gathered me up in his arms and rolled me over, pinning me with his body. "I'll plan on it." His eyes traced my face as if he was memorizing it, and his hand slid along the line of my jaw until it rested in his palm. "I'm going to miss you," he said with unspeakable longing.

"Not as much as I'll miss you," I echoed softly. "I'm a little jealous that you'll be so busy. I'll just be stuck in New York, doing nothing."

"Cecelia Beaton would never say her parties consisted of doing nothing."

"Ugh, I'm going to have parties planned for the next three years just to keep myself occupied."

"Hey, as long as you aren't occupied with some other guy, I approve." I heard the worry in his voice beneath the joke.

"Impossible. Why settle for ground chuck when I've got filet?"

"I dunno. Hamburgers are convenient."

"I'll wait for the steak, thank you."

He let out a long breath, thumbing my cheek. "I wish I could ask you to promise you won't."

"You don't have to ask—I'm yours. There's no *maybe* about how I feel about you. There's no *if*. Just you and me and the countdown to when I'll see you again."

"Think we'll make it?"

I gave him a look. "Have you ever seen me not get something I want?"

"Nope."

"Exactly. And I want you. So kiss me, Levi Hunt, and make me forget I'm about to miss you."

"Only if you remind me again how much you love me."

My heart swelled until it hurt. "You know the longing we all share? The searching we do for that piece of us that's missing?"

He nodded.

"If you took my picture now, if you looked for my truth, you'd only find satisfaction. Because I found what I'd been longing for when I found you. I couldn't let you go without cutting out a piece of my heart. And I don't want to do without you again, not after a whole lifetime of searching. So kiss me and fly away so you can hurry back to me. I'll be waiting." My lips curled in a smile. "How was that?"

"A-fucking-plus," he said with a smile of his own before kissing away every thought but the promise of our future.

I'd bet every penny on that future.

And I'd be right.

EPILOGUE

STELLA

Six months later

EVERYTHING IN THE ROOM GLITTERED.

It felt like standing inside a disco ball, from the mirrored ceiling and walls to the sparkle and shine of every person at the Galaxy party.

Stars were everywhere, from constellations to the celebrity variety, and as I scanned the crowd with a smile on my lips, I found the happy faces of all the people I loved. Betty in a minidress composed strictly of glimmering silver beaded fringe. Joss in a ballroom gown made of silver taffeta, stars in her finger waves and a diamond necklace of constellations around her neck. Z in white chiffon threaded with LED lights, a celestial headdress dotted with dangling stars. Ash in a silver suit and even Tag in a custom suit of faintly glinting gold as he tried and failed to dance with my cousin Sadie, who'd just moved in with us from Texas.

Yes, everyone I loved was here, everyone except the one I loved most.

I sighed, my happy smile fading to that longing one I hated so much. Not longing for something unknown, just the simple longing of a woman who missed her man.

It had been six months since Levi and I'd said goodbye in Paris and two months since I'd seen him in Dubai last, which basically meant an unbearable eternity I'd spent without him. We hadn't gone a day without talking except twice when he was so deeply entrenched in a war zone, he couldn't risk compromising his position.

Those were the days I got zero sleep and spent every waking hour scouring the news for anything that would make me feel better, which, unsurprisingly, was always fruitless. But we videoed at least three times a week, and just the shortest glimpse of his smile was enough to power me through any time spent without him. And though I'd told myself it was going to be impossibly hard to be without him, I found waiting for him easy. Not that I didn't miss him—I did, and with a desperation that had worn my friends to the bone. But that I never once faltered. Never found myself frustrated, never even considered that it wasn't going to work.

I'd wait a lifetime for him, if that was what it took.

But we'd finally gotten word that he was coming home, his bosses calling him back to New York to cover the mayoral election, which had heated up to *Fahrenheit 451* proportions. That, and Warren's trial was about to begin, and since Levi had broken the story for *Vagabond*, Marcella had tapped him to cover the trial too. Honestly, I couldn't give a shit why he was coming home and could have kissed Marcella on the mouth for giving him a reason to stay. Because he was, and I'd been counting the seconds until he was home.

I had big ideas for a blowout party to welcoming him home, and just as soon as I knew when his flight would be, Genie was ready to book the whole thing. Parties had been back on since Warren's arrest, and we'd been blissfully left alone—until a month ago. The mayor had appointed a new commissioner who looked like a bulldog in a uniform and made a habit of barking publicly at us whenever the opportunity arose. And when the raids started again, our suspicions were confirmed.

Warren was nothing more than a mini-boss, and someone was still out for us.

And as soon as Levi came home, we'd pick up the chase where we left off.

I slid my hands into the pockets of my dress—a champagne affair with a corseted top and mid-length layers of tulle, the whole thing covered in shimmering rose-gold glitter and stars of all sizes. I looked like a chic version of Glinda the Good Witch and was low-key obsessed with myself tonight.

I just wished Levi were here to see me.

Z swished toward me, her cheekbones—dusted with glitter and stars—high with her smile. Betty giggled from her arm, hooking my elbow when she approached. Z split off to sandwich me between them, and we stood on a platform in the back of the venue, surveying our domain with the pride of a trio of queens.

"Why aren't you dancing?" Betty asked.

"Just wanted to watch for a minute, that's all."

"This dress deserves to be twirled," Z noted. "If you need someone to twirl you, I volunteer as tribute."

I chuckled. Then sighed.

"You miss him?" Betty asked.

"Don't I always?"

"You are such a puppy," Z said. "A mopey little basset hound puppy who keeps tripping over her ears."

"I can't help it, especially now that I know he's coming home. I feel like I could crawl out of my skin waiting. I've never been a patient woman."

"You're like Veruca Salt without the attitude," Betty said.

"The Oompa-Loompas would stamp you a good egg even if you *do* want it all now."

"What's the first thing you'll do when you see him?" Z asked with a curious smile on her face.

"After wrapping myself around him like an octopus?"

"Yes, after that."

"Take him to bed for a week. I have six months of canoodling to make up for. I just want to ... I don't know. Reconnect. But is it weird that I'm nervous too?"

"Not at all," Betty answered. "It's been a minute since you were in the same place for more than a week, and when you *were*, it was basically a train wreck."

"It really was," I said on a laugh.

"What are you nervous for?" Z asked. "It's not like he's a stranger."

"No, it's not that, I don't think. Well, maybe a little. It's been so long since we were in New York together, and what if ... what if it's weird? Or what if ..." I shook my head. "Never mind."

"What?" Betty bumped my hip, but I shook my head again.

Z pinched my ass hard enough to elicit a squeal and a jump. "Spill."

I sighed. "What if he realizes he doesn't want me anymore?"

Betty and Z shared a look before busting out laughing.

"You are a crazy person, Stella Spencer," Betty assured me.

I made a face. "Am not. That's a valid concern."

"No, it's not," Z said, her eyes flicking behind me and a smile rising on her face. "That boy is so gone for you, if he doesn't propose within a year, I'll eat Charlise."

I gasped in mock surprise. "Your favorite wig?"

"That's how sure I am. And if you don't believe me, how about you ask him yourself?"

My face quirked, but before I had a chance to ask, Z grabbed me by the shoulders and turned me around.

Levi stood a few feet before me in a suit of cobalt velvet,

his hair a little long and his eyes a little tired but his smile bright enough to power a solar system.

I didn't know if he moved or I moved, but in a breath, I was in his arms, our lips a seam and my dress flying as he spun me around.

And my heart beat the words, *he's home, he's home, he's home.*

I broke away to gape at his smug, beautiful face in shock. "You're home!" I said stupidly, my heart sighing. "You didn't tell me!"

"Yara got my ticket yesterday, and I wanted to surprise you. Did it work?"

"I am so fucking surprised, I can't close my eyelids. You might disappear."

"I'm not going anywhere, Stell. I'm home for good."

"Until you get another foreign job."

He shrugged one shoulder, his smile tilted and his eyes sparkling. "I'm home for a good long while, at least until Warren's trial and the mayoral election is over."

"Well, then I'll have to enjoy you while I have you."

"I learned a lot over there, about life, humanity, the world. I learned a lot about myself too, about the things I want and the things I love." He held my face, looked down at me as if he were dreaming. "I have new plans. Big plans."

"How big?"

"So big, I can't tell you yet."

I pouted. "That is such a cruel tease, Levi Hunt. You know I'll lose sleep over it."

"I'll give you a hint. You know how I wanted a taste?"

"And you got the bottle?"

"I'm planning to call the whole vineyard mine."

I stilled, my eyes widening. A flush warmed my cheeks in a tingling rush.

"Not just yet—don't freak out. But when the time is right, I'm putting in an offer, Stella Spencer."

"But what if … what if we settle in and I'm … I'm not what you want? You shouldn't have told me, Levi, not until you'd put up with me for enough time to know you could stand it."

He watched me for a beat. "Is that how you feel about me? Do you need to make sure you still want me?"

"Not even for a second."

"Then, we're on the same page. You waited all this time for me. And if we survived that, I think we can do just about anything. Don't you?"

Smiling, I shook my head in disbelief. "Did you just ask me to ma—"

He descended for a kiss, a possessive promise on his lips, branding me with his name. "Don't say it. That's not how this is going to happen. But one day, it's going to happen. So heads up."

"Well, one day, I'm going to say yes."

It was him who flushed, but before I could tell him I loved him, he kissed me again.

And I wished upon a star for the future we'd have.

Turns out, wishes do come true.

THANK YOU

What a ride this was.

Writing through a pandemic and a civil rights movement was no easy feat, but escaping into the world of the Bright Young Things was the shining spot in a dark and emotional time. It inspired me, as I hope it inspired you.

My husband Jeff always gets this first spot simply because he's the reason I'm able to follow my dreams and write from my heart. He's also the reason I write romance, something I often say and will always say. Thank you, babe. You're my hero.

Kandi Steiner always gets the second spot simply because she's my rock every day. If you loved Stella, you should know Kandi, because they are so much alike, I would sometimes ask myself during writing, *What would Kandi do?* Follow her on social media and bask in her shine. Kandi, thank you for being my support and my diary. I love you.

The third spot always goes to Kerrigan Byrne, because if Kandi is my right leg, Kerrigan is my left. She's always down to plot, always ready with big ideas and bigger laughs. She's the one I turn to when it all feels impossible, and she always reminds me that I can do anything. Kerrigan, I couldn't do this without you, not for one second. Thank you.

The next of the K-crew is Kyla Linde, the smartest of cookies who always has an answer to any random question I might have and an abundance of conflict to offer when I need to throw a wrench at my characters. She's my Kylencyclopedia, one of my dearest friends, and one of the people who helps me survive this crazy career with my head on straight.

Tina, my friend and assistant, makes the world go 'round. Dani Sanchez is always there to help keep me on track and to offer her advice. My alpha readers: Abbey Byers, Sasha Erramouspe, Amy Vox Libris, Becky Barney—you were instrumental in the execution of this book and in helping make it look like I knew what it was doing. To my beta readers: Danielle Legasse, Sarah Sentz, Nadine Killian, Chase Coe, Jenny Ellis, Melissa Brooks, Sam Schumpf, and Julia Heudorf—you helped me put the shine on what has turned out to be one of my favorite books to have written. And last but certainly not least, I'd like to thank Amanda Punchfuk, the drag queen of the hour, for putting her stamp of approval on my favorite baby: Zeke.

Jovana Shirley, you are the editor everyone needs in their lives. To my typo hunters, you are a godsend.

Bloggers, you are the motor to this whole operation, and your support, hard work, and dedication to the community are worth more than you'll ever know.

Readers, it's all for you. Thank you for spending these hours with my heart.

ALSO BY
STACI HART

CONTEMPORARY STANDALONES

Bad Habits
With a Twist (Bad Habits 1)
A ballerina living out her fantasies about her high school crush realizes real love is right in front of her in this slow-burn friends-to-lovers romantic comedy.

Chaser (Bad Habits 2)
He'd trade his entire fortune for a real chance with his best friend's little sister.

Last Call (Bad Habits 3)
All he's ever wanted was a second chance, but she'll resist him at every turn, no matter how much she misses him.

The Austens
Wasted Words (Inspired by Emma)
She's just an adorable, matchmaking book nerd who could never have a shot with her gorgeous best friend and roommate.

A Thousand Letters (Inspired by Persuasion)
Fate brings them together after seven years for a second chance they never thought they'd have in this lyrical story about love, loss, and moving on.

A Little Too Late (Follow up to A Thousand Letters)
A story of finding love when all seems lost and finding home when you're far away from everything you've known.

Living Out Loud (Inspired by *Sense & Sensibility*)
Annie wants to live while she can, as fully as she can, not knowing how deeply her heart could break.

The Tonic Series
Tonic (Book 1)
The reality show she's filming in his tattoo parlor is the last thing he wants, but if he can have her*, he'll be satisfied in this enemies-to-lovers-comedy.*

Bad Penny (Book 2)
She knows she's boy crazy, which is why she follows strict rules, but this hot nerd will do his best to convince her to break every single one.

The Red Lipstick Coalition
Piece of Work
Her cocky boss is out to ruin her internship, and maybe her heart, too.

Player
He's just a player, so who better to teach her how to date? All she has to do is not fall in love with him.

Work in Progress
She never thought her first kiss would be on her wedding day. Rule number one: Don't fall in love with her fake husband.

Well Suited
She's convinced love is nothing more than brain chemicals, and her baby daddy's determined to prove her wrong.

The Bennet Brothers

Coming Up Roses
Everyone hates something about their job, and she hates Luke Bennet. Because if she doesn't, she'll fall in love with him.

The Hardcore Serials
Hardcore: Complete Collection
A parkour thief gets herself into trouble when she falls for the man who forces her to choose between right and wrong.

HEARTS AND ARROWS
Greek mythology meets Gossip Girl in a contemporary paranormal series where love is the ultimate game and Aphrodite never loses.

Paper Fools (Book 1)
Shift (Book 2)
From Darkness (Book 3)

ABOUT THE AUTHOR

Staci has been a lot of things up to this point in her life: a graphic designer, an entrepreneur, a seamstress, a clothing and handbag designer, a waitress. Can't forget that. She's also been a mom to three little girls who are sure to grow up to break a number of hearts. She's been a wife, even though she's certainly not the cleanest, or the best cook. She's also super, duper fun at a party, especially if she's been drinking whiskey, and her favorite word starts with f, ends with k.

From roots in Houston, to a seven year stint in Southern California, Staci and her family ended up settling somewhere in between and equally north in Denver. When she's not writing, she's reading, gaming, or designing graphics.

www.stacihartnovels.com

staci@stacihartnovels.com

Made in the USA
Coppell, TX
27 July 2020

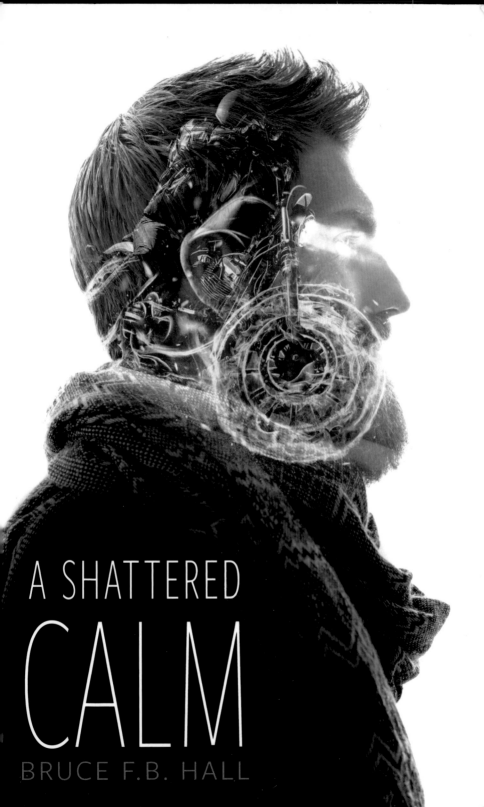

A SHATTERED
CALM

BRUCE F.B. HALL